PRAISE FOR THE NOVELS OF

#1 NEW YORK TIMES BESTSELLING AUTHOR
BARBARA FREETHY

"I love *The Callaways*! Heartwarming romance, intriguing
suspense and sexy alpha heroes. What more could you want?"
-- *NYT Bestselling Author* **Bella Andre**

"I adore *The Callaways*, a family we'd all love to have. Each new
book is a deft combination of emotion, suspense and family
dynamics. A remarkable, compelling series!"
-- *USA Today Bestselling Author* **Barbara O'Neal**

"Once I start reading a Callaway novel, I can't put it down. Fast-
paced action, a poignant love story and a tantalizing mystery in
every book!"
-- *USA Today Bestselling Author* **Christie Ridgway**

"In the tradition of LaVyrle Spencer, gifted author Barbara Freethy
creates an irresistible tale of family secrets, riveting adventure and
heart-touching romance."
-- *NYT Bestselling Author* **Susan Wiggs**
on Summer Secrets

"This book has it all: heart, community, and characters who will
remain with you long after the book has ended. A wonderful story."
-- *NYT Bestselling Author* **Debbie Macomber**
on Suddenly One Summer

"Freethy has a gift for creating complex characters."
-- **Library Journal**

"Barbara Freethy is a master storyteller with a gift for spinning tales about ordinary people in extraordinary situations and drawing readers into their lives."

*-- **Romance Reviews Today***

"Freethy's skillful plotting and gift for creating sympathetic characters will ensure that few dry eyes will be left at the end of the story."

*-- **Publishers Weekly** on The Way Back Home*

"Freethy skillfully keeps the reader on the hook, and her tantalizing and believable tale has it all– romance, adventure, and mystery."

*-- **Booklist** on Summer Secrets*

"Freethy's story-telling ability is top-notch."

*-- **Romantic Times** on Don't Say A Word*

"Powerful and absorbing…sheer hold-your-breath suspense."

*-- NYT Bestselling Author **Karen Robards***
on Don't Say A Word

"A page-turner that engages your mind while it tugs at your heartstrings…Don't Say A Word has made me a Barbara Freethy fan for life!"

*-- NYT Bestselling Author **Diane Chamberlain***
on Don't Say A Word

Also By Barbara Freethy

The Callaway Family Series
On A Night Like This
So This Is Love
Falling For A Stranger
Between Now And Forever
All A Heart Needs
That Summer Night
When Shadows Fall
Somewhere Only We Know

The Wish Series
A Secret Wish
Just A Wish Away
When Wishes Collide

Standalone Novels
Almost Home
All She Ever Wanted
Ask Mariah
Daniel's Gift
Don't Say A Word
Golden Lies
Just The Way You Are
Love Will Find A Way
One True Love
Ryan's Return
Some Kind of Wonderful
Summer Secrets
The Sweetest Thing

The Sanders Brothers Series
Silent Run
Silent Fall

The Deception Series
Taken
Played

To my wonderful husband Terry for his never-ending love and support!

SOMEWHERE ONLY WE KNOW

The Callaways

BARBARA FREETHY

HYDE STREET PRESS
Published by Hyde Street Press
1819 Polk Street, Suite 113, San Francisco, California 94109

Printed in the United States of America

Cover design by Damonza.com
Interior book design by KLF Publishing

ISBN 978-0-9906951-7-2

One

The cold wintry night was eerily similar to the one three years ago when thick clouds of fog had swept into San Francisco just after dusk, shutting out the last bit of daylight, holding the city in the icy fingers of late January. And just like that night, Burke felt a chill run down his spine, an uneasy feeling that was heightened by the sirens that suddenly lit up the air.

As a firefighter, he was used to sirens, to emergencies, to the unthinkable happening in a second, but nothing had prepared him for *that* night.

He tried to force the horrific images out of his mind.

It wasn't the same, he told himself, but three years had done little to erase the memories, which was why the last thing he wanted to do was attend yet another memorial dinner in honor of his late fiancée Leanne Parker. But Chuck and Marjorie Parker insisted on remembering their only daughter's death every year since the tragic car accident had taken her life. As Leanne's former fiancé, he could do nothing but support them. It was his duty to attend, and he'd never been a man to shirk his duty.

As a cold blast of wind rocketed through the tall

buildings that surrounded him, he zipped up his jacket and proceeded up the steep hill to the Hanover Club. Originally a private gentlemen's establishment started by one of San Francisco's first families, the Hanover Club now catered to high-powered executives and politicians of both genders interested in holding parties or meetings. Tonight was something in between...

"Burke, wait up."

He stopped, surprised at the sound of his sister's voice. He turned around to see Emma and his younger brother Sean walking quickly up the hill behind him. Emma was a slender blonde with snapping blue eyes that reflected her sparkling, often stubborn personality. A fire investigator for the San Francisco Fire Department, she'd obviously come straight from work, wearing her navy blue slacks and matching jacket.

Sean wore dark jeans under a black wool coat, and like all the Callaway men, he had brown hair and blue eyes. But while Sean looked like everyone else in the family, he was in many ways the odd man out: the musician, the soulful, emotional singer/songwriter in a family of overachievers, many of whom were firefighters.

"What are you guys doing here?" Burke asked.

"Supporting you," Emma said with a purposeful smile, as if she was expecting to get an argument from him. "You should have told us about the dinner, Burke."

"I didn't tell you, because I didn't want you to come." Bluntness was the only thing that worked when it came to his stubborn younger sister. "How did you find out?"

"Mrs. Parker called Mom to see who from the family would be attending. You can imagine how thrilled Mom was that you hadn't told her."

Now he knew why he had four voice messages from his

mother that he had yet to listen to. He'd also been avoiding his text messages, which had been pinging away all day. He glanced at Sean and frowned. "And you—this is what you decide to show up for? The guy who misses almost every family event? This one you have to make?"

Sean gave him an understanding look. "Emma insisted. Drew and Ria are on their way as well as Aiden, Sara and Mom. Jessica and Nicole send their regards, but they had a school function with Brandon and Kyle tonight. I'm not sure what's up with Shayla or Colton."

"They're both stuck at work," Emma put in. "And Dad had a dinner meeting he couldn't miss."

"Thank God for that," Burke muttered. While he was close to his father, Jack Callaway had a huge personality, and Jack had never gotten along that well with Leanne's dad. Chuck was a white-collar investment banker and staunch conservative. Jack was blue collar all the way, although he now served as Deputy Chief of Operations for the San Francisco Fire Department.

"How are you doing, Burke?" Emma asked, her blue eyes filled with worry.

"I'm fine, and you really didn't have to come."

"We all loved Leanne. She was going to be part of the family."

"It seems like a long time ago now."

"There's Mom." Sean tipped his head toward the top of the hill where his mother, his brother Aiden and Aiden's wife Sara were getting out of a car. "Don't fight it," Sean advised. "We're going to be here for you whether you like it or not. It's the Callaway way."

He knew it was the Callaway way. Usually, he was the first one to support a sibling or parent or cousin in need, but he wasn't used to being on the receiving end of the attention, and he didn't like it. As the oldest of eight siblings, he'd always been the one to take care of everyone else, to be the strong, independent leader of the family. It was a role he both loved and hated. It was tiring to always have to set the bar high. On the other hand, as his brother Aiden liked to remind him, he did have the chance to set the bar while the rest of his siblings had to follow.

They walked up the hill together, meeting up with his other family members outside the entrance to the club.

His mom Lynda gave him a hug. Aiden nodded, concern in his eyes, and Sara sent him a warm smile and told him that Drew and Ria were on the way.

"Great," he muttered. "I guess we should go in."

As they walked through the lobby and into the private dining room, he saw Leanne's family and friends chatting around tall cocktail tables while waiters served champagne and appetizers. Despite the party set-up, there was a somber air in the room, and Burke felt better having some members of his family walking behind him.

Chuck saw him and immediately came over to shake his hand. Dressed in a dark suit, Chuck had aged in the last few years, his gray hair now completely white, and the shadows under his brown eyes had become permanent fixtures.

"Burke, I was beginning to think you might not make it," Chuck said.

There was a hint of censure in his voice, but that was Chuck. He was always demanding and often disappointed in the people around him. Leanne had told him many times that she just couldn't seem to make her father happy.

"Don't give him a hard time," Marjorie interrupted with a smile that was very much like her daughter's, and that smile made his heart squeeze a little tighter. "It's nice to see you, Burke. It's been a long time."

"Yes," he admitted. "I like your hair." Her normally brown hair was now a deep rich auburn.

She gave him a dimpled smile. "I decided to go red. Leanne always used to tell me I should change things up every once in a while, so today I decided to finally do that." Her gaze swept across the rest of his family. "I'm so glad you could all come. It means so much to us."

Burke stepped back as his mother and Marjorie exchanged a hug and Chuck shook hands with the rest of his siblings.

As he looked around the dining room, he saw four of his coworkers at one of the tall tables. Apparently, they'd also heard about the event. Since his cousin and fellow firefighter Dylan Callaway was at the table, Burke wasn't surprised they'd found out about the event. Next to Dylan was Frank Harding, who'd been friends with him since the fire academy, Rachel Briggs, a paramedic at their firehouse, and Shelby Cooper, one of their long-time dispatchers who also worked out of the firehouse.

He was touched by their attendance and not that surprised by their presence. His firehouse family was as close as his Callaway family.

Rachel and Shelby both gave him hugs while Frank slapped him on the shoulder and Dylan gave him a nod.

"Thanks for coming," he said.

"No problem," Dylan replied. "I remember last year the Parkers put on a good spread."

"You're always looking for your next meal," he said, appreciating Dylan's attempt to lighten the mood.

"Are you all right, Burke?" Shelby asked.

Shelby was a dark-eyed brunette in her mid-thirties who worked dispatch with a calm coolness that always kept them on track. Since Leanne's death, Shelby had offered him a friendly ear on more than one occasion. She'd also been friends with Leanne, so it was easy to share memories with her, not that they spent much time talking about Leanne anymore. It had been three years, but tonight it felt like yesterday.

"I'm fine." He wondered how many more times he would say those words tonight.

"Are you?" Rachel challenged. A tall, slender blonde, Rachel could have been a model if she'd had any interest in posing in front of a camera. But she was a tomboy at heart, a girl who loved action sports and pushing herself to the limit.

"I'd just like to get this over with," he told her.

She nodded in understanding. "I'm sure."

"We're going to Brady's after this," Shelby added. "You should come with us after you pay your respects to the Parkers."

"I'll think about it."

"Looks like the buffet table is open," Dylan said. "Anyone want to get some food?"

"You guys go ahead." He wasn't the least bit hungry.

As his friends moved over to the buffet, Aiden crossed the room and put a bottle of beer into his hand.

"Thanks," he said, taking a long swig of cold beer.

"What do you figure? Give this a half hour, then say goodbye?" Aiden asked.

"Definitely not longer than that." He looked towards the front of the room and saw Leanne's smiling face gazing back at him from a large poster. Her parents had set up the same photos that they'd had at the funeral—a display of Leanne's life in photographs. He shook his head in bewilderment. "What are they thinking? When does this end? When do we stop celebrating the worst day in all of our lives?"

"They're thinking that they don't want anyone to forget

their daughter," Aiden said quietly.

"I don't need a poster to remind me of Leanne."

"Maybe they do," Sara suggested, joining them. "Sometimes memories start to fade and people worry that they'll forget. I remember feeling that way after my mom died. As the years went by, I couldn't see her face as clearly. I couldn't hear her voice in my head. I couldn't remember her laugh. To tell you the truth, it scared me. I felt like she was slipping away. Perhaps the Parkers feel like that, too."

Sara's words rang true in his head. Leanne had been fading in his mind. While he hadn't been in a serious romantic relationship since then, he had dated other women. He had gone on with his life. Maybe that was why he hadn't wanted to come tonight. He felt like the Parkers were trying to pull him back into the darkness, and he didn't want to be there anymore. He'd gone through the anger, the guilt, the sadness and the multitude of *what ifs* that could have changed the outcome if only he'd done something different. He was over all that.

He looked away from the pictures, his gaze coming to rest on the newest arrival to the gathering—Mitch Warren. His heart sank. This was not going to go well.

Mitch was in his mid-thirties and was a fellow firefighter. Mitch had also been a good friend of Leanne's long before Burke had met her. In fact, Burke had always thought that Mitch had felt a lot more than friendship for Leanne, but Leanne had always dismissed that idea with a laugh, saying they were just good friends.

As much as Mitch liked Leanne, he did not care for Burke. And that dislike had only grown after Leanne's death. Mitch was convinced that Leanne's death was not an accident, that somehow Burke was to blame. He could understand that Mitch needed someone to blame, because he'd looked for a scapegoat himself, but some accidents were just that—unexpected, unexplainable and tragic.

Next to Mitch was Burke's youngest brother Colton.

Burke could see the worry in Colton's eyes. His brother worked under Mitch at a firehouse on the other side of the city, but he was caught in the war between Burke and Mitch, and there was nothing Burke could do about it. Colton would have to find his own way to a relationship with Mitch Warren.

He stiffened as Mitch saw him and headed in his direction. The last thing he wanted was a confrontation here, but there was nowhere to run, and it seemed obvious from the aggressive look in Mitch's eyes that he wanted to make a scene. He was itching for a fight.

"I can't believe you had the nerve to show up," Mitch ground out, anger burning in his eyes.

He told himself not to react. Mitch's anger came from a place of grief, and that was something they had in common. It wasn't something to fight over.

"Let's get something to eat, Captain," Colton suggested.

"Not yet. I'm done letting your brother act like he had nothing to do with Leanne's death, when we all know he did."

As Mitch spat out the words, Burke could smell the liquor on Mitch's breath. There was no question that alcohol was fueling his fire.

"Why don't we go outside?" Burke suggested calmly, seeing Chuck and Marjorie approaching, tense looks on their faces.

"I'm not going anywhere with you," Mitch replied. "You and I are going to have it out. I'm tired of playing your games. You don't want to answer my questions, but tonight you're going to have to do just that."

"Captain," Colton began again.

"Get out of my face, Callaway," Mitch said forcefully, shoving Colton away.

"What's going on?" Chuck Parker asked.

"It's Burke's fault, Chuck," Mitch said, looking at Leanne's father. "I know you don't want to hear that, but it's true."

"I don't understand." Chuck sent Burke a sharp look. "What's he talking about?"

"I'll tell you what I'm talking about," Mitch answered, not giving Burke a chance to explain. "Ask Burke why Leanne was on the road that night. Ask him why she was so close to the firehouse. Ask him why there didn't happen to be any security cameras in that particular neighborhood. Go on, ask him."

"Leanne was going to her yoga class," Marjorie cut in. "We already know that, Mitch. She went there every Thursday night."

"And it's not far from the firehouse," Chuck said.

"She wasn't going to yoga. That wasn't the way to the studio."

"She took a shortcut," Marjorie interrupted. "Leanne was always cutting through back alleys."

"I don't believe that. Leanne was upset with him." Mitch pointed an accusatory finger at Burke. "Leanne left me a message that day. She was crying. She said she had to talk to me about him."

Marjorie put a hand on Mitch's arm. "Mitch, we understand that you're upset. You and Leanne were so close. But this isn't going to solve anything. We'll never know what Leanne wanted to talk to you about."

"We'd know if he'd talk," Mitch said, glaring at him again. "But he just stands there and says nothing."

Burke had more than a couple of reasons for why he'd

never responded to Mitch's questions, but there was no point in trying to explain that now…or ever. Nothing would bring Leanne back or change the past.

"Let it go," Chuck said firmly.

Mitch shook his head. "So he gets a free pass? No, he needs to pay. He needs to feel some of the pain that the rest of us are in."

Burke saw Mitch pull his hand back a split second too late. He tried to duck, but he was pinned in. Mitch's fist connected with his jawbone, the force of the man's anger making it a solid, purposeful punch.

He stumbled backwards, his head spinning, and knocked into one of the waitresses handing out glasses of champagne. He tried to stop himself from falling, but he got tangled up with the woman, and the next thing he knew he was on his ass on the floor with champagne splashing into his eyes and across his stinging face.

"Oh, my God," the waitress said, on her knees next to him. "I'm so sorry. Are you all right?"

He looked into a pair of emerald green eyes framed by thick dark lashes and felt like he'd been punched again. "Maddie Heller?"

"Burke Callaway?" she asked, the same amazement in her voice.

As he stared into Maddie's face, he didn't know whether his night had just gotten better or a whole lot worse.

Two

—➤➤◄◄◄—

Maddie stood up as two men helped Burke to his feet while several others hustled the man who had punched him out of the club. A busboy came to clear the broken champagne glasses while Pamela, the director of catering, suggested Maddie return to the kitchen and change her wet server's blouse for a dry one.

She was moving in that direction when Emma Callaway intercepted her, a happy, surprised smile on her face. "Maddie Heller? Is it really you? I thought you were living in Europe."

"I was for a while," she said as the always affectionate Emma gave her a quick hug.

While she'd been better friends with Emma's older sister Nicole, she'd gotten to know Emma in high school. Once Nicole had her driver's license, she'd often been tasked with driving her younger siblings around, and Maddie had accompanied Nicole on many of those trips.

"So you're back now," Emma began. "And you're..."

"Working here part-time," she finished.

"What are you doing the rest of the time?"

"Still figuring that out."

"Last I heard you were dating some handsome Italian

restaurateur and living on the Amalfi Coast."

"That was a couple of years ago. It didn't work out."

"Sorry about that."

"Nothing to feel sorry about." She paused as her gaze came to rest on the diamond ring on Emma's left hand. She grabbed Emma's hand and pulled it up to take a better look at the ring. "This is beautiful. You're married?"

"Over a year now. His name is Max. He's a police detective, and we're amazingly happy."

"I'm so glad," she said, thinking Emma looked really happy. There was a sparkle in her eyes and a glow to her skin.

"I should make sure Burke is okay," Emma said, glancing over her shoulder. "Where did he go?"

"I think he left. Who was that man who hit him?"

"A friend of his former fiancée, Leanne Parker. She died a couple of years ago. They were planning their wedding at the time."

"That's so sad," she said, her heart twisting a little for the pain Burke must have gone though.

"It was horrible. Burke has had a rough time since then. He didn't want to come tonight. I guess he should have followed his instincts."

She nodded, then saw her supervisor sending her a pointed look from across the room. "I'm sorry, Emma. I would love to catch up, but I need to get back to work."

"Give me your number," Emma said, pulling out her phone. "Nicole would love to catch up with you."

"Sure, that would be great," she said, giving Emma her number. "I'll see you soon."

She hurried back to the kitchen where her friend Alicia stopped her with a wide-eyed expression of curiosity. "What is going on out there? I heard you got in the middle of a fight."

"Wrong place, wrong time—story of my life." She moved toward the dressing room to change her shirt. She'd hoped that returning to San Francisco would change her luck, but trouble seemed to follow her around. She tossed her damp shirt into the laundry basket and quickly put on another one.

"Do you know why those men were fighting?" Alicia asked.

"I have no idea. It's a memorial celebration, so I guess grief must have had something to do with it."

As she took a quick look in the mirror, she wished now she'd put on a little more makeup, that her blonde hair wasn't pulled back in a tight ponytail and that she wasn't wearing a white shirt, black skirt, black nylons and a pair of really ugly but practical and comfortable black pumps. It would have been nice to show Burke that she was looking better these days. But for some reason she and Burke always seemed to meet up at the oddest times, in the most unusual places.

Not that anything romantic had ever happened between them. Well, almost nothing…

"Who are you primping for?" Alicia asked curiously.

"No one." She quickly turned away from the mirror and made her way back into the dining room.

As she took up her new post at the buffet table, she looked around for Burke, but he was gone, as were the rest of his family members. She felt a wave of disappointment, which was ridiculous. She should be glad Burke was gone. He'd rarely seen her at her best, and she was nowhere near her best right now, so it was just as well he was gone.

Maybe the next time they ran into each other there would be less drama and she'd be wearing better clothes.

—➤➤◄◄—

After ditching his family and friends with assurances that he was fine, Burke went home, changed out of his champagne-drenched shirt and put an ice pack on his rapidly swelling left eye. He was pissed that Mitch had gotten the jump on him. He had five brothers; he knew how to fight, but he hadn't wanted to fight Mitch or ruin the Parkers' memorial or celebration or whatever the hell it was.

He sat down on the couch, tried to watch some television, then opened his computer and read through some of his favorite news sites, but nothing grabbed his attention. He felt restless and distracted, his mind replaying the evening's events, and it wasn't just the sucker punch that had left him feeling unsettled, it was seeing Maddie Heller again.

How crazy was that? He hadn't even known she was in the city. And there she was—right there to break his fall.

He smiled at that thought. He wished he'd had a second to talk to her, but his family had urged a speedy departure, and he'd gone along, thinking it would be good to put some distance between Mitch Warren and himself. He'd thought that situation was resolving, but it seemed to be getting worse. Mitch was completely blind when it came to Leanne's accident. He couldn't seem to see any picture but the one he'd created in his head.

Burke couldn't help wondering what the Parkers thought about their exchange. He really should apologize to Leanne's parents.

That thought ran around his head for another few minutes. Then he jumped up from the couch, grabbed his keys and headed out the door. He could probably catch the end of the party.

Ten minutes later, he pulled up just down the block from the Hanover Club. Now that it was almost nine, the street had cleared out and there were plenty of parking spots. As he got out of his car, he saw a crowd of people come through the front door, including Marjorie and Chuck. The party was obviously over.

He jogged up the hill as Chuck placed the posters of Leanne in the back of his sedan.

Marjorie gave him a surprised look. "Burke. You're back."

"I wanted to apologize. I hope you know that the last thing I would ever want to do is ruin a memorial gathering for Leanne."

"You didn't start it," she said, but there was a hint of uncertainty in her voice. "What was Mitch talking about? Is there something we don't know?"

"Mitch is just stuck in a circle of anger and grief. I wish he could get himself out of it. Leanne wouldn't have wanted him to be so unhappy for so long."

Marjorie slowly nodded, but there were shadows and a little doubt in her eyes, as if she was starting to wonder if Mitch knew something she didn't.

"Anyway, I'm sorry," he said.

"It's not your fault," she replied. "I'm just glad you came. I wasn't sure. You seemed hesitant this year."

"It's a hard day for me," he admitted.

Chuck nodded grimly. "For all of us. We miss our girl."

"I miss her, too."

"Come to dinner one night," Marjorie said. "We'll catch up. It's been too long, Burke."

"I'll do that."

He stepped back as they got into their car. He was about to leave when his phone rang. It was Shelby. "What's up?"

"You sound better than I thought you would. How's the eye?" she asked.

"It's fine. I've taken worse hits in my life."

"I still can't believe Captain Warren hit you. We were shocked. What's between you two anyway?"

"It's a long story. I don't want to talk about it."

"No problem. Listen, Rachel, Dylan and I are at Brady's. Why don't you come over for a drink?"

"Thanks, but I'm going to head home."

"I thought you went home a long time ago," she said, a question in her voice.

"I did, but I came back to the club to speak to Leanne's parents. I wanted to apologize to them."

"You're always so considerate, Burke."

"I'll see you next shift."

"See you then."

He had just slipped his phone into his pocket when he saw some of the wait staff exiting the building. His heart skipped a beat as Maddie waved goodbye to a friend, then headed in his direction. She hadn't seen him yet. She was checking something on her phone, and he liked having a moment to just look at her.

She'd changed into jeans and a pink sweater under a dark blue wool coat. She'd also taken the band out of her hair, letting the long, blonde waves fall over her shoulders and halfway down her back. She'd always had the silkiest hair, even when it had been streaked with red or purple or blue. He'd been tempted to run his fingers through her hair on more than one occasion, but he'd always managed to stop himself, because Maddie Heller was a free spirit, a troublemaker and the kind of girl who could get a guy off track.

He had a feeling she was still that girl.

Maddie looked up, her jaw dropping in surprise when her gaze connected with his.

"Burke. What are you doing here?"

"I came back to apologize to the Parkers. How did the

rest of the event go?"

"There weren't any more fights, so I guess it was a success." She paused. "You have a nasty black eye."

"It looks worse than it is."

She stared back at him, her expression somber. "I'm sorry about your loss, Burke. Emma told me that you were engaged to the woman being honored tonight."

"Yes, I was."

"I guess she was the one you told me about a few years ago, when we ran into each other in Times Square on New Year's Eve."

"I don't remember telling you about her." What he did remember was the shock he'd felt when he'd run into Maddie there. He'd been grumbling about freezing his ass off in a crowd of idiots who thought gathering in a square to watch a ball drop in ten-degree weather was a good idea. And then Maddie had appeared right in front of him with her mischievous smile, her pretty green eyes, and his heart had literally stopped. But they'd barely had a second to talk.

"You said you were seeing someone—that's all," Maddie replied, drawing his attention back to the present. "You didn't mention it was serious or that you were thinking of getting married."

"I didn't know at the time. And it wasn't like we had a real opportunity to talk. The ball was dropping, and you were with someone—a guy with a ponytail."

She grinned. "Jeremy."

"Boyfriend?"

"Not really. Just someone I went out with a few times. He'd always wanted to do Times Square on New Year's Eve, and it was on my list, too, so we went. You were the last person I expected to run into there."

"I was at a family wedding in the city. My cousin Dylan

talked me into going to Times Square."

"That makes sense. I didn't think that was your scene."

"But it was definitely yours. You always liked big parties."

"Most people do. It's strange how we keep running into each other, isn't it? The airport in Los Angeles—I was on my way back to Europe. You were heading to San Francisco—"

"After a fire symposium. I remember. You were practically giddy with excitement about your upcoming trip."

"And you looked tired but happy to be learning new fire prevention strategies."

"Did I say that?" he asked, thinking how boring he must have appeared to her back then.

"You did. We also met up at Nicole's twenty-sixth birthday in Lake Tahoe," she continued. "You came up with Aiden for the dinner."

"And you were there with some guy who had a long name."

"Hal Weatherington the Third," she said with a laugh. "He was not as impressive as his name."

Burke grinned. "And then there was the basement of Viper Club."

"I forgot about that one. I was home for two days and my girlfriend insisted we go hear a hot local band. I didn't know it was your brother's band until we got there. How is Sean?"

"Still playing music, but he also runs a music studio now in the Haight."

"Is he single?"

"No, he's seriously involved with a single mom."

"Good for him." She paused. "I always liked how Sean went after his dream of being a musician."

She would like that because she was as big a dreamer as anyone he'd ever met. "So are you living in San Francisco now?" he asked. "What are you doing?"

"Well, in between breaking up fights with a tray of champagne glasses, I'm waitressing and figuring out my next move."

"You told me you were figuring out your next move the last time I saw you."

"That was four years ago. It's time for another plan. Not everyone has their life planned out from birth. I assume you're still a firefighter?"

"I am," he admitted.

"And you like it as much as you always did?"

"I do."

"And you're still a man of few words," she said with a smile. "I should go. I need to catch the next bus, or I'll have to spring for a cab."

"Where are you headed?"

"Home."

"Which is where?"

"Hayes Valley—temporarily. I'm subletting an apartment for three months until I can put a few paychecks together and—"

"Figure out your next move," he finished.

"Exactly."

"I'll give you a ride home."

"Really?"

"It's not a big deal."

She hesitated, then said, "If you're sure you don't mind, I wouldn't mind giving the bus a pass."

"It's the least I can do after knocking a tray of champagne glasses onto you. I'm just glad you didn't get cut."

"Only wet, and now I have a nice champagne smell to my hair. It's better than my usual shampoo."

He smiled to himself as they made their way to his car.

Maddie always found a way to look at the bright side, and tonight he wouldn't mind if a little of her positive attitude rubbed off on him. It had been a long while since his side had looked even close to bright.

Once they buckled up, he pulled out into traffic and headed across the city to Hayes Valley. With Maddie sitting so close to him, he could smell the champagne clinging to her skin, but there was another scent that he'd always connected to her and that was lavender. "You still wear that perfume," he murmured. "Something with lilacs, right?"

She gave him a surprised look. "You remember my perfume?"

"I remember that you doused yourself in it, and I had to open the windows in my car when I gave you a ride home after tutoring you in algebra."

"I was a little too liberal with the perfume back then. Lavender is a calming scent, and I was looking for some calm."

"Seriously?" He gave her a quick glance. "I thought you were always looking for trouble. What did they used to say about you—Maddie Heller likes to raise hell?"

She groaned. "I can't believe you remember that, too. Don't you forget anything?"

There were a lot of things he wanted to forget, but he couldn't.

"I didn't like to raise hell," she added defensively. "I was just looking for adventure, excitement—that's what life is all about, isn't it?"

"I suppose."

"Tell me about your family. What's up with the Callaways?"

"We would need a much longer ride for me to cover everyone in the family."

"So give me the highlights. I saw Emma at the party. She said she's married to a police detective now. What about Nicole? Are she and Ryan still together? I think I heard something about their little boy being sick."

"Brandon is autistic but there's been some improvement in the past year. Nicole and Ryan went through some difficult times, but they're stronger than ever now."

"I'm glad. I always liked them together. What about Drew? Is he still in the Navy?"

"No, he flies helicopters for the Coast Guard now. He recently got married, and his wife's eighteen-year-old niece lives with them when she's not at college."

And Aiden?"

"He married the girl next door, Sara Peterson."

"Really? Sara? I wouldn't have put the two of them together."

"They complement each other. They have a little girl named Chloe."

"Is Aiden still a firefighter?"

"He quit smokejumping when he met Sara. He'd been injured on the job, so it was a good time to try something else. He's working in construction for my Uncle Kevin now, and he got his contractor's license a few months ago."

"What about the twins, Shayla and Colton?"

"Shayla is a doctor and Colton is a firefighter, both also romantically involved."

"Wait, are you telling me that you're the only unattached Callaway?" she asked.

He sighed at the question. It wasn't the first time someone had reminded him of that fact. "It looks that way. What about you? Anyone in your life?"

She let out a little sigh. "There was someone, but not anymore."

"What happened?"

"Maybe I'll tell you sometime, but that's my building," she said, pointing to the three-story building on the corner. "You can just drop me off."

"There's a parking spot. I'll walk you in."

"I can make it upstairs by myself."

"I'm sure you can, but I'll come with you just the same."

"Suit yourself."

As they got out of the car, he looked around and said, "This is a nice neighborhood."

"It is. I've only been here three weeks, but everyone seems friendly. I got lucky finding such a deal. The person I'm renting from had to go to work in Australia for three months and needed a subletter on short notice. Luckily, I saw the ad online and was able to snag it before anyone else beat me out. It's hard to find housing in the city."

"Is it? I haven't looked in a while."

She opened the gate and led the way up the stairs to the second floor. "Where do you live?"

"Russian Hill."

She paused. "That's on the other side of town. I thought you said you were coming this way."

He shrugged. "I said it was no big deal to give you a ride. I wasn't doing anything."

"Well, thanks again."

"You're welcome."

She led him down the hall, stopping abruptly at the sight of a yellow piece of paper taped to her door with two large words written across the top: *Eviction Notice*. "What is this?" she asked in shock.

"It looks like you're being evicted."

"That's impossible. I paid first and last month's rent when I moved in." She grabbed the padlock on the door and stared at it. "I can't believe it. I'm locked out."

"Who did you pay rent to?"

"The person who sublet me the apartment."

"Not this guy, Hector Ortiz?" he asked, reading the name on the notice.

"No, I've never heard of Hector Ortiz."

"He appears to be your landlord. You need to call him."

"I know I need to call him," she muttered in frustration, pulling out her phone. "I cannot believe this is happening." She punched in the number on the notice, then waited. "Voicemail. Dammit." She tapped her foot impatiently, then said. "This is Maddie Heller. I am subletting the apartment at two-twenty-seven Robinson and I've paid rent to Carter Hillyard. I need to get into my apartment. Call me back as soon as possible so we can straighten this out." She left her number, then ended the call. "Well," she said, letting out a breath.

He waited for her to continue, but for a woman who usually didn't run out of ideas, she didn't seem to have an immediate plan of action. Instead, she looked shocked and tired.

A voice inside his head reminded him that this was typical Maddie. She was always getting herself into situations that seemed to take her by surprise. But she should have grown up by now. She should have a better handle on her life.

On the other hand, it didn't appear that she had done anything really wrong, except perhaps to trust the wrong person.

"Do you want me to drop you off at a hotel?" he asked.

"Um, maybe a motel." She pulled her wallet out of her bag and checked her cash. "A cheap motel."

"Don't you have a credit card?"

She shook her head. "I lost those with the last boyfriend."

She frowned and waved her finger at him. "And don't give me that judgmental Burke Callaway look. You have no idea what I've been through."

"I wasn't judging, Maddie." Although maybe he had been doing that—a little. "What about your parents? Do they still live in the city?"

"No, they moved to Portola Valley about ten years ago. They're out of town until Tuesday, and their house is being remodeled while they're gone."

"Friends?"

"I've only been back in town a few weeks; I haven't reconnected with my old friends. There is one woman I know. She was going to her boyfriend's house tonight, but I guess I could call her."

"I have a couch." The words came out of his mouth before he could stop them. "It's not super comfortable, but you can have it if you want. And it's free."

She stared back at him with nothing but doubt in her eyes. "Really?"

"You don't seem to have many options, Maddie."

"You're right, I don't. So I accept, but I'll pay you back, Burke."

"No pay back necessary. I've seen your wallet."

"I can do something else for you. I'll cook for you one night."

"Would that be on a camp stove under a freeway overpass?"

She raised an eyebrow. "Wow, Burke Callaway cracks a joke. Back in high school, I never thought that would happen. I will get my living situation straightened out. I know I'm not coming across really well right now, but I can take care of myself—most days. I've just had some surprisingly bad luck in the last year."

"Don't worry about it," he said as they returned to his car.

He actually liked the idea of having Maddie on his couch. Ever since he'd collided with Maddie at the party, he'd felt charged up and more interested in what tomorrow might bring than he had in a very long time.

Three

Going home with Burke Callaway was probably a bad idea, but Maddie needed time to regroup and figure out what to do next. She was still reeling in shock at the eviction notice. There had to be some mistake. Carter Hillyard seemed like such an honest person. And she had paperwork—somewhere—although she hadn't really read through the contract. She needed to do that. Unfortunately, their agreement was in the apartment behind the padlock.

Sighing, she couldn't believe the mess she'd gotten herself into. She seemed to be making a lot of bad decisions lately, and they almost always involved trusting the wrong people. And those wrong people were usually men.

She was trusting Burke now, and that might be another mistake, but she didn't think so. Burke had always been honest, straightforward and responsible—the perfect guy.

He'd also always been the one man who could make her blood run hot with one look, and that look didn't even have to include a smile—which it usually didn't.

In high school, she'd been an annoyance to Burke, and on the few occasions they'd met since then, there had been an odd tension between them. They weren't really friends. They weren't really anything, except two people who used to know each other.

If she hadn't been so desperate, she would have tried to make another arrangement, but it was just one night. Tomorrow, she'd get back on track.

After parking in the underground garage, Burke ushered her into his apartment building. His place was a short walk up the stairs to the second floor. The building was definitely well-maintained, with plush carpeting in the halls and freshly painted walls.

As she stepped into Burke's home, she was expecting neat and organized, maybe a rather sterile environment, but that was not what she found. Instead, she was immediately charmed by sleek hardwood floors covered by colorful area rugs and warm lighting from carved wooden lamps that sat on either side of the oversized dark blue couch with an assortment of fluffy pillows. There was a comfortable armchair adjacent to the couch, two bookshelves filled with books and a large flat-screen TV taking up most of one wall.

The adjacent kitchen had a small breakfast nook with a round oak table upon which sat a coffee mug and a newspaper. A bike hung on the wall in the wide hallway leading to the bedrooms, reminding her that Burke had not just been super smart, he'd also been an athlete.

"My bedroom is at the back," Burke said. "The second bedroom is, unfortunately, an office/storage room at the moment."

"It's fine. I don't mind the couch. I'm happy to have anywhere to sleep tonight." She frowned. "Why is it you're the one around when I'm at my worst?" she wondered, realizing too late she'd said the words aloud.

"I've asked myself that same question," he said lightly, meeting her gaze.

"I did pay my rent. I'm not a deadbeat."

"You already told me that."

"I'm not sure you believe me. You've never had a high opinion of me."

He cocked his head to the right, giving her a speculative look. "Why would you think that?"

"You've been fairly vocal at times. You told me once I was lazy."

"That was in reference to your study habits. I was trying to teach you algebra at the time, and you never had your assignments ready when we got together."

"I hated math," she said defensively.

"You hated a lot of things, but you did love to break rules. Do you know that I spent only one day in detention during all my years in school? And that one day I spent in detention was the first day I was assigned to tutor you."

"It was not my fault we were late getting back from lunch. There was traffic."

"But you're the one who talked me into going off campus. You're the one who said you weren't going to do your tutoring session if we didn't get burgers from Caldwell's first. You didn't think you could do equations without a chili burger first."

She smiled at the memory. "Those were really good burgers. And you didn't have to agree to go."

"You threatened to get me fired, and I needed the cash. Your parents paid well."

"I'm sure I didn't actually threaten you," she protested, although that did sound a little like her.

"It was implied. Anyway…make yourself comfortable. Do you want something to drink?"

She was thrilled with the change of subject. "What do you have?" she asked following him into the kitchen.

"Beer, cola, water, orange juice," he said, looking into his fridge.

"I'll take some juice."

As Burke took out the carton and poured two glasses of juice, she couldn't help thinking how attractive he was, even with a swollen eye and a dark purple bruise along his jaw. In fact, he looked even sexier, which hardly seemed possible, considering Burke had always been one of the most good-looking guys she'd ever met. His dark hair and blue eyes were a striking combination, not to mention the broad shoulders and athletic build. Add in a confident, sometimes cocky, attitude, and Burke was not a man who would ever be ignored.

He'd been the leader of everything in high school—the student body president, the star athlete, the straight-A student. It was crazy how he was so good at everything—except maybe having fun. He'd always been a little too serious, a little too focused, for her taste. She'd pushed him sometimes just to see if she could get him to loosen up. She'd never really been successful.

Burke handed her the juice. "Sorry I don't have any vodka to add to that."

"I haven't drunk vodka since my twenty-first birthday."

"I'm guessing there's a story behind that statement."

"Let's just say it was a memorable birthday."

"So you actually remember it?"

She smiled. "I do. It was at the Eiffel Tower in Paris." She leaned against the counter. "I studied abroad my senior year of college. I went to the Tower with a bunch of friends just before midnight and toasted my birthday with way too many drinks. It was magical."

"Vodka makes a lot of things magical."

"Not that night. The magic came from the lights, the fact

that I was in Paris, exactly where I was supposed to be."

"You always wanted to be in Paris on your twenty-first birthday?"

She nodded, thinking back to all the conversations she'd had with her sister about the perfect place for them to turn twenty-one.

"It was a dream Dani and I had when we were little girls. When I had a chance to get into a study abroad program that would put me in Paris on my birthday, I jumped at it." She finished her juice, thinking that the only thing wrong with that night had been the fact that her twin sister had died long before that birthday.

"Are you okay?" Burke asked, a somber note in his eyes. "I'm sorry if bringing up your birthday made you think about your sister—"

"It's fine," she said, cutting off his apology. "I like to talk about Dani, but it's been a long day, and I'm tired." She set her glass down on the counter.

"I'll get you a pillow and some blankets."

"Thanks." She went back into the living room while Burke disappeared down the hall. She sat on the couch and took off her coat, then pulled off her boots and set them by the coffee table as Burke returned with a pillow and two blankets.

"You should be warm enough, but if you want to turn up the heat, the thermostat is right over there," he said, pointing to the far wall.

"I really appreciate this, Burke. Tomorrow I'll get out of your hair."

He sat down in the armchair next to the couch. "So what do you think your next move will be?"

"Call my landlord again in the morning, try to reach Carter Hillyard. I'm guessing that won't be easy."

"He probably used your money to get out of town, Maddie."

"He seemed like a nice man. He dressed like an executive. I never imagined he wasn't paying his rent. But I'll figure things out. I'll bounce back. I always do."

"I'm sure your parents would help."

"I'm sure they would, but I don't like to worry them. I'm getting a paycheck from a catering job I did last month. It should clear my account by tomorrow, so I can find another place to stay."

He frowned. "Why are you so broke, Maddie? What happened to all your money?"

"It's a long story."

"You said that before, but we seem to have time."

She hesitated, knowing that her story would not improve Burke's opinion of her, but he seemed determined to understand her circumstances.

"I moved to Las Vegas a year ago to take a job as a line cook at a casino restaurant. Vegas was one of the last places on my list of cities to see. I met a great guy the first week I was there."

"Of course," he said dryly. "Isn't there always a guy in your life?"

She made a face at him. "There haven't been that many men. At any rate, Paul was athletic, funny and great with kids. He ran an indoor rock-climbing center. We had a whirlwind romance. Two months into it, he told me he was ready to get married and have a family and when he asked me if I was ready, too, I found myself saying yes."

"After two months?"

"I'd been traveling for almost ten years. It was time to settle down somewhere. We moved in together and opened a joint checking account. That was a big mistake."

"He cleaned you out."

"Yes. I didn't realize that Paul had a gambling addiction. But after we'd been living together for three months, he'd run up all my credit cards and cleaned out my bank account. I broke off the engagement as soon as I realized what was happening, but that didn't end my problems."

"Why not?"

"Paul had gotten himself into trouble with a loan shark whose goons showed up at my work. They told me they were going to get the money from someone. If they couldn't get the cash from him, it would be from me. I told them we weren't together anymore and there wasn't any money. They didn't believe me. For the next few weeks, I found myself always looking over my shoulder. I couldn't shake the feeling that I was in danger, so I quit my job and came back to San Francisco three weeks ago." She paused. "I thought I was putting my troubles behind me. I never expected to get taken again. I really need to figure out a way to read people better."

"I'm sorry, Maddie."

She saw the pity in his eyes and disliked it almost as much as the judgmental glint that often turned his gaze to blue steel. One day she would like to see something else in his eyes—maybe a little respect. "I'm going to be fine," she said, wishing she felt as hopeful as she sounded, but even her optimistic outlook on life had taken a beating the past year. "If you're not making mistakes, you're not trying hard enough, right?"

"Who told you that?"

"I don't know. I heard it somewhere. It made me feel better." She took a breath and decided to change the subject. "What about you? Any women in your life since Leanne?"

"No one serious." A shadow passed across his face, then he stood up. "I'm going to let you settle in. Do you need anything else?"

Apparently, their conversation was over. Just as well. She'd already told him way too much about herself. "Maybe a T-shirt?" she asked tentatively.

He hesitated. "Yeah, sure. I'll get you one of my shirts. Hang on."

As he disappeared down the hall, she took a deep breath, wondering why her pulse was suddenly beating so fast and why the idea of sleeping in Burke's T-shirt was making her feel very hot.

She got to her feet as Burke came back into the room with a T-shirt and a new toothbrush.

"Here you go."

"Thanks," she said, taking the items out of his hand.

He looked at her like he wanted to say something.

"What?" she asked.

His blue gaze darkened. "What you said earlier, you were wrong."

"About what?"

"That I didn't have a high opinion of you. It's true that I thought you were crazy a lot of the time, and a little self-destructive, but I also admired you."

Her stomach did a somersault at his unexpected words. "What did you admire about me?"

He thought for a moment. "You were never afraid to fail, so you'd try anything. You were fearless, Maddie. If you did fail, you just got up and moved on—like you're doing now. You have an incredible spirit. The man you were engaged to might have taken a lot from you, but he didn't take that." He gave her a warm smile. "Good night, Maddie."

"Goodnight," she murmured, a little shocked at his words.

She sank down on the couch, her arms wrapped around

his T-shirt, amazed by what Burke had just said. She wished she felt as resilient as he'd just suggested. The truth was she'd been running on empty for a while, and she was tired of failing, tired of having to get back up again, but now there was no way she could give up. Not with Burke watching.

So tomorrow she would start over—again.

After a restless night of intense dreams that all seemed to star a handsome blue-eyed firefighter wearing the same navy blue SFFD T-shirt that hugged her bare breasts, Maddie woke up a little after seven feeling restless, tingly and annoyed with herself all at the same time. She hadn't dreamt about Burke since—well, since the last time she'd seen him in Times Square.

She'd gone to bed that night wishing it were Burke who had kissed her at midnight instead of the man she'd been with. But Burke had never kissed her.

Over the years there had been a couple of moments between them, a sizzling electric charge, a feeling that they were very, very close to falling into each other's arms, but it had never actually happened. They'd always said goodbye. And then years would pass before they saw each other again.

Only, this time was different. She wasn't leaving San Francisco anytime soon. But she would be leaving Burke's apartment, she told herself. And she probably wouldn't be hanging out with Burke after today.

Getting up, she used the bathroom in the hall to wash her face, brush her hair and change out of Burke's T-shirt, then she returned to the living room, folded up the blanket and tucked the pillow underneath it.

Grabbing her phone, she called her landlord's number

again; it went to voicemail. She left another pleading message for him to return her call as soon as possible so she could straighten out her rental situation. She also called the number she had for Carter Hillyard, but it had been disconnected, which wasn't surprising.

Sighing, she set down her phone and debated her options. She needed to get to the bank and see if she could get her last deposit to clear, but she couldn't do that until nine. Maybe she'd make breakfast.

When she entered the kitchen, she felt immediately better. This was the one room where she always knew what to do and how to do it. Cooking had always been her therapy, her passion, her escape. It had been that way since she'd made her first batch of oatmeal raisin cookies after her sister got sick.

She opened up Burke's refrigerator and was happy to find eggs, bacon and vegetables. Within minutes, the air was sizzling with the delicious smell of coffee brewing and onions sautéing. She worked with quiet efficiency, enjoying every moment, slicing and chopping vegetables with a joy that reminded her that this was the place she needed to get back to.

She just had to find a way to get back into a kitchen and get paid to cook. While she would always cook for the love of it, she needed to live, to pay bills, to get her own place and to rebuild her life.

She would figure out how to do all that—just as soon as she finished cooking breakfast.

For a moment Burke thought he was back home in his parents' house, the smell of bacon tempting him out of sleep.

As he blinked his eyes open, he realized he was in his apartment, in his bed, and the person cooking had to be Maddie.

He rolled over onto his back and stared at the ceiling. He hadn't slept much the night before. He'd been thinking far too much about Maddie, about their past, the girl she'd been and the woman she appeared to be now. However, the Maddie of today was as much of a puzzle as the Maddie of yesterday.

How did a smart woman not only get involved with a deadbeat boyfriend but also a fraudulent rental deal? Was she naïve or too trusting? Did she act too impulsively? She was smart, but sometimes she didn't weigh out the consequences before she acted. Whatever the reason, she'd certainly ended up in a mess.

She'd owned up to her mistakes, though. He liked that she hadn't offered excuses or been defensive.

That's the way she'd always been. She'd loved breaking the rules, but if she got caught, she took responsibility for her actions.

Of course, she'd have an easier time in life if she stopped breaking rules and making mistakes, but maybe she'd been right when she'd said if you weren't making mistakes, you weren't really living.

He rarely broke a rule and he rarely made a mistake. He'd thought that was a good thing, but sometimes he wondered what he was missing by keeping such tight control over his life.

Still, he preferred rules and structure to chaos, which made him Maddie's opposite. She loved chaos. Or maybe it was chaos that liked her, he thought with a smile.

Who wouldn't like Maddie?

She was beautiful, had a quick wit, a positive attitude, a friendly, warm smile. God knew that smile did amazing things to his body every time she turned it on him. He'd found it an annoyance in high school, because he didn't want to be tempted to do anything that didn't jibe with his plans for his life.

Since high school, on the few occasions that they'd run into each other, Maddie's smile had always given him an odd sense of regret, as if he'd missed out on something while they'd been apart. That was crazy, because they'd been apart more than they'd ever been together. They were barely friends. And it had been years since high school. They were both in their thirties now. They'd lived separate and very different lives.

But he couldn't help thinking that for the first time in fifteen years they were both in the same place and both single at the same time. Not that that meant anything. He wasn't going to date Maddie. She hadn't been right for him as a teenager, and she wasn't right for him now. They were opposites, and while opposites might attract, they didn't last. In the end, they would drive each other crazy.

Still, he couldn't help thinking it might be fun for a while.

Hell, he knew it would be fun for a while. But then what?

A knock came at his door, and he jolted into a sitting position, his pulse taking a crazy leap. He'd been hoping for a knock ever since he'd said good-night, thinking that maybe, just maybe, the free-spirited Maddie would suggest they share his bed. But that hadn't happened—until now.

Four

—➤➤◀◀◀—

"Burke?" Maddie called. "Are you awake? I made breakfast."

He cleared his throat. "Yeah, I'll be right out."

"No hurry, but I thought if you're hungry, you might want to eat while it's hot."

"I'll be right there." Okay, so she was offering breakfast and nothing else. He'd take it.

He scrambled out of bed, threw on some sweats, and went out to see what Maddie had cooked up for him.

As he sat down at his kitchen table, in front of the most beautiful plate of eggs he'd ever seen, he was once again surprised. He had not anticipated an omelet stuffed with red peppers, mushrooms, onions, and spinach. Crisp bacon was layered across a piece of sourdough toast, and chunks of oranges, apples and strawberries made up a bright bowl of enticing fruit.

"This is amazing. Did you go to the store?"

"No, I just raided your refrigerator." She sat down adjacent to him. "I was thrilled to see you had vegetables."

"I try to eat healthy, but the vegetables usually go bad before I have a chance to cook them. And if I had cooked them, I definitely would not have come up with this."

"It's just eggs," she said lightly, but there was a gleam of pride in her pretty green eyes.

"They're really good," he murmured swallowing his first bite. "I haven't had more than cereal for breakfast in a while."

"Not even at the firehouse?"

"Unfortunately, our best cook got transferred about three months ago. Since then we have not been eating very well."

"You should make cooking part of your hiring requirements."

"Believe me, that's been discussed before."

"Tell me about your job. Have you been involved in any really scary fires?"

"A few, but I don't go inside the way I used to. I'm a battalion chief now, so I'm usually working the fire from the outside."

She nodded, a knowing gleam in her eyes. "I'm not surprised you're in charge, but I would have thought that battalion chiefs were older."

"I am one of the younger ones, but I worked hard to get my position. It wasn't because I'm a Callaway."

She raised an eyebrow. "I never thought that for a second, Burke. You've always held yourself to high standards. Even as a teenager, you were not susceptible to peer pressure. You knew who you were, and you didn't give a damn what anyone else thought about you."

"I don't think you cared very much about what other people thought of you, either, Maddie. You changed your hair color every week. You wore crazy clothes to school. Hell, you dyed the mashed potatoes in the school cafeteria pink."

She laughed. "I totally forgot about that. It was a Valentine's Day special. I figured not everyone was going to find candy hearts, carnations or valentines in their locker, so it was my love letter to the nerdy kids, the wallflowers, the people like me who didn't fit in."

He didn't think she'd fit into any of those categories, either. She hadn't been a nerd or a wallflower, but she had definitely been one of a kind.

"I got in trouble for those pink mashed potatoes," she added. "I was barred from the kitchen after that, and I had to do detention for two weeks."

"So was it worth it?"

She grinned. "Totally worth it."

"You definitely marched to your own beat, Maddie," he said, popping a piece of toast into his mouth.

"I was actually trying to find my beat. After Dani died, I was lost. Being twins, we were super close. We'd shared literally every moment of our lives together. When she wasn't there anymore, I felt like half of me was missing."

"When did your sister get sick?" He knew a little about Dani's story since the Hellers had belonged to their church, but he didn't remember the details. He hadn't gotten to know Maddie until after her sister died.

"She was eleven when they discovered she had leukemia. She fought really hard for three long years, but it got her in the end. It's a horrible disease. Dani suffered so much, but she had an incredible spirit. She'd never get down for too long, which made it easier for us, for me especially. I used to feel guilty when I'd go to see her and she'd end up making me feel better. I was supposed to be the one cheering her up."

"I'm sure you did."

"She was an amazing person. I wish you could have known her."

He saw the moisture in her eyes, and he put his hand over hers. "You don't have to talk about her."

"No, it's fine. I like to talk about her," she said, squeezing his fingers. "And these days there are not many people in my life who even know I had a sister."

"It sounds like you and Dani were a lot alike," he murmured, thinking how right it felt to have her hand in his.

"In some ways, but not in others. Dani was more responsible than me. She was a little more like you. She liked to plan things out. During her chemo treatments, she would work on what she called her *scrapbook of dreams*. It was a really pretty bucket list, and it was filled with all the things she would do when she got better, when she got older. She'd put in pictures, blogs about places she wanted to see, recipes of things she wanted to cook. She had a whole timeline planned out. We used to spend hours dreaming up adventures, thinking about what the future would hold, what we wanted to do with our lives."

"What did Dani want to be?"

"She wanted to be a nurse. She wanted to take care of kids who were sick like her. It's too bad she never got that chance, because I think she would have helped a lot of people." Maddie paused. "When Dani died, it didn't feel real, and going out into the world was somewhat terrifying. For months, we'd been so isolated in Dani's illness that the outside world barely existed. I was behind in school, because I'd missed so many days, and when I had gone to school, I hadn't cared about learning anything. I just wanted to finish the day so I could get back to Dani. I was angry at anything that took me away from her, and after she passed away, I was angry with the whole damn universe."

He was beginning to understand what had driven Maddie through her rebellious high school years.

"In the end, Dani was the one who pulled me out of the dark sea of grief I was drowning in," Maddie said.

"How did she do that?"

"It was spring of my freshman year. We were being forced to go to all those seminars about planning for college. At the time, the last thing I wanted to worry about was college. One night my dad came into my room with Dani's scrapbook of dreams. He insisted that I open it. I hadn't looked at it since Dani died, and I didn't want to look at it then, but my father was more determined than I'd ever seen him. I told him that the book was filled with her dreams, but he reminded me that my dreams were in that book, too."

She took a breath, then continued. "Dani and I had planned a lot of our adventures together, and one of the first ones was to go to college. At first, Dani wanted to go back East, to an Ivy League school, but as she got sicker, she was always cold. She wanted sun and heat, so we started looking at universities in southern California. San Diego State was perfect—a school by the beach with plenty of sun and lots of parties." She smiled at Burke. "Suddenly, I had a goal. I started studying a little harder. I agreed to let my parents hire a tutor so I could get through algebra."

He smiled. "You might have agreed, but you weren't on board right away."

"I was still fighting against fulfilling dreams that Dani couldn't fulfill, but eventually I gave in and started to embrace my new plan. I would graduate. I would go to San Diego State. I would join a sorority, date a cute boy, play volleyball on the beach and go skinny dipping in the sea."

"You went skinny dipping?" he asked, his brain caught on the sudden image of Maddie running into the sea, her long blonde hair dripping down her naked back.

"I did everything we'd talked about. I had a great four years there. It was like Dani was guiding my way. She was with me on every adventure. It was fun."

"I don't doubt that."

"But I have to say that some of her bucket list ideas were a little out there. I almost didn't do a couple of them."

"Like what?"

"Like zip lining across a Costa Rican jungle. That was pretty terrifying."

"But you did it."

"I screamed the whole way."

"And then you wanted to do it again."

She laughed, letting go of his hand as she sat back in her seat. He found himself immediately missing the warmth of her touch.

"You're so right. I did want to do it again. It was exhilarating. Have you ever zip lined?"

"I did it in Hawaii one summer, but it was a tourist attraction and very safe."

"Well, you probably don't need a zip line to get your heart beating, not with the kind of job you do, or used to do."

"True."

"Does your pulse leap every time the alarm goes off? Or are you used to it by now?"

"You never get used to it. There is always that moment of excitement and trepidation. When we first arrive on the scene, we never know what we're going to find, what kind of fire we'll encounter, if there will be victims, obstacles, chemicals."

She shook her head, admiration and amazement in her eyes. "I don't know how you do what you do. You run into a situation where everyone else is running out. That takes tremendous courage."

"I suppose." The truth was he hadn't felt that brave in a long time. Maybe it came from being the one to stand outside and send others in. Maybe it was because he'd been in some kind of hibernation since Leanne died. Maybe it was just that

Maddie's free-spirited, adventurous thinking made him feel like he hadn't been living very much at all.

Not that he wanted her life. No way. Living like a gypsy, drifting from job to job, not having money in the bank—all that would make him totally crazy.

Maddie jumped at the sound of her phone. She got up and retrieved it from the kitchen counter. "Hello? Mr. Ortiz? Thank you so much for calling me back. There's been a terrible mistake. I'm subletting the apartment at two-twenty-seven Robinson, number six." She paused. "Well, I didn't know that the tenant wasn't allowed to sublet the apartment. I paid him to stay there."

As she took a breath, Burke could hear Hector Ortiz rambling in a mix of rapid English and Spanish.

"Look, I need to get into the apartment and get my things," she said. "You can't just lock me out." She blew out a breath. "Okay, thank you. I'll be there in an hour." She set down the phone. "He said I can get my stuff, but I can't stay there, because I didn't sign a rental contract, and he had no knowledge of the sublet. That was apparently illegal."

"At least you'll be able to get your things."

"I need to meet him in an hour. I'll clean this up, and—"

"I'll give you a ride," he finished.

"I want to say no because it's really an imposition," she said, a frown on her face. "But I don't have a car, and it's going to be difficult to take my things on the bus."

"It's fine, Maddie. I don't mind helping you."

"You don't have to work?"

"I'm off until tomorrow." As he finished speaking, his doorbell rang. He was startled. Rarely did anyone drop by without calling first and rarely did anyone get through the secured front door without having to buzz first. He got up from the table and opened the door.

Shelby greeted him with a smile, a coffee and a bag from his favorite bakery. "Good morning. I thought you might like a little breakfast. And I wanted to see how you were feeling. Your eye doesn't look too bad."

"It's better. How did you get into the building?"

"Your neighbor was coming out, so I just came up. I hope that's okay."

"Sure."

Shelby moved past him, then stopped abruptly when she saw Maddie. "Oh, I'm sorry. I didn't know you had company."

"This is Maddie Heller."

"Hi," Maddie said, coming forward with a friendly smile. "And you're not interrupting. I'm a friend of Burke's from high school."

"Really?" Shelby said, giving Maddie a speculative look.

"It's a long story, but I got locked out of my apartment," Maddie explained. "Burke let me crash on his couch." She glanced at Burke. "I'm just going to clean up the kitchen."

"You can leave it. I'll take care of it later."

"It's the least I can do."

Shelby turned her gaze on him as Maddie disappeared into the kitchen. "She looks familiar. Has she been at the firehouse?"

"No, but you might have seen her yesterday at the club."

Awareness dawned in Shelby's eyes. "She's the waitress you knocked over. I saw you talking to her, but I didn't realize you knew her."

"I hadn't seen her in years. She was leaving the club last night when I went back to speak to the Parkers, and we got to talking. I gave her a ride home, but there was a problem with her place." He didn't want to embarrass Maddie by getting into the specifics.

"Well, it was nice of you to let her stay here. You've

always been a knight in shining armor."

"I hardly think offering my couch to an old friend qualifies me for knighthood," he said dryly.

Shelby handed him the bakery bag. "I see you already had breakfast, but you might want these later."

"Thanks. I really appreciate your coming by. How was Brady's last night?"

"Same old, same old. What's on your schedule today?"

"I'm going to help Maddie get her living situation straightened out. I might work out later. Nothing big planned. What about you? Are you still seeing that guy you met in Hawaii last month?"

"Not really. The more I see of him, the less exciting he becomes."

"Not a good sign," he said with a commiserating smile. He and Shelby had been exchanging bad date stories for years.

"I'll see you tomorrow at work," she said.

He walked her to the door. "Thanks again, Shelby. You're a good friend."

"I am," Shelby agreed with a smile. "Don't forget that."

"I couldn't," he said with complete sincerity. Since Leanne's death, his entire work family had been there for him with Shelby leading the way.

Shutting the door behind her, he headed down the hall for a quick shower.

❧⚜❧

While Burke got dressed, Maddie quickly cleaned the small kitchen, returning it to the state she'd found it in. As she did so, she couldn't help thinking about the woman she'd just met. Shelby was an attractive woman in her mid-thirties, and she'd made a special trip to Burke's place to bring him coffee and pastries, so she was obviously a good friend, but was she more than a friend?

Shelby had definitely flinched when she'd seen her. That's why Maddie had made a point of telling Shelby that she and Burke were old friends. It had seemed important to reassure the woman. Shelby had certainly looked a lot happier when she'd discovered they were not having breakfast together after a night of sex.

Burke had told her he wasn't seriously involved with anyone, but she couldn't imagine he didn't get a lot of interest. He really was a gorgeous man.

When he'd walked out of his bedroom with his dark hair mussed, his blue eyes hazy with sleep and a sexy growth of beard on his jaw, her hormones had jumped into overdrive. And it was all she could do not to suggest they have breakfast in bed.

She smiled at the foolish thought. Burke would have probably given her one of his trademarked looks of shock and disdain. He wasn't very good at hiding his feelings when it came to things or people he didn't like or didn't respect. And while he might not dislike her, she knew he didn't respect her. Why would he? Every time they were together, she was digging herself out of some mess.

Well, that was going to end today, she told herself firmly. She just needed Burke's help for a little while longer. Then she'd regain control of her life.

After wiping down the stove, she started the dishwasher and returned to the living room, relieved to see Burke fully dressed now—not that he didn't look just as hot in his jeans and V-neck sweater.

"Are you ready?" he asked, grabbing his keys off a side table.

She nodded. "Yes. Do you want the coffee Shelby brought you? It's on the kitchen counter."

"No, thanks, I'm good."

"So is Shelby someone you're seeing?" she asked as they made their way down to the parking garage.

"She works with me. She's a dispatcher. We've known each other for years. She's just a friend."

"Are you sure she doesn't want to be more?"

Burke opened the car door for her. "Why would you ask that?"

"She didn't like seeing me in your place."

"I didn't get that impression."

"Because you're a man and I'm a woman, and I can tell when another woman thinks I'm on her turf."

"You're not on her turf." He shut her door, then walked around to his side of the car. As he buckled his seatbelt, he added, "We're a close-knit group at the firehouse, like family. There's nothing going on between anyone."

"Okay." She wasn't entirely convinced, but it was none of her business.

"Shelby has a big heart. She likes to take care of people."

"Now you sound like you're trying to convince yourself and not me."

He gave her a dark look. "You like to stir things up, Maddie."

"I just made an observation."

"An incorrect one."

"Fine." She dug out her phone as it rang again. The number made her stomach churn.

"What's wrong?" Burke asked.

"It's a Las Vegas area code. I'm afraid it's Paul or one of his loan sharks."

"Only one way to find out."

She was afraid to answer the call and afraid not to. She didn't want to talk to Paul or see him, unless he was going to pay her back the money he'd stolen from her. On the other hand, running away from her problems never made those problems go away.

"Hello?" she said, catching the call before it went to voicemail.

"Thank God," Paul said, relief in his voice.

There was a time when Paul's voice had made her heart leap with excitement. Now she just felt wary of what he would have to say. "What do you want?"

"I'm in trouble, Maddie."

"I already knew that."

"You have to help me."

"With what, Paul? You took everything I had. I have nothing left."

"You could borrow some money from your parents."

She was truly stunned at his request. He'd met her parents once when they'd come to Vegas specifically to meet the man their daughter was going to marry. "Do you really think my parents would want to help you? Are you high? What is wrong with you? You destroyed my life, and they know that."

"I have an addiction, Maddie. It's a disease, but I'm getting help for it. I just want to stay alive long enough to finish the program. I need a couple of thousand, and then I'm free and clear. We'll both be safe."

She hated that he was dumping her into the danger he'd gotten himself into. He was supposed to be the man who was going to love and protect her. What an idiot she'd been.

"Please, just ask your parents for a small loan," he begged. "I promise it will be the last thing I ever ask of you. I'll get back on my feet and I'll make it up to you."

"There's nothing you could ever do to make up for what

you did to me." She drew in a breath for strength and said the words she needed to say. "I can't help you, Paul." She almost added that she was sorry, but she cut herself off. She wasn't sorry; she was determined to move on. "I hope you can find a way to help yourself."

"Maddie, wait," he pleaded. "You're the only one I have left. I know I hurt you, but you have to understand that these guys I owe money to are dangerous. They will come after you. I'm not just protecting myself; I'm trying to protect you."

"I can take care of myself. Don't call me again." She ended the call before he could say anything else. Then she put her phone on silent. Glancing over at Burke, she saw his mouth drawn in a hard line. He must think she was a total loser getting involved with a man like Paul. And she couldn't blame him.

"He wanted more money," Burke said, making it a statement and not a question.

"Yes."

"I'm glad you told him no."

"Even if I'd wanted to help him, I wouldn't have been able to."

"But you didn't want to—did you?"

"No, of course not. That would have been another mistake. I just hope he doesn't try to contact my parents directly."

"Would he go that far?"

"He sounds desperate, and I can understand that. I met two of the guys who were threatening him, and they were terrifying. I have no doubt that they will hurt him if he doesn't come up with money to pay off his debt." She felt a little sick to her stomach at the thought. She was angry with Paul, but she didn't want to see him get hurt.

"You're not responsible for whatever happens to him,

Maddie."

"Logically I know that."

"But you have a soft heart."

"It's getting harder by the minute. Anyway, hopefully he'll find a way to get himself out of trouble."

"I'm not worried about him, but I am concerned about you. Maybe you should ditch that phone and get a new number. Does Paul know where you live?"

"I don't even know where I live right now," she said with a sigh.

"Right. I almost forgot." He squeezed the car into a tight spot down the street from her building. "Your landlord might be willing to work something out with you once he meets you. You can be hard to say no to."

"I'm not sure I have that much charm, but I'll give it a shot."

Five

Hector Ortiz was definitely not impressed by her impassioned plea to rent the apartment from him directly. Two minutes into her speech, he cut her off, saying it was too late. He had another tenant moving in the next week. He just needed her to get her stuff and go so he could clean out the apartment.

Burke also tried to help out by telling Hector what a good person she was, but Hector brushed him aside as well, telling them both they had one hour to move her things before he came back with a cleaning crew.

"That's that," she said to Burke as Hector left them alone. "Thanks for trying to help." She looked around the small apartment, feeling a little flustered and not sure where to start. "I don't know what to do. I don't even have any boxes. I threw them out after I moved in."

"Trash bags should work," he said, moving into the kitchen. "Where do you keep them?"

"There are some in the cupboard under the sink."

He returned a moment later with the box of large plastic bags. "Why don't we start in the bedroom? You can tell me what's yours, and I'll help you pack up."

"Okay." She felt a little relieved to have him take charge. She'd been spinning in a dozen different directions since Paul's treachery had been revealed. She'd been trying to stay positive, to fight back, but losing this apartment was putting her very close to the edge of defeat.

She followed Burke into the bedroom. He stripped the bed while she moved into the closet and transferred her clothes into another bag. Then she moved over to the dresser and emptied that as well.

As she reached the bottom of the first drawer, her hand closed around the two-inch-thick scrapbook that her sister had so lovingly put together so many years ago.

She pulled it out, feeling immensely relieved that she hadn't lost it. Everything else could be replaced, but not this. She pressed the thick book against her heart, feeling an immediate connection to her twin. She could almost hear Dani's voice telling her to suck it up. Things weren't that bad. She could do it. Dani had never had a lot of patience with people feeling sorry for themselves, especially when their problems weren't going to be fatal.

"Is that the book?" Burke asked, coming around the bed.

She nodded and showed him the cover, which featured Dani and herself in one of her favorite pictures. They were about six years old, and they were lying on their stomachs, their heads barely peeking out from under the couch where they loved to hide. They hadn't been identical twins, but they had looked very much alike.

Burke smiled at the picture. "You were both cute."

"I can't believe I almost lost this. If Hector had cleaned out the apartment before I could reach him—"

"He didn't," Burke said quickly.

"But it was close."

"I'm sure you've had close calls before. Just focus on

what did happen and not what didn't happen."

"I'm trying."

"What else do you have to pack?"

"Just some kitchen things," she said, keeping the scrapbook in her arms as they went into the living room.

"What about the furniture?"

"It all belonged to Carter. I rented the place furnished. I don't know why he left it all behind. He must have known that he wasn't coming back here."

"Who knows who he ripped off before you? It might have been someone else's furniture."

"True."

She moved into the kitchen and set down the scrapbook long enough to grab her case of knives and dump her favorite pots and pans and a couple of treasured cookbooks into yet another plastic bag.

"That's it," she said a moment later, taking one last look around the apartment that had only been home for a few weeks.

"Four bags, not bad," Burke said.

For some reason his words made her feel emotional. Her whole life could be put into four garbage bags. How sad was that?

Burke's gaze narrowed on her face. He quickly crossed the room and after a moment's hesitation, he put his arms around her.

She was shocked at his action.

"It's going to be okay, Maddie," he said, patting her back somewhat awkwardly. "You're going to get past this."

She closed her eyes for a second, savoring the feel of his solid body against hers. She'd been independent for so very long...

It felt good to lean on someone, but she couldn't let the

hug go on too long. If she did, she might never want to leave the circle of Burke's arms. And he just felt sorry for her. She didn't want pity to be the reason he was holding her, although what other reason could there be?

She stepped out of his embrace and gave him what she hoped was a confident smile or at least an attempt at one. "Thanks. I'm going to be okay. It was just seeing everything in garbage bags..." She shook her head. "Let's get out of here."

They divided up the bags and then walked back out to Burke's car.

The bags filled up the trunk with the last one going into the back seat. She got into the front seat with Dani's scrapbook on her lap. The book had always given her strength and courage, two things she really needed right now.

A few minutes later, she realized that Burke hadn't asked her where she wanted to go. Which was probably good, since she didn't know where she wanted to go, but it was also bad, because he was heading back to his apartment, and she'd already imposed on him too long.

But where else could she go? Alicia lived with another girl in an apartment no bigger than a shoebox, and her parents wouldn't be back until Tuesday. Which left a motel.

"I need to go to the bank," she said. "If I can get my check cleared, I can go to a motel and get out of your hair."

"I'm happy to take you to the bank, Maddie, but I think you should stay with me for a few days. I'll be moving into the firehouse for forty-eight hours starting tomorrow morning. That will give you a few more days to figure out your next move."

"That's really generous, but I can't just stay at your apartment."

"Why not?" He gave her a challenging look. "Why spend

money you obviously don't have on a motel room when I'm not even going to be in my apartment for two days? You only have to put up with me today, then I'll be gone." He gave her a smile. "Think you could do that?"

"I could probably manage that." She was very tempted to take him up on his offer. "Why are you being so nice to me?"

"I'm a nice person. You just never saw that side of me before."

She was beginning to think there were a lot of sides to Burke that she hadn't seen before.

"What you said before about me judging you—you judged me, too, Maddie," Burke added a moment later. "Back in high school."

"I did?"

"You know you did. Maybe we both want a second chance to be seen for who we really are."

She couldn't imagine why he would care what she thought, but she was a little touched that he did. "Okay, I'll stay at your place, but I do want to go to the bank if you don't mind. It shouldn't take too long."

"No problem. Which one?"

"The Wells Fargo at Broadway and Fillmore."

"Got it."

As they drove across town, another idea began to form in her mind. Burke was being so generous, she wanted to do something for him in return. "What are you doing the rest of the day?" she asked.

"I don't have any specific plans. Why?"

"My parents gave me a gift certificate for my birthday, and I haven't had a chance to use it yet."

He stopped the car at a light and glanced over at her with a wary look in his eyes. "What's it for?"

"It's a certificate for an adventure, for two people. Want

to go with me?"

"You're going to have to give me more details."

"It will be more fun if you're surprised." Actually, she thought he'd be more likely to go if she didn't tell him exactly what they were going to do. "It's one of the few things on Dani's bucket list that I haven't had a chance to do yet."

He hesitated, then gave a nod. "Why not? I'll go."

"Great. It's the perfect day for it. And if I can get my money to be released, I'll even buy you lunch."

--->>>-<<<--

Burke waited in the car while Maddie entered the bank, wanting to give her a little privacy for what would probably involve more pleading on Maddie's part. He hated to see her in such dire financial straits. But he also could see that she was trying very hard to make the best of a bad situation. He wished he could get his hands on her ex-fiancé, though. He'd like to give him a little pain for everything he was putting Maddie through.

He really hoped that Maddie was far enough from her ex's reach to be safe. While he didn't doubt that Paul had been playing up the danger to get help from Maddie, he knew it wasn't that big of a leap for someone to try to get Paul's former fiancée to pay off his debts.

His phone rang, and his sister Nicole's number flashed across the screen. "Nic, what's up?"

"I heard you got into a fight at Leanne's memorial last night."

"It wasn't much of a fight. It was over with one punch, and unfortunately I was on the receiving end of that."

"Emma said you didn't try to hit back."

"I'd like to say that was because I was exercising self-control, but I didn't have a chance to hit back. I got tangled up with a waitress and a tray of champagne glasses."

"I heard that, too. I can't believe you literally ran into Maddie Heller. How is she? Emma gave me her number, but I haven't had a chance to call her yet."

"You should call her." He thought Maddie could probably use another friend these days. "I'm sure she'd like to hear from you."

"We were good friends in high school, but that was a long time ago. We lost touch after that. We went to different colleges. I got married, had Brandon, and from what I know Maddie went off and had adventures all over the world."

"Well, she's back in town now." He didn't tell his sister that Maddie had spent the night at his apartment. The last thing he wanted was to get his sisters into his business. He saw Maddie coming out of the bank and added, "I have to get going, Nicole."

"Before you go," Nicole interrupted, "I'm trying to get a head count for tonight, and you haven't responded. You are not going to try to tell me that you're not coming to Mom's birthday party, are you? We specifically picked this day because no one was working."

He inwardly groaned. He'd forgotten about his mom's birthday. "I'll stop by," he quickly promised.

"Good. You know you can bring a date if you want."

"I'll see you later." He hung up before Nicole could start suggesting possible dates for him to bring. She and Emma had been trying to set him up the past year, and while he appreciated their intent, he could find his own woman—when he wanted to, when he was ready.

As Maddie slid into the seat next to him and flashed him a triumphant smile, he had a feeling he'd passed *ready* about twelve hours ago.

He might be ready for a woman, but he wasn't at all ready for what Maddie had in mind. He'd never been a fearful person. While he wasn't as impulsive as Maddie, he took risks. He ran into burning buildings. He dove into dangerous waters. He scaled tall buildings, but there was something about the massive black horse with the proud stance and the suspicious eyes that made him more than a little uncomfortable.

"What's wrong?" Maddie asked, coming up next to him.

"We're going riding?"

"That's right."

He looked around the stables, seeing two long barns filled with horses, but no designated riding area. "I don't see a ring."

"Well, that wouldn't be much fun would it? Just going around and around in circles? We're going to ride on the beach, watch the waves breaking over the rocks. It will be great."

"Yeah, sure—great." He tried not to let her see how much he didn't want to get on that horse.

Her narrowed, thoughtful gaze told him he wasn't succeeding.

"You're not afraid of horses, are you?" she asked.

"I wouldn't say I've ever had an opinion, one way or the other."

"So you've never been riding before?"

"When I was seven I rode a pony at the pumpkin festival. It went around in a small circle."

"Well, this is going to be a little different," she said with a laugh. "You're going to love it. Dani and I shared a horse when we were little. Her name was Lulu. She was the sweetest thing. She lived in the barn at my grandparents' property in Portola Valley, where my parents live now. We loved riding her, but we never got to leave the property. We always thought it would be fun to ride on the beach, feel the wind in our hair, taste the salt on our lips and feel as free as a bird. Unfortunately, Dani got sick and never made it to the beach. But it was on her bucket list. Today, I get to make that dream come true."

He was beginning to realize just how strong of an influence Dani had had on Maddie's life. "I'm surprised you haven't done it before now."

"Me, too. I've done pretty much everything else." She paused. "You know, I don't usually talk about Dani this much. I think it's because I'm in a stressful place. That's when the memories come back. Anyway, if you don't want to ride with me, you don't have to. I can do it another time."

"No, I'm good to go." He could see the need in her eyes to escape from reality for a little while, and he wanted to make that happen for her.

Relief moved through her eyes. "Great. We'll get you a good horse, I promise."

"Not that one." He tipped his head to the black stallion who was eyeing him like the enemy. "He doesn't like me."

She smiled. "I think you and he would make a great pair. He actually reminds me of you—tall, impatient, annoyed that he has to be here at all."

He grinned. "You think you have me pegged."

"Am I wrong?"

He couldn't say that she was, so he simply shrugged.

Maddie nodded, a knowing gleam in her eyes. "We'll get you a mare. You were always good with the ladies. You had a lot of girlfriends in high school."

"Every guy had a lot of girlfriends in high school. Relationships lasted three days," he said, as they walked toward the stable office to redeem Maddie's gift certificate.

"That might be true if your last name was Callaway. Some guys were not lucky enough to make out with Rebecca Mooney at lunch every day."

He laughed as Maddie's words took him back in time. Rebecca Mooney had been a busty blonde cheerleader who had certainly helped his reputation, not to mention what she'd done for his hormones. "I haven't thought about Rebecca in years."

"Too many girls to remember?"

"It was a long time ago. I'm sure you had your share of make-out sessions back then."

"Nope. I was not in the popular group."

"You had a lot of friends."

"Who were also not popular, except for your sister Nicole. She used to say that she was only popular because of you, Aiden and Drew. The girls wanted to hang out with her, hoping she'd invite them over to your parents' house so they could accidentally run into you or your brothers."

"There were a lot of people around our house. It was rare to sit down to dinner without a few extra bodies squeezing in at the already crowded table. But my parents were always happy to make room for one more."

"I know. I used to be a little jealous of your big family. You always seemed like you were having so much fun."

"It was fun, most of the time. It was certainly better when my dad and Lynda got together. After my mom died, the air in the house was dark and heavy for a few years."

She frowned. "I totally forgot that you lost your mom when you were—how old?"

"I was seven when she got sick, eight when she died,

almost ten when my dad and Lynda got together."

"So you probably remember your mom better than any of your siblings."

"Aiden and I have the most memories. Drew has a few. Sean doesn't remember anything about her."

"Did you like Lynda right away? Or were you angry that your dad had fallen for someone else?"

"I did like her, but I felt torn. I wanted to be loyal to my mother. It didn't seem right that my dad was laughing and smiling again. On the other hand, it was a lot worse when he was sad, so I warmed up to the idea of them being a couple. And Lynda was great. She took things slow, let us adapt."

"You got two sisters, too."

"Emma and Nicole definitely added some excitement to the crew. We were four wild boys before they showed up. Then the twins were born. It was all good. I'm glad my dad found a way to move on."

"Maybe you should follow his lead. It's been a few years since Leanne died, hasn't it?"

"Yes, it has."

"Do you think you'll be able to fall in love again?"

He looked into her eyes and had the strange feeling that was already happening.

"Someday," he said shortly. He opened the door to the stable office and ushered her inside, happy to put an end to what was turning out to be a very personal conversation. As a teenager, Maddie had always asked him the tough questions, challenged him about his attitudes, his feelings. She'd never been afraid to call him out. It had been a while since he'd been with anyone like that, especially a woman.

He and Leanne had had a completely different kind of relationship. They'd been very compatible and in some ways very alike. There'd been no reason to challenge each other.

They'd always been on the same side—until a few weeks before she died when suddenly they seemed to be at odds over the smallest things. He'd chalked it up to the wedding plans. Leanne had wanted a big wedding, and while he'd gone along with most of her ideas, he'd started to balk at over-the-top suggestions like filling the pond at the country club with live swans or leaving the ceremony in a horse-drawn carriage.

His friends had laughed and told him to relax and just let it all happen. The wedding was for the woman. His job was to let her do whatever she wanted. But it had started to feel as if Leanne was more interested in the wedding than in the actual marriage. Things had gotten so strained between them he'd actually talked to her about calling the ceremony off, reconsidering what they really wanted. Leanne had cried at the suggestion. He'd hurt her, and he'd felt bad, but he'd also felt like someone needed to cut through all the bullshit and figure out what was going on with them.

Unfortunately, that hadn't happened, and one of the last conversations he'd ever had with Leanne had been punctuated by her tears.

His gut twisted at the memory. He'd had to live with his words for a long time, and he'd given up trying to wish them away. He'd said what he'd said, and he hadn't been wrong, but his timing had definitely been bad.

"We're all set," Maddie said, turning to him with a happy smile. "I told them to make sure you have a good horse."

"Great."

They walked out to the stables. A few minutes later, he mounted a beautiful gray horse while Maddie hopped onto a chestnut horse that pranced restlessly, eager to get on the trail. A young man named Derek came up next to them and told them he would be their guide. All they had to do was follow along behind him.

Burke hoped his horse was on board with that idea, because he had a feeling that wherever his horse wanted to go, that's where they would be going.

"Do you want to go second?" Maddie asked.

"I'll follow you."

"Okay." Maddie nudged her horse into a walk, falling in behind Derek with Burke bringing up the rear. It seemed awkward at first, but once he got into the rhythm of the ride, he started to relax and enjoy the view.

They first trekked across a wide grassy meadow heading toward the ocean, then down a narrow path to the beach. There were two guys and a dog playing football near the water, but otherwise the beach was empty. The sea was a sparkling blue, sunbeams bouncing off the waves, but the prettiest view was right in front of him.

Maddie's long blonde hair flew out behind her as she encouraged her horse into a faster trot. She was totally immersed in the riding experience. He doubted she even knew he was behind her.

He found himself urging his own horse into a gallop. He wanted to keep up with her, and as they flew down the beach, he felt more alive than he had in a very long time. The sea, the sun, the wind and the amazingly powerful animal that ran so effortlessly through the sand actually made him feel like he was flying. Maddie was right. It was a freeing experience.

He was leaving the past behind, forgetting about his problems, throwing off the pressures of work and life and constantly trying to do the right thing, be the best he could be. He'd been so focused for so long he'd forgotten what it was like to let go, relax, just breathe. This ride was exactly what he'd needed.

He hoped the experience was making Maddie feel better, too. She'd had a rough time the last year, and the past two days hadn't been good, either. She was trying hard to put on a brave face, but she was reeling on the inside, shocked that she'd ended up out on the street after she'd thought she was making a change for the better. She'd barely held it together when they'd left her apartment with all of her life dumped into a few big garbage bags. But she had fought off the tears. In typical Maddie fashion, she'd squared her shoulders, lifted her chin and kept on moving. He couldn't help but admire that.

Ten minutes later, Derek headed off the sand, leading them up a winding dirt path, finally bringing them to a halt on a secluded bluff about fifty feet up from the crashing waves below.

As he came up next to Maddie, she flung him a smile of pure joy, her green eyes bright, her cheeks red, her lips pink and parted with pleasure.

Something inside of him turned over. He could almost hear the ice around his heart cracking.

"Wasn't that amazing?" she asked. "Have you ever had this much fun in your life?"

He stared back at her. "No, I don't think I have."

Her expression sobered as her gaze clung to his for a long minute. "Then you were due," she said lightly.

"I was," he agreed.

She looked out at the sea. "I feel like we're in our own private world, a place only we know."

"Well, us and our friend," he said, tipping his head to Derek, who'd moved a few feet away to give them some privacy. He was texting someone on his phone and not paying any attention to the magnificent view in front of them.

"True," she said with a laugh. "But you know what I mean."

He did know what she meant, because Derek barely

registered on his radar. This moment belonged to Maddie and him.

It was crazy to think that twenty-four hours ago he didn't know she was about to come back into his life. But that was Maddie. She always showed up when he least expected it. She usually left pretty quickly, too. This time was different. This time she was planning to stay—at least he thought she was. She was still figuring out her next move, and hopefully that move would be in San Francisco. He was never ready to say goodbye to her, but he felt even less inclined to do that now. They were just getting to know each other again. He wanted that to keep going for a while.

Maddie let out a sigh. "I wish we could stay out here forever. I feel like my problems are a million miles away."

He felt exactly the same way. "I know what you mean." He shifted in his seat as his horse bent down to eat some grass. "I think the horses might get hungry, though."

"Always so pragmatic. Are you ready to go back?"

"Not yet." He wasn't ready to go back to the barn or to his life. For the first time in as long as he could remember, he didn't know what he wanted to do next.

Actually, that wasn't true. He knew what he wanted to do. He wanted to take Maddie's hand, breach the gap between them, taste her sweet lips.

He also knew that he shouldn't do that, because one taste wasn't going to be enough.

Maddie gave him an odd look, as if she could read his mind.

He started to lean in, thinking he'd spent all of his life doing what he should do. Maybe it was time for a change.

Unfortunately, Derek took that moment to bring his horse over and ask them if they wanted a picture.

Maddie, of course, said yes, and extended her hand. He

took it, happy to have at least one part of his fantasy come true. As her fingers curled around his, the rest of the ice around his heart melted away.

Six

It was after one o'clock when they got back to the barn. Maddie was a little sad that the ride was over. She gave her horse's nose a loving pat as she got off. The horse whinnied and nudged her hand, asking for more.

"I think you made a friend," Burke said, walking over to join her.

She smiled as Derek led her horse back to its stall. "She was a good ride. She liked to run. Your horse did, too."

"She needed a little more urging than yours."

"Maybe she was taking her cue from you."

"Possibly," he conceded. "So, I'm starving. What about you?"

"I could definitely eat. I saw a café down the road on our way in."

"Let's check it out," he said, falling into step with her as they walked out to his car. "Thanks for sharing your gift certificate with me. It was an experience I will not forget."

"I'm glad you had a good time. I wasn't sure you would."

"I wasn't sure, either, but it was better than I expected."

She laughed. "It's nice when things go that way instead of the other way."

"Very true."

The café was a mile down the highway and had a beautiful deck overlooking the ocean. After ordering at the counter, they took their drinks to an outside table and sat down. It was past the lunch hour, so they had the deck to themselves.

"It's difficult to believe it's January," she said. "It's seventy degrees and not a cloud in the sky."

"It's California."

"I have missed this state." Out of all the places in the world she'd traveled, there was nothing that made her feel as happy as this part of the California coastline.

"Maybe you should have come back sooner."

"I definitely could have skipped the Vegas part of my travels."

"Where else have you been in the last decade?" he asked.

She winced at the question. "The word *decade* makes me feel really old."

"You're two years younger than me," he said dryly. "So let's not talk about who's feeling old. I know you went to San Diego State and you were in Paris on your twenty-first birthday. Then where did you go?"

"After I finished my study abroad and graduated from college, I decided to stay in Europe and travel with two other girls. We lived in hostels, met some great people, took the train everywhere we could think of. It was quite an adventure. After six months, one of the girls went home, and then it was just the two of us. We decided to leave Europe and go down under. We went to Australia and New Zealand and managed to snag a work visa there for a year." She paused in her story as the waiter set down their food. She'd opted for a turkey club while Burke had ordered a tri-tip sandwich.

"What did you do for a job?" Burke asked a moment

later.

She swallowed the first bite of her sandwich. "This is good. How's yours?"

"Perfect."

"I waited tables in a café," she said, answering his earlier question. "I tried to get into the kitchen whenever one of the cooks was sick or late, which wasn't as often as I liked. The girl I was traveling with fell in love and went back to the states to get married, so it was time for me to move on, too. I decided to go back to Europe and really learn how to cook. I spent some time in France at a cooking school there. Then I went to Italy and spent two years traveling and cooking my way through the country." She paused. "Am I boring you yet?"

"Not at all. Keep going."

"After Italy, I went to Boston and got a job in a restaurant there for a couple of years. Then it was on to New York where I worked as a sous chef. I was doing that when I ran into you in Times Square four years ago. It was a good job, but the restaurant changed hands and the new owner brought in his own staff, so I was sent packing. I left New York and headed for India."

"Why India? Wait—it was on the bucket list."

"Yes, it was. Dani and I had always talked about India. It seemed like a romantic and exotic place. So I went to New Delhi and learned how to do yoga and make every kind of curry imaginable."

Burke shook his head, amazement in his eyes. "You're a gypsy."

"I was a gypsy. I liked traveling, meeting new people, trying new things. Every day was an adventure. But after I passed thirty and then thirty-one, I started to feel like it was time to do something else." She took another bite of her sandwich, remembering how indecisive she'd felt. "After leaving India, I wanted to try somewhere else that was new, so I went to Las Vegas. You know the rest."

He nodded, tilting his head to the right as he gave her a thoughtful look.

"What?" she asked.

"Las Vegas wasn't a random choice. It was the last place on the list, wasn't it?"

She shifted a little uncomfortably under his piercing gaze. "Maybe."

"No maybe about it. You ran out of Dani's dreams."

"Not just Dani's dreams; mine, too," she reminded him. "I wasn't living her life. I was living the things we'd talked about together. It's important for you to get that."

"I get that, but like you said before, you wouldn't have done some of those things if you hadn't done them for her."

"That's true, but it was good I did them, because every experience was life-changing in some way—even the bad ones."

"Was getting a husband on the list? Having children? Buying a house with a white picket fence?"

She frowned, seeing where he was going with his questions and not wanting to go there with him, but she also didn't see any point in lying about it. "Dani and I did put those on the list."

"That's why you got engaged after two months," he said with a satisfied nod, as if he'd just figured everything out. "You wanted to check the final items off the list. It was time to settle down, get married, have kids."

"That is not why I got engaged, Burke. I fell in love."

"Did you, Maddie?"

"Yes. Why would you doubt that?"

"There was something in your eyes when you said you

hit thirty and thirty-one and felt like it was time to settle down somewhere."

"Everyone feels that way when they hit their thirties. Didn't you get engaged around thirty-one?"

"We're talking about you."

"Aren't we *done* talking about me?" she asked, a little exasperated with his intense questions.

"Not yet."

"What do you want from me, Burke?"

"I want you to admit that Paul was another checkmark on the bucket list."

"I'm not going to admit that. I wouldn't have gone that far," she said, frowning at the thought. Had Paul been part of her drive to complete the bucket list?

"You don't sound that convinced, Maddie."

She sighed. "The truth is—I don't really know anymore. I thought I loved Paul. He was one of those relationships that started out fast and hot and you don't stop to think, at least I didn't. I should have been more careful, but I wasn't. It all feels like a bad dream now."

"I'll bet. You know what I think?"

"I'm pretty sure you're going to tell me," she said dryly.

"I think you were starting to panic. The bucket list was running out. The dreams of a fourteen-year-old girl ended at falling in love, getting married. No one thinks beyond that point as a teenager. You didn't know what to do with the rest of your life; you'd reached the end of the book that had been driving your decisions for more than a decade. Maybe you were in love with Paul. Maybe he just wasn't the right one. But putting all that aside, what now? What do you do now that you've finished living out the dream list?"

She'd been asking herself that question for a while. "I get a job and find a place to live, put money in the bank, do what everyone else does."

"Wrong answer."

"Really? You don't think I should focus on getting a job and straightening out my life? You? The most practical person I've ever met. Now I've heard everything."

He leaned forward, determination in his gaze. "You should get a job. But you have to keep dreaming, Maddie. If you're a chef, why are you working as a waitress at the Hanover Club? Why aren't you trying to be a chef?"

"That's a part-time job. I am hoping to get hired in a restaurant. I have an interview on Monday at a restaurant called 311 Post."

"Well, good, because it sounded a little like you'd given up."

"I don't give up. Sometimes I retreat. But I always get back out there."

"Good. I don't want you to settle."

"Why do you even care?"

"You've had an amazing life so far. You've done incredible things. I'd hate to think you couldn't come up with new dreams just because some asshole kicked you in the teeth. That wouldn't be the Maddie I used to know."

Was that admiration in his eyes? A tingle ran down her spine as she sat up a little straighter in her chair. "I'm trying to get back to that Maddie as we speak."

"Good. And by the way, 311 Post is an excellent restaurant."

"I know. If they take me on, I'll be set." She paused. "Even though I traveled for a long time, I was pretty frugal. You'd probably be surprised to know this, but I used to put away ten percent of everything I made. My father had ingrained that in me at a young age. He's a little bit like you when it comes to making long-term plans. While most of what he advised me to do didn't stick, that did. I had quite a bit of money in my accounts when Paul ripped me off. I had hoped to buy a food truck or put the money towards an ownership interest in a restaurant." She paused, feeling once again the sting of that betrayal. "Anyway, that's not going to happen now. I'm going to have to start at the bottom and work my way up again. But I want you to know that I didn't end up on the streets with no money because I didn't do anything to protect myself. I just didn't realize that the danger would come from someone so close to me."

His gaze hardened. "Did you turn Paul in to the police?"

"No. I didn't see how I could. I gave him access to my accounts. It wasn't like he illegally broke into anything."

"I think you could have made a case in some way."

She took a sip of her drink. "It wasn't the loss of the money that hurt the most; it was the breach of trust. I never thought Paul would hurt me like that. I was a fool. I don't know if I'll ever be able to trust anyone again."

"I can understand why you wouldn't, but somehow I think you'll find a way."

"Why would you say that?" she asked curiously.

"Because your instinct is to trust, to think the best of someone. That's who you are, Maddie."

"Who I used to be," she corrected. "I'm hard now. I'm cynical and jaded. I don't believe in forever. In fact, I hate that word. For me, it's about right now. Nothing else matters."

He smiled. "Right now isn't bad. But I don't think you're as cynical as you'd like to believe. I saw your face when you were riding down the beach. No one who is that jaded about life can be that happy."

"Well, I'm not cynical about horses. Anyway, that's enough about me. It's your turn to talk."

"I can't come close to your story. I've been a firefighter

since I was twenty-one years old. I have fourteen years on the job. I haven't been much of anywhere, except New York, Hawaii and a weekend in Cabo."

"Do you ever want to go to Europe?"

"I wouldn't mind taking a trip someday. I have to admit my world has felt a little small the last few years."

"What was Leanne like?"

A shadow immediately crossed Burke's face. "I don't want to talk about her."

"Come on, tell me something. It doesn't have to be too personal. What did you like most about her?"

He thought for a moment. "She was intelligent, well-read, wanted to work hard and make something of herself."

"What did she do for a living?"

"She worked in advertising. She put together slogans and campaigns for the food and wine industry."

"I probably saw some of her work then. I read the online food magazines every week."

He smiled, but there was a distance in his eyes now, as if he'd gone back to the past.

"You miss her, don't you?" she asked softly.

He drew in a heavy breath and blew it out. "We were fighting before she died. We never fought before we got engaged, but somehow planning our wedding brought out the worst in us. I don't really even know what happened. Little things got blown out of proportion. We were constantly at odds. I felt like we went from being on the same page to not even being in the same book."

"Weddings are stressful. I've catered a few. I've seen people get into some big knock-down, drag-out fights over flower arrangements."

"I think it was more than the wedding. There was something bothering her—or maybe I was just annoying her.

But we were out of sync. It was so bad that I suggested we think about whether or not we wanted to get married. She looked at me with so much shock in her eyes, I tried to take it back. I tried to smooth things out with her, but it was still awkward and tense. A day later, she was killed in a car accident."

She caught her breath, seeing the pain and guilt in Burke's eyes. "I'm sorry."

He drank the rest of his water, then set down his empty glass. "It is what it is. I can't change it."

"You can't," she agreed. "When my sister was dying, I was constantly wondering if this conversation was going to be the last, and when I wasn't wondering that, I was just talking, sometimes being a brat. Dani got so much attention, and she deserved all of it, but I was a kid, and sometimes I was selfish. I wanted my parents' attention, too. So I'd say something I didn't mean or get mad about nothing. Afterwards, I'd feel horrible. One time I went running into Dani's room just to make sure that I could tell her I loved her and I was sorry for calling her annoying. She just gave me this tired smile and said she was annoying to herself, too. That's the kind of person she was."

"What was the last thing you ever said to her?"

"I think I'll make oatmeal raisin cookies tomorrow. That was it. That was what our relationship ended on. It wasn't bad, but it wasn't great, either."

"It was actually very—you," he said with a warm smile.

"That's what I told myself. I tried to remember if she smiled when I said it. I think she did. Oatmeal raisin cookies were her favorite." She paused and drew in a breath, focusing her attention on Burke. "But the point is no one ever knows what their last words to someone will be. You can't put everything on a moment. Relationships are built over time, and they're always changing. You were being human. So was Leanne. If the situation had been reversed, she'd probably feel guilty that she'd been fighting with you, too."

He slowly nodded, obviously thinking about her words. "I never thought of it that way."

"So why did that man hit you last night? What was that about?"

"Mitch Warren was in love with Leanne, but she thought of him as a long-time friend. He was devastated by her death, and to make himself feel better, he's been trying to prove that Leanne's death was not an accident."

Her eyebrows drew together as she puzzled over that comment. "How does he get to that conclusion? I thought it was a car accident."

"It was a hit-and-run. They never found the other driver."

She stared back at him, her imagination kicking into overdrive. "Mitch thinks that someone deliberately crashed into Leanne's car?"

"Yes. He thinks I was involved in the accident in some way, but I wasn't. I was working that night, Maddie. I didn't cause the accident that happened five blocks from the firehouse, but when a bystander called 9-1-1, we got the call."

"No," she breathed, shocked by the thought of Burke being the first on the scene.

He nodded, his gaze grim. "I was the one who pulled her body out of the car."

She swallowed a knot in her throat at the terrifying image his words brought forth. She couldn't begin to imagine how Burke could have gotten past that horrific moment.

"It was weird," he said. "Her face was perfect, not one cut on it. All her injuries were internal." He blew out a breath, his gaze turning toward the sea, as if he were looking for some peace. Finally, he turned back to her. "I've never talked about that night with anyone."

She didn't know how to react to that statement. She was happy that he felt he could trust her, but she didn't have any idea what to say, how to help him or comfort him. In the end, she said, "You're a strong person, Burke."

He shook his head. "I've felt a lot of things in the last three years, but strong isn't one of them."

He was being incredibly hard on himself, she thought, but that was Burke. He'd always tried to control everything and everyone around him. Over the years, he must have run through a million scenarios in his mind: If he'd only gotten to the scene faster, if they'd gotten Leanne out of the car a minute earlier, if they hadn't been fighting that week, would she have been in the car?

That last question gave her pause. "Wait a second. You said that Mitch thinks you're responsible for Leanne's death. But he knows you were at work, so you obviously weren't driving the car that hit her."

"He blamed me for Leanne being on the road that night. He knew she was upset about something. Apparently she left him some cryptic phone message. He keeps asking me what she was upset about, as if that will provide some magic answer or make everything better."

"You've never told him that you and Leanne were fighting?"

"I've never told anyone, not Mitch, not Leanne's parents, not one of her friends—just you." He sighed. "I probably shouldn't have told you."

"You can trust me, Burke. But I am a little curious about your silence. Why not just tell Mitch what happened, that you were fighting about the wedding?"

He sat back in his seat and folded his arms across his chest. "Leanne and I had our problems, but they were ours.

She was a private person, and so am I. If she'd wanted her family or Mitch to know that we weren't getting along, then she would have told them."

"It sounds like she might have wanted to tell Mitch something that day—if she left him a message."

"Who knows? He could be making a lot out of a simple call-me-back voicemail."

His words made sense, but she could see that the secret, the guilt, had been festering inside Burke for far too long. "Do you know why Leanne was on the road that night?"

He met her gaze. "She usually went to yoga on Thursday nights, at a gym not far from the firehouse, but she'd told me earlier that she was too upset to go. She'd said she was going to stay home and think about us—about our future." He drew in a breath and let it out. "Obviously, she changed her mind. I think she was coming to see me, to try to talk me into continuing the engagement."

"So you blame yourself for Leanne's death, too." It was more of a statement than a question, because she could already see the truth in Burke's dark blue gaze.

"It's possible that our fight put her on that road at the worst possible time," he conceded.

"Or...Leanne might have decided to go to yoga and try to de-stress. What was she wearing?"

"She had on her yoga pants, but she wore those a lot even when she wasn't going to yoga. She was very active—loved to run, dance, go to the gym—so it wasn't unusual for her to be in workout gear." He paused. "I'm never going to know why Leanne was on the road that night. And neither is Mitch. He's going to have to find a way to live with that, just as I have."

"He doesn't appear to be doing very well in that regard considering it's been three years and he's still very angry."

"It does seem that time is making everything worse for him."

"I feel like there's something you haven't told me, Burke."

"What do you mean?"

"Mitch gets a message from Leanne indicating she's upset about something and later that night she dies in a hit-and-run. He blames you because he's jealous of you or he thinks she was upset about you. But it seems like a big stretch for him to think you actually drove Leanne off the road."

"I never said it made sense, Maddie."

"It's strange that there were no witnesses to the accident. Where is the firehouse?"

"We're in a somewhat industrial area. There's no foot traffic and it was nighttime. No one was out. There weren't any security cameras in the area. The person who called in the accident said she turned the corner and saw the car flipped on its roof. She got out and called 9-1-1. She said she didn't see anyone leave the scene. The only thing that indicated there was another car involved was that the investigators found paint on Leanne's car, but whoever hit her obviously didn't sustain serious damage to their car or any severe injuries. The police checked the hospitals and body shops for days after that."

He shook his head in frustration. "Mitch is trying to find someone to blame. I understand that. But he's not going to get anywhere. And he should know that by now. The last private investigator he hired quit after spending a lot of Mitch's money and coming up with nothing."

"Maybe you should just talk to him, Burke."

"I don't want to talk to him. I didn't like the guy before Leanne died, and I like him less now. And it's none of his business what was going on in our relationship."

She could see by the steel in Burke's eyes that his mind was completely made up when it came to Mitch Warren, and she couldn't really blame him. She did think he could defuse the situation by being more open, but he obviously didn't see it that way. She knew from experience that when Burke made his mind up, it was difficult to sway him in another direction.

They finished eating in silence. The waiter had just cleared their table when her phone rang. It was not a number she recognized, but the area code was local so hopefully the call had nothing to do with Paul. "Hello?" she said warily.

"Hi Maddie. It's Nicole. Remember me?"

"Of course I remember you," she said, a warm pleasure running through her at the sound of Nicole's voice. "How are you?"

"I'm great. I would love to catch up with you. Emma said you're back in town."

"I am."

"Well, it's about time you decided to come home."

She didn't really know if San Francisco was home anymore, but maybe it could be.

"Listen, I know it's super short notice," Nicole continued, "and you're probably busy, but I'm hosting a family birthday party for my mom tonight, and Emma and I both want you to come."

"But it's a family thing," she protested, her gaze moving to Burke who was listening to her side of the conversation with a curious look in his eyes.

"There will be lots of people there, not just Callaways," Nicole said. "And it's my party, so I can have whoever I want. I have to tell you I'm not going to take no for an answer. The party starts at seven, and I'll text you my address. Okay?"

"Uh, I'm really not sure."

"Please come, Maddie. It's been ages. I want you to meet

my son Brandon. And I know Ryan would love to see you again."

"Could you hang on one second?"

"Sure."

She put her hand over the phone and looked at Burke. "Nicole wants me to come to a party tonight."

"So that's who you're talking to."

"What should I say?"

He hesitated, then said, "Say you'll go."

"Are you going to be there?"

"It's my mom's birthday, so yes."

"It wouldn't bother you if I went with you?"

"No, it's fine, unless you have something better to do."

She was a little surprised at his answer. "Obviously I don't. But would it be awkward for you?"

"Actually, it would probably be less awkward for me if you're there. More attention on you will mean fewer questions for me about what happened with Mitch at the club last night."

"Okay." She took her hand off the phone. "I can come, Nic."

"I'm so happy."

"What should I bring?"

"Just bring yourself. Actually, if you're seeing someone, you could bring him, too."

She looked across the table at the very handsome Burke and felt her stomach tighten, but when she replied to Nicole, she just said, "I'm not seeing anyone, but I will see you tonight. Thanks for the invitation." She set down her phone and said, "Looks like we're going to be spending a little more time together, Burke."

"It looks that way." He met her gaze, a small smile playing around his lips. "It might actually be fun to show up at the party with you. It will shock the hell out of my family, and it's been a long time I've surprised anyone with anything."

"They might get the wrong idea about us—why I'm staying at your place. They might think we're—you know..."

His smile broadened. "I don't really care what anyone thinks. You and I know what's going on."

She stared back at him and said the first thing that came into her mind. "Do we?"

Seven

Burke thought about Maddie's question all the way home. Did he know what was going on with Maddie? He liked spending time with her. Today had been one of the best days he'd had in a long time. Maybe that's all he needed to know right now. He'd been planning every step of his life for far too long, and where had those plans gotten him? His career was on track, but his personal life was a mess.

So he was going to wing it for a while.

Maddie lived on the edge, and he felt embarrassed to say he hadn't been close to the edge of anything in forever. He'd been hibernating, playing it safe, staying within the bubble of his life—until today.

Riding on that beach with Maddie had lit a fire inside of him. He wanted more days like this. He wanted to be free, to have fun, to enjoy his life.

"Uh-oh," Maddie said, pointing her finger toward the front of his apartment building.

His heart sank at the sight of Mitch Warren. "What the hell does he want?"

"Are you going to talk to him?"

He was tempted to drive straight into his underground

garage and not answer the door, but Mitch had already seen him and was flagging him down.

Deciding to get it over with, Burke pulled into the loading zone in front of his building. "Stay here."

As he exited the car, he heard Maddie's door open and close. He turned to give her an angry look. "You don't need to be part of this."

"I'm already part of it, and you should have a witness for whatever is about to be said. Save your breath. I'm not getting back in the car."

"Fine," he grumbled, turning to face Mitch.

Mitch looked haggard and exhausted, dark shadows under his eyes and an unhealthy pallor to his skin.

"What do you want?" Burke asked.

"Who's she? The new girlfriend?" Mitch tipped his head toward Maddie.

The last thing he wanted was for Maddie to get tangled up with Mitch. "It doesn't matter. I repeat—what do you want?"

"You know I hired a private investigator."

Burke's gut tightened at the sudden gleam in Mitch's eyes. "And he found nothing. Yes, I know that."

"That was the first guy. I hired another one a few weeks ago, and he's managed to find some information that I think you'll find interesting. I know I did."

"About the accident?"

"No, about Leanne." Mitch reached into his jacket pocket and pulled out a piece of paper. He handed it to Burke. "This is a copy. I have the original."

"What's this?" He stared down at what looked like a page from a medical chart. There was a stamp at the top of the page that said West Bay Medical Center.

"Read it," Mitch ordered.

Burke felt strangely reluctant to move his gaze down the page, but he was also too curious not to look. Leanne's name appeared at the top of the chart. A date was followed by vitals: height, weight, blood pressure. It was the words that followed that almost stopped his heart. *Bloodwork confirms a pregnancy of 7.1 weeks. Patient wishes to discuss options for termination.*

His vision blurred as his head began to spin. Leanne was pregnant?

He tried to refocus, his gaze seeking the date of her appointment. She'd seen the doctor two weeks before her death. Why hadn't she told him?

The last line of the report danced in front of him again: *Patient wishes to discuss options for termination.*

What options? What the hell was she thinking—that she wouldn't have his baby? That was unimaginable.

He slowly lifted his gaze to Mitch, shocked to see a gleam of triumph in his eyes. "Where did you get this?"

"My investigator found it. Now I know why you and Leanne were fighting. She told you she was pregnant, but she wasn't sure it was yours. You found out that Leanne and I slept together and that she might be having my baby. So you decided to get rid of the baby."

"You're out of your mind," he said, reeling from the shock of Mitch's accusation.

"Maybe you didn't think Leanne would die. Maybe you just thought she'd be injured and would have a miscarriage."

He swallowed a knot in his throat as he began to understand exactly what Mitch was saying. Mitch's words finally began to make sense in a horrifying, unacceptable way. "You slept with Leanne?"

Mitch met his gaze. "She finally realized she was in love with me."

"You son of a bitch."

Blind rage ran through him at Mitch's suggestion, at everything he'd just learned, and this time he was the one to throw the punch. His fist cracked against Mitch's jaw.

Mitch stumbled backward, bouncing off a nearby parking meter. He put a hand to his bloody nose. "You didn't think anyone would ever figure it out, did you? But I know the truth. I know she was having my baby. I know you got someone to hurt her, and I'm going to prove it."

"Leave me the hell alone," Burke bit out, ripping up the chart note and throwing the shreds of paper into the street.

He walked back to his car and got in, gunning the motor. He pulled into the parking garage with a protesting squeal of his tires. It wasn't until he was in his space that he let out a breath and realized that he'd left Maddie on the street with Mitch.

"Shit!" He hit the steering wheel with his hand, fury and shocked confusion sending his blood pounding through his veins.

Leanne was pregnant?

Leanne had cheated on him? With Mitch?

He didn't want to believe any of it.

On the other hand…it was hard to dismiss the medical chart, the statement that Leanne wanted to discuss options for termination. Why would she do that? Was it possible everything Mitch had said was true? That she'd cheated on him, found out she was pregnant and decided to get an abortion to hide what she'd done? Was that why she'd been distant, why they'd been fighting about nothing? Had she been holding in a terrible secret?

He felt sick at the thought.

How could Leanne have slept with Mitch?

They were in love. They were getting married.

When would it have happened?

Hell, it could have happened at any time. In his job, he was gone several nights a week. It would have been easy to cheat on him. But opportunity didn't explain the motivation.

He drew in a breath and slowly let it out, trying to calm down so he could think more clearly.

Even if Leanne had cheated on him with Mitch, even if she'd been pregnant with another man's child...none of that explained the accident. Because he had known nothing and he had done nothing. Mitch was wrong about that.

Maybe he was wrong about the other stuff, too. Maybe he was making up the fact that Leanne had slept with him. She was the only one who could disprove that, and she was gone.

The baby she was carrying might not have been Mitch's; it might have been his baby.

A whole new wave of pain ran through him. Had he not only lost his fiancée but also his unborn child?

He sat in the car for another fifteen minutes asking himself questions for which he had no answers, letting the anger run around inside of him until it finally began to disappear. He thought he'd known everything there was to know about Leanne, about her accident, but now he felt like he knew nothing.

So he would find out. He would get the answers he needed—somehow. He just didn't know how he would do that yet.

Forcing himself to get out of the car, he took the stairs to the lobby level and then walked across the entry to open the front door.

Maddie was sitting on a low brick wall outside. There was no sign of Mitch.

"Are you all right?" she asked. "That was quite a scene."

"I'm sorry I left you out here with him."

"Don't worry about it," she said, getting to her feet. "He's gone."

"Did he say anything to you?"

"Not much. He left pretty quick."

There was something about her manner that suggested she was holding back. "But he didn't leave without saying something. What was it?"

"It doesn't matter—"

"Maddie, just tell me. I can't handle any more secrets."

Her lips tightened. "He told me you were dangerous. If I valued my life, I'd get away from you as soon as possible. I told him I didn't know what was going on, but I knew one thing for sure, that you would never ever be responsible for getting someone hurt."

He stared back at her unwavering gaze. "Thank you."

"I was speaking the truth."

"I don't know what the truth is anymore. Come on in."

They didn't speak on the way up to his apartment. Once inside, Maddie gave him an uncertain look and then sat down on the couch. He paced restlessly around the living room, his mind still racing.

"So what do you think?" Maddie asked finally.

"I don't know what to think." He perched on the edge of the chair. "If I believe that Leanne was pregnant, do I have to believe she cheated on me with Mitch?"

"No. While there may be proof she was pregnant, there wasn't anything on that paper about the father, was there?"

"I don't think so. I shouldn't have ripped it up. I should have hung on to it. I should go down to that clinic and talk to that doctor and find out the truth." He jumped to his feet. "What was the name of that place? It was something with Bay in it."

"Burke, you need to take a breath."

"What I need is information, Maddie."

"Which you'll get. But you'll have a better chance of getting it if you take a minute and think about everything you've learned. You have to consider the fact that this information is all coming from a man who doesn't like you and is apparently still very obsessed with Leanne."

He stared back at her. "Is he obsessed because she slept with him? I thought it was all one-sided. I thought I could trust her. We were engaged."

"I don't know, Burke. Mitch could be lying."

"Or he could be telling the truth, and that's why Leanne and I were suddenly at odds with each other. Maybe she felt guilty. Maybe was trying to find a way to drive me away or punish herself." He paused, drawing in a much-needed breath. "The medical chart said that she wanted to discuss options for termination. That's what makes me think Mitch is telling the truth. Because why would Leanne want to terminate our baby? We were going to be married. We were going to start a family."

"Was there an autopsy?" Maddie asked.

He stared back at her, surprised by the question. "There was a toxicology report. Leanne was not under the influence at the time of her death, but it was obvious what injuries contributed to her passing, so I don't think anything else was done. To be honest, the Parkers dealt with all that. Leanne and I weren't married. I wasn't her official next of kin at that point."

As he finished speaking, he wondered if the Parkers might have known Leanne was pregnant and chosen not to tell him.

He sat back down in the chair and pressed the tips of his fingers together. "I'll have to talk to them."

"When you've had a chance to consider everything."

He frowned. "I can't believe you're the one who's telling me to slow down. Aren't you usually full speed ahead, to hell with the consequences?"

"So learn from my mistakes," she said evenly.

He let out a breath. "Sorry."

"You know, Burke, even if Leanne cheated and was pregnant with Mitch's child, that doesn't make what happened to her anything more than an accident, because you didn't hurt her. Mitch is wrong about that. Maybe he's wrong about the other stuff, too."

"He has to be wrong. I should talk to his investigator."

"That might be wise. His words won't be clouded by jealousy and rage."

"True."

"But you still need to breathe through this a little first."

Maddie had a point. There was too much adrenaline running through his body, and he felt pinned in by the four walls of his apartment. The freedom and happiness he'd felt a few hours earlier had completely vanished. Now he felt restless, angry and confused. He needed to take some action, but he didn't need to go off half-cocked.

"I have to get out of here," he said, standing up again. "I need to go for a run."

"That's a good idea," she agreed, relief passing through her eyes. "Do you happen to have an extra key to this place, to your car? I need to get something out of my bags in your trunk."

"Of course." He grabbed his extra set of keys out of the top drawer of his desk and handed them to her. "Get your stuff, spread out, hang your clothes up in whatever space you can find. Don't worry about crowding me."

"Thanks."

"I'm going to change."

He went into his bedroom, put on shorts, a T-shirt and running shoes, then headed out the door. He broke into a jog as soon as he hit the sidewalk, and he didn't stop running until he reached the walkway directly under the Golden Gate Bridge.

By then his breath was coming short and fast and his legs were aching from the speed of his sprint across town. He put his forearms on the railing and stared up at the majestic bridge. The sun was sinking lower in the sky, but there was no fog on the horizon. The sky was clear. He just wished his brain was as clear as the view.

The run had calmed him down a little. He knew there were still things to figure out but he didn't have to race to the truth. Whatever Leanne had done or not done didn't really matter now. He couldn't change it. She was gone. Her baby was gone. Maybe that child had been his—maybe not. He should let it all go. That would make the most sense.

On the other hand, he couldn't just forget what he'd heard. He hated the idea of Mitch spreading rumors about Leanne that might not be true. She wasn't here to defend herself.

But how the hell was he going to find out the truth? Mitch would only share his version, and he was acting crazy now, leaping to conclusions Burke knew weren't true.

He needed to talk to other people, the Parkers, Leanne's friends. He didn't want to stir everyone up, but what other choice did he have?

He supposed he had the choice to do nothing, but just because he didn't talk didn't mean Mitch wouldn't have a lot to say.

He looked up at the sky and murmured, "Why didn't you tell me, Leanne? Why didn't you talk to me if you were unhappy, if you wanted out, if you wanted someone else? What were you afraid of?" He paused. "I'm going to try to find out what happened. Maybe you wouldn't want that, but I need to know. I need to move on."

He let out a sigh, then turned around and ran back home.

—————

While Burke was gone, Maddie grabbed some clothes out of Burke's car and took a long shower. It had certainly been a wild twenty-four hours and not just for her, for Burke, too. Her shocking eviction was starting to pale in comparison to the secrets his fiancée had kept from him. She didn't know exactly what was going on. She'd been trying to piece together the facts from what both Mitch and Burke had told her, and so far the picture was very fuzzy.

One thing she did know was that Burke was stunned, completely knocked off his feet. He'd always been a man to have control over his emotions, his situation, everything. But that had been shattered today. The pain in his eyes when he'd learned about the baby, about Leanne's possible infidelity, had been so agonizing, it had been hard to look too closely at him.

She wished there was something she could do to help him.

She knew what it was like to be betrayed by someone you loved, someone you thought you knew as well as you knew yourself.

After Paul had taken her money, she'd realized that she'd ignored a lot of red flags in their relationship. Had Burke done the same thing with Leanne?

When the water ran cold, she got out, dried off, dressed and dried her hair. Then she went back out to the living room and debated her next move. She had a key to Burke's apartment. She had some cash from the bank. And she was invited to a potluck that evening. She wasn't sure Burke would want to go after the news he'd just received, but she did want to see Nicole. It would probably be better for Burke to be surrounded by family tonight than to sit at home and stew about what Mitch had told him. Hopefully, his run would bring some peace and he'd be willing to go out later.

Grabbing her bag, she decided to run out to the market she'd spied a block away. Nicole had told her not to bring anything, but she'd feel better showing up with a dish to contribute.

When she left the building, she couldn't help looking around for Mitch. She didn't see him anywhere, but that didn't mean he wasn't lurking in the shadows somewhere. As she walked to the market, she couldn't shake the feeling that someone was watching her, but it was probably just her imagination. Mitch didn't care about her.

But Paul did. Or at least he cared about her money and the possibility of her helping him.

Sighing, she realized she should be focusing on her own problems. Paul's earlier phone call had disturbed her, but she reminded herself that Paul didn't know where she was staying in the city. Even if he somehow tracked her to the apartment she'd sublet, she wasn't there anymore. Her parents were safely out of town for a few more days, so there was no way Paul could reach them. And they didn't know where she was, either.

Despite all those reminders, she felt a little better when she stepped into the market.

It was a gourmet market with organic vegetables and meats and local wines from the nearby Sonoma and Napa vineyards. It was expensive, but it was convenient. She grabbed some vegetables, deciding to make some vegetable tarts to take as an appetizer. They were usually a big hit at parties.

After checking out, she walked quickly back to the apartment. The sun was going down, the late afternoon shadows getting longer and once again goose bumps ran unexpectedly down her arms as she moved toward Burke's apartment building.

She was not ordinarily a fearful person. She'd been all over the world. She'd traveled in dangerous areas by herself. There was nothing to fear on this residential block in San Francisco's Russian Hill neighborhood.

Still, she quickened her pace. When she got to the front door, she juggled the bags in her hand so she could get her key out.

Steps came up behind her, and her heart leapt into her throat as a hand came down on her shoulder. She gasped, whirling around to see...Burke.

"You scared me," she said breathlessly.

"Sorry. I saw you struggling to get the key out." His gaze narrowed. "What's wrong?"

"I don't know. I just had a bad feeling walking to the market and back."

Burke glanced around. "I don't see anyone."

"It was just a feeling. Probably my imagination." She stepped back as Burke opened the door for her. He grabbed one of her grocery bags from her as they headed up the stairs.

"What's all this?" he asked.

"Just a few things. I thought I'd make something to take to Nicole's potluck, if you still want to go."

"I'm not really in the mood for my family."

"They might take your mind off things. How was your run?" she asked, as he let her into the apartment.

"It was good. I feel better now."

"You seem calmer." She set her groceries on the kitchen counter.

"I don't know about calm, but I do know that I need some answers."

"Are you going to talk to Mitch again?"

"Not if I can help it. I need a more objective person to speak to."

"Any ideas?"

"Leanne's parents, her friends, someone must know something."

She liked his renewed sense of determination, although she couldn't help wondering if getting to the truth would make him feel better. "What if you don't like the answers? Would it be better not to ask the questions?"

He gazed back at her. "I don't think I can do that."

"You might want to try. While I know you're more focused on the personal aspects of your relationship with Leanne, I'm worried that Mitch thinks you had something to do with Leanne's death. He might try to get revenge, Burke. If you start questioning his relationship with Leanne, that might set him off even more."

"I'm not worried about Mitch. I can handle him. In the meantime, I'm going to take a shower."

"Okay." As Burke left the room, she finished unpacking the groceries.

While she appreciated Burke's fearless attitude, she was a little worried that he was underestimating the depth of Mitch's anger.

Eight

Burke hadn't really wanted to go to Nicole's party. It had been a long, stressful day, and he knew there would still be questions about his black eye, which didn't look as bad as it had but was visible enough to remind everyone what had happened on Friday. But Maddie had looked so eager to see Nicole again, and she'd made some kind of appetizer that smelled like heaven, so how could he say no?

It might be good to get his mind off of Mitch and Leanne and remember that whatever had happened between them had occurred three years ago. The truth might bring him clarity, but it wasn't going to change the end game. Nothing would change that.

"Having second thoughts?" Maddie asked.

"No, I'm good."

"You're thinking a lot."

He gave her a brief smile. "I've been known to do that."

She smiled back at him. "True. I forgot."

He turned down Nicole's street and found a parking spot a few houses down. Judging by the cars he passed, most of his family was already at the party.

"Should we go in separately?" Maddie asked. "Pretend

we just happened to arrive at the same time?"

"I don't think we need to make a plan. We'll just see what happens."

Her eyebrow shot up. "Seriously? Not only do you think a lot, as you just reminded me, but you love to make plans."

"Maybe you're rubbing off on me." The truth was he couldn't begin to think of an explanation as to why he and Maddie were together—at least not in the next five minutes.

"So is everyone going to be here?" Maddie asked as they walked down the block to Nicole's house. "All your siblings—all their significant others?"

"I think so. It's hard to keep track. We've practically doubled in size the last two years."

"Just wait until everyone starts having kids."

"It's going to be a madhouse," he agreed, trying not to let the mention of kids remind him of Leanne's pregnancy, but it was too late, he'd already gone there. He forced his mind back to the present. "There will be more than the immediate family present today. My mother's birthday is one of the family events that no one misses, not unless they want to get on my father's bad side, and no one does. He's not only the leader of our family, he's also the oldest of his siblings, so my aunts, uncles and cousins all tend to make appearances at events mandated by my father."

She smiled at his words. "Your dad always had such a big personality. I remember his bright blue eyes and booming voice. He loved to tell stories and when he laughed, it came from down deep in his gut. If he was in the room, you always knew it."

"That's for sure. He's always been bigger than life, and he's always had high expectations for his kids."

"You've obviously lived up to those expectations."

"I've certainly tried. My father drilled into me at an early age that as the oldest I had to set the example."

"Was that a burden?"

"Yes," he said, happy to see that she understood that. None of his siblings seemed willing to admit that he'd had to play under different rules. "My brothers and sisters wouldn't agree with you, though. They always complained how it was much harder to come after me, especially Aiden."

"You and Aiden were really different as teenagers. Talk about hell raisers…Aiden spent more time in detention than I did."

"That's true. I hope his daughter Chloe gives him as much trouble as he used to give our parents."

"My mother loves to say the exact same thing to me."

At her words, he realized how much Maddie was like Aiden, and for some ridiculously strange reason, he was kind of glad that Aiden was already married.

As Maddie reached for the doorbell, he put his hand on her arm. She gave him an enquiring look.

"Don't say anything about Mitch or Leanne," he said.

"I wouldn't dream of it. Maybe you could leave my eviction out of any stories, too?"

He smiled. "Your secrets are my secrets."

She smiled back at him. "Likewise."

The look that passed between them was almost intimate. His pulse began to race as he stared at her in the shadowy moonlight. He'd felt a pull to her for a very long time, but it had never been as strong as it was right now. But this was absolutely the worst possible time to give in to that pull.

"Burke?" she asked, a questioning note in her voice. "Is something—"

"Nothing." He shook his head and rang the bell.

A second later, Nicole threw open the door and gave her a happy smile. She quickly pulled Maddie into a hug.

"I am so glad you decided to come," Nicole said with genuine delight. "It's been ages, Maddie. You haven't changed a bit."

"Neither have you," Maddie said.

"That's sweet of you to say, but a complete and utter lie," Nicole retorted.

Burke cleared his throat, and his sister gave him a surprised look. "Burke, I didn't even see you there."

"I noticed."

"Come in, come in," Nicole said, waving them into the house. "Everyone is here."

"I brought a little something for your potluck." Maddie handed Nicole the covered platter.

"I told you not to worry about that, but thank you."

"It's nothing, just some vegetable tarts."

Nicole took a whiff. "They smell delicious. I remember how well you could cook, even as a teenager, so I'm sure they're going to be great."

"Where's Mom?" Burke asked.

"She's in the living room."

"I'll go say happy birthday."

Nicole gave him a dismissive shrug as she led Maddie down the hall toward the kitchen. His sister had been so happy to see Maddie she hadn't noticed that he and Maddie had arrived together.

He wasn't going to have to explain anything—well, at least not until it was time to leave.

⇒ ≫ ≪ ⇐

Nicole's big country kitchen was filled with Callaways. Maddie was immediately swept up in a flurry of introductions and hugs: Emma and her attractive husband Max; Aiden and his wife Sara and their cute toddler daughter Chloe; Drew and Ria and an exotically pretty teenager named Megan; Shayla, who'd grown into a beautiful young woman in the years since Maddie had last seen her and Shayla's boyfriend Reid, who could definitely hold his own in the looks department; and finally Colton and his girlfriend Olivia.

Burke was right. All of his siblings were paired up. As the oldest, it must be strange for him to be the last of his siblings to be single. Not that he would be single if Leanne hadn't died. Or maybe he would have been. She couldn't help wondering if they would have actually made it down the aisle now that she knew there were problems and maybe even cheating.

"What will you have to drink?" Nicole asked her as the large group broke into smaller conversations. "We have wine, beer, sodas, water..."

"Red wine is good. Whatever is open."

"We're so glad you came," Emma said, joining them by the makeshift bar set up on the kitchen counter.

"Me, too. Your family seems to have tripled in size."

"Add in significant others and lots of cousins and that happens," Nicole said, handing her a glass of wine. "Let's go out to the back deck. We have the heat lamps on, so we'll be warm, and there will be fewer people."

"I don't want to take you away from your mom's birthday party," she protested.

"Oh, it's just getting started," Emma said, leading the way outside. "We can't start eating until Grandma and Grandpa arrive, and they won't be here for another half hour."

"How are your grandparents?" she asked, following them out to the deck.

"My grandmother has Alzheimer's," Nicole replied as they sat down at a round table.

"Oh, I'm sorry. She was such a nice lady. She always had freshly baked cookies for you when you came home from school. And remember that day when she taught us how to make old-fashioned wedding cookies?"

Nicole laughed. "I think I bailed out on the lesson in about five minutes, but I do remember you loving every second of it."

"I always think of your grandmother when I make those cookies."

"You should tell her that," Nicole said, her gaze soft and a little sad. "I think she'd love to hear it. But don't feel bad if she doesn't remember you. Sometimes she doesn't remember anyone, including herself."

"That must be so difficult."

"It makes us appreciate the good days."

"So tell us about your life, Maddie," Emma said. "I think you're the most adventurous person I know."

"I've had a good time," she admitted.

"Like?" Emma persisted. "What was the most fun?"

"Traveling throughout Italy and learning to cook the foods of the different regions was probably my most memorable experience."

"Wasn't there an Italian restaurateur in the mix?" Nicole asked, a curious light in her eyes.

"There was, and he was quite handsome with dark eyes and a charismatic smile, but in the end he was much more in love with himself than with me."

"Has there been anyone serious in your life?" Emma asked.

"I was engaged last year, but it didn't work out, so I'm as single as can be."

"We'll have to find you someone. I work with a lot of single firefighters, and some are very good-looking."

She could believe that. Most of the firefighters she'd met were Callaways, but they were all very attractive, especially Burke. Her heart squeezed at the thought of him. The way he'd looked at her just before they'd rung the bell tonight…It had almost seemed like he wanted to say something or that he wanted to kiss her.

One of these days she wanted one of those moments to actually happen, not to almost happen.

"Emma loves to matchmake," Nicole put in. "So beware."

"She's right, and I've run out of siblings, well, except for Burke. But he wouldn't let me set him up in a million years." Emma paused. "And I wouldn't want to set him up until he was really over Leanne. No woman wants to come in second to a memory."

That was true. Probably another reason not to let one of those *almost* moments happen.

"What's happening with you two?" she asked, changing the subject. "How's your son, Nicole?"

"Brandon is seven years old now. He was diagnosed as being autistic when he was three, and it's been a struggle dealing with his issues, but he's improved in some areas the last few years. It's a long story, and I want to tell you all of it, but tonight is probably not the best night for that."

"Another time then. But you and Ryan are good?"

"Stronger than ever," Nicole said. "In fact…" She licked her lips. "I wasn't going to say anything yet, but I'm pregnant."

"Oh, my God," Emma squealed. "Are you serious?"

"Yes. I'm only nine weeks, and I was going to wait until I got through the first trimester to tell anyone, but it's too hard to keep the secret."

"I'm so happy for you," Maddie said, seeing the joy in

Nicole's eyes.

"Thank you. For a really long time I was afraid to have another child. Brandon's problems have just worn me out. But since Ryan and I started working as a team, when we remembered how much we love each other, and since Brandon and his twin were reunited—that's another story I'll have to tell you—I've felt like another baby would be a blessing. I don't want to take anything away from Brandon, though. I do worry that he'll react negatively to a sibling."

"I don't think he will," Emma cut in. "He's adjusted really well to Kyle. This is just such amazing news, Nic. Do you know what you're going to have?"

"I have an ultrasound appointment next week. I think we'll be able to find out the sex then if we want to know. I'm not sure if I do."

"Why on earth would you want to wait?" Emma asked. "Let's find out if we can start buying some little girl clothes. Actually, if you have a girl, you can get Chloe's hand-me-downs. And it would be fun for Chloe to have a little girl cousin to play with."

"Stop," Nicole said with a laugh. "We'll figure it all out, but not right this second."

"You need to tell everyone tonight," Emma said. "It will be the perfect present to give Mom. She'll be over the moon."

"I was thinking about it, but I don't want to steal the attention from her birthday."

"Are you kidding? Come on, she would love it. You have to do it."

"Ryan wants to make the announcement, too," Nicole admitted. "We'll see how things go."

As Emma and Nicole talked about baby names, Maddie couldn't help but feel a little envious of their happiness. They were both settled with men that they loved, and they were surrounded by extended family. She and her parents made up a very small group of three. And the one set of cousins she had lived out of state.

"Do you want to have kids, Maddie?" Nicole asked.

She started as the focus turned back to her. "I do—someday. I have to find the right man first. But you've already found your man, Emma. So are you next?"

"We've actually just started trying," Emma said.

"Really?" Nicole asked. "Wow, we might have kids close together then."

"We'll see. I don't know how long it will take."

"What about your job?" Maddie asked.

"I want to keep it. I'm planning on working after I have a baby. Basically, I want to have it all."

"What are we talking about, ladies?" Sara interrupted, joining them at the table.

"Emma is trying to have a baby," Nicole said.

"Hey, I wasn't planning to announce that to the world," Emma protested.

"I'm not the world. I'm your friend and your sister-in-law, and I'm thrilled," Sara said. "I need some kids for Chloe to play with."

"Then you might want to talk to Nicole," Emma said.

Sara's gaze swung to Nicole." Is there something you want to tell me?"

"Later. We'll talk later," Nicole promised.

Sara hesitated, then shrugged. She turned to Maddie. "It's so good to see you again. I remember when you and Nicole drove Emma and me around. You actually encouraged Nicole to drive the getaway car when we TP'd Ronnie Hartman's house."

"I forgot about that," Maddie said with a laugh.

"That's right," Nicole said. "I was so nervous; I thought

we were going to get caught." She wagged her finger at Maddie. "You were a bad influence on me."

"She was a good influence," Emma said. "She showed you how to have fun."

"Well, that's true," Nicole said with a grin.

"Hey, Nic," Ryan said from the doorway. "Your grandparents are here, and everyone is in the living room. I'm thinking this is a good time..."

"Okay," Nicole said, getting to her feet.

"A good time for what?" Sara asked with interest.

"Come inside and you'll find out," Nicole said.

"You're such a tease," Sara complained.

Maddie followed the other women into the house. It took a while to get into the living room, and when they did so, she could see Callaways perched on every available piece of furniture with some of the younger generation sprawled on the floor.

While Nicole, Emma and Sara moved into the room, Maddie paused in the doorway. She saw Burke across the room. He was standing next to his father. His gaze met hers, and neither one of them could seem to look away. It felt sexy and a little exciting to have a secret relationship. She silently laughed at herself for that thought. What relationship did they have? She was just crashing on his couch, she reminded herself. But there was still something in his gaze that made her shiver just a little.

"Before we get started on the birthday festivities," Ryan said, quieting the chatter in the room. "Nicole and I have an announcement." He put his arm around his wife and gave her a loving smile. "Do you want to tell them or—"

"I'm pregnant," Nicole said.

Cheers broke out in the room followed by hugs and high-fives and questions about due dates. There was so much love in the room, Maddie felt overwhelmed and a little emotional. She hadn't thought about family much in the last ten years, but now she couldn't help feeling like fun and adventure were great, but wasn't family what it was really all about?

She moved back a few steps to get out of the way, and a moment later Burke came over to join her.

"I wasn't expecting that," he said. "You didn't look too surprised."

"Nicole told me outside. I'm really happy for her. It sounds like she's had a difficult few years."

"That she has, but she's a strong woman."

"With a strong family behind her. That helps. You're really lucky, Burke, to have all these people who love you and have your back."

"They're okay," Burke said lightly, but she could see the pride in his eyes.

"Burke?" An elderly woman interrupted their conversation. She had white blonde hair, light blue eyes and her smile lit up the room. Maddie would have known Eleanor Callaway anywhere.

Burke stepped back to let his grandmother into their conversation. "Hi Grandma. How are you doing?"

"Well, I'm very excited to know I'm going to have another great-grandchild." As she finished speaking, she turned to Maddie. "I know you, don't I? You're Nicole's friend, the one who liked to make cookies with me."

"I am. I'm Maddie Heller. You taught me to make old-fashioned wedding cookies."

"You got more sugar on yourself than you put on the cookies."

"I was a pretty sloppy cook back then."

"But very enthusiastic. Do you still cook, dear?"

"As often as I can."

Eleanor patted her on the arm. "I am so glad. I always felt good when I was cooking. It's something I miss these days. But I have a little problem remembering things, so no one likes me to go near the stove."

Maddie smiled. Eleanor might be sick, but tonight she was very much like the woman Maddie had known in high school: vibrant, cheerful, with a dry wit. Cooking with Eleanor had not just been about the cookies; Eleanor had also cheered her up after Dani died. Their conversations had not been all about butter and sugar.

"So are you married, Maddie?" Eleanor asked.

"Not yet."

"You'll meet the right person, probably when you least expect it."

"I'm not worried."

Eleanor gave Burke a sly look. "You should take Maddie out sometime. Introduce her to some of your single friends."

Maddie enjoyed the uncomfortable look that crept into Burke's eyes and decided to play along. "You should do that, Burke. I'm sure you must know some single men around our age."

"Not anyone worthy of Maddie Heller."

"Oh, I bet you know someone," Eleanor persisted.

"I'll have to think about it," he replied.

"Or you could take her out yourself," Eleanor suggested, a wicked gleam in her eyes.

"We could go on a date," Maddie agreed. "Unless you're still holding that detention against me." She looked at Eleanor. "I got Burke his first and only detention in high school. I don't think he's ever forgiven me."

"Were you doing something fun when you got in trouble?"

She said, "Yes."

Burke said, "No."

Eleanor laughed. "I think I'd like to hear this story."

"Some other time," Burke said. "It looks like dinner is ready. Can I get you a plate, Grandma?"

"Your grandfather always takes care of that. You two have fun," Eleanor said, then made her way back to her husband.

"Did you enjoy that?" Burke asked her.

"Yes. Your grandmother is a sweetheart. I've loved her since the first day I met her. She always had great stories to tell."

"That's true," he said quietly, his gaze turning reflective. "I wish now I'd been a better listener."

"Nicole told me about your grandmother's diagnosis. I'm sorry."

"She's hanging in there. Some days are better than others."

"Those are the days you have to savor," she said, knowing firsthand what it felt like to watch someone slowly disappear.

"Yeah. Let's get something to eat."

"Okay."

As they filled their plates, Maddie was happy to see her vegetable tarts were a popular item among the crowd. It was also the first thing Burke put into his mouth when they sat down together at a table on the back deck.

"Amazing," he got out, as he downed the tart in two bites. "I've been wanting to eat one of those since you took them out of the oven. You need to be in a restaurant, Maddie."

"I'm working on it," she said, pleased with his obvious enjoyment of her food.

"Does your upcoming interview involve you cooking? If

it does, I think you'll blow them away."

"You've only tasted my omelet and my tarts, and this restaurant is very high brow. So I don't know if I'll impress them."

"I've seen you raise your brow," he said with a laugh. "You can compete."

"Very true." She liked this lighter side of Burke. She would have thought after the revelations he'd heard earlier, he would be in a down mood, but since his run and getting together with his family, his tension had definitely eased. She also liked to think that maybe she was a tiny bit responsible for his happier mood, or at least her tarts were doing that job.

"Are we interrupting?" Emma asked as she and her husband Max sat down at the table.

"Not at all," Burke replied. "Haven't seen you in a while, Max. What's going on?"

"Not much. How's your eye?"

"It's fine."

"Emma filled me in. Do you want to file charges?"

"No, I'm going to handle the situation on my own."

"I told you that's what he'd say," Emma said, sighing as she met her husband's gaze. "He's stubborn."

"It seems to run in your family," Max said dryly.

"How did you two meet?" Maddie asked. "Was it love at first sight?"

"Maybe on Max's part," Emma said with a wicked sparkle in her eye. "But not for me."

Max rolled his eyes. "Or me, either. Emma was annoying as hell."

"Because you were in my business."

"My business," he retorted.

Emma looked at Maddie. "Max was working a murder investigation, and I was working an arson case. They met in the middle and so did we. Eventually, we realized some of the tension between us was attraction."

"You left out the part where you were being stalked and Max had to save your life," Burke interjected.

"Oh, that," Emma said with a wave of her hand.

"It sounds terrifying," Maddie put in.

"Emma doesn't scare easily," Max said, slinging his arm around the back of his wife's chair. "Do you, babe?"

"No, but that was pretty scary I have to admit."

"You Callaways certainly have a lot of drama," she said.

Burke laughed. "You don't know the half of it, Maddie." He stood up. "I'm going to get seconds. Anyone need anything?"

After everyone said no, Burke moved toward the house.

"I'm worried about Burke," Emma said as soon as her brother was out of sight. "He thinks he can handle Mitch, but the man looks like he's lost his mind. And Colton told me that Mitch has been missing work the last two weeks."

"Burke can take care of himself," Max told her. "You need to stay out of it, Em."

"You know I don't like to do that."

"This time you should," Max said. "But it probably doesn't matter what I say, does it? When it comes to your family, you're a force of nature. Actually, when it comes to anything, you're a force."

"I can't help it. I love my family and Burke is the only one of us who doesn't have someone." Emma paused, her expression changing slightly as she gazed over at Maddie. "You and Burke seemed awfully friendly when we came out here. Is there something between you two?"

"We're friends," she said. "He used to tutor me in high school."

"That was a long time ago."

"Leave her alone, Em," Max said. "You have to stop trying to match Burke up with someone."

"Fine, but I'm still going to worry about him. If you don't want me to butt in, I think you should, Max. Why don't you go talk to him? Maybe you can make him see that he needs our help."

"I seriously doubt that will be the outcome, but I will give it a shot." Max kissed Emma on the cheek, smiled at Maddie and returned to the house.

"You have that man wrapped around your finger," Maddie said.

"Not really. Max and I have our moments. We're both pretty strong-willed, but it works. I like that he challenges me, and hopefully he feels the same way."

"He looks at you like he adores you, so I think it's safe to say he definitely feels the same way."

"I'm lucky. I had a bad relationship before Max. I wasted a lot of time on a loser."

"I know what that feels like."

"Live and learn, right?"

She sighed. "I think I've done enough learning. I'm ready for everything to work out now."

Their conversation was interrupted by Nicole, who popped out on the deck long enough to tell them to come inside for cake and presents.

As they got up to go inside, Emma gave Maddie a sly look. "Even if there's nothing going on between you and Burke now, that doesn't mean there couldn't be. You're friends. That's a good start."

"I would drive your brother crazy in a second. We are very different people."

"That could be a good thing. And maybe it would be an interesting kind of crazy."

Maddie laughed. "I've had interesting. I've had crazy. I think the combination could be deadly."

"Or amazing. Aren't you the girl who isn't afraid of anything?"

"I used to be," she said. "Sometimes I wonder what happened to that girl."

Nine

❯❯❮❮

Burke was sitting on the front porch railing in front of Nicole's house when Max came out to find him. "Emma sent you out here to talk to me, didn't she? You're not really going to jump every time she says jump, are you?"

"Only when warranted, or when I want to have a really good night—later."

"Too much information," Burke drawled.

"Then let's talk about you. What's going on between you and the firefighter that attacked you last night?"

Burke hesitated, torn between wanting to say nothing and knowing he might need Max's help to get to the truth. "Up until today, I thought Mitch was just caught in a circle of grief, but now I know it's more than that."

"What happened?"

"I'd like to tell you, Max, but I don't want Emma involved. Can we have a conversation that doesn't go back to her?"

Now Max was the one who hesitated. "I don't like to keep secrets from Emma, especially when it comes to her family."

"Then we shouldn't be talking."

Max stared back at him. "I'll keep this conversation between us. But if we need to have another one, we'll have to renegotiate."

"Fine. Mitch came to my apartment building with some new information about Leanne. He told me that he and Leanne had an affair and that she was pregnant when she died, possibly with his child."

"What?"

"Yeah, he dropped a bomb on my head."

"Do you believe him?"

"I don't want to, but he showed me a medical report stating Leanne was pregnant. So that part seems to be true. The rest I have to figure out." He took a breath. "Mitch believes that Leanne's hit-and-run was deliberate and that I hired someone to take her out, kill her, kill the baby that wasn't mine."

Max's gaze hardened. "That's unbelievable."

"Not according to Mitch. He was obsessed with Leanne, and now he's obsessed with making me pay for her death, a death he believes I'm responsible for. He has a private investigator working with him. Apparently, that's who dug up Leanne's medical records. I don't know where they're going next."

"They're going to the night of the accident," Max said. "When I get into work tomorrow, I'll see if I can pull the reports from that night."

"I've seen those reports. There's nothing on them. The police had no clues, no witnesses, nothing."

"Well, sometimes a fresh eye helps when you're talking about a cold case."

"I'd appreciate the help," he said. "I still think it was an accident, because I didn't do it, and who else would have a reason to hurt Leanne?"

"Aside from you and Mitch, I can't think of anyone. Unless there are other things you didn't know about her."

"I hope not," he murmured. But if Leanne had not told him she was pregnant, or that she'd cheated on him with Mitch, it was more than a little possible that she had other secrets. Had one of those secrets killed her?

"Emma saw us leave together," Maddie said as Burke drove them back to his apartment just after ten. "She came out on the porch right after I got in the car."

"Then I'm sure one or both of us will be getting a text message very soon."

"You don't seem too upset about it," she said lightly, unable to gauge his mood.

"I don't really care what Emma thinks. Do you?"

"No. You disappeared for a while. Where did you go?"

"I was talking to Max. He's going to look at the police reports from the night of Leanne's accident."

"That's good, I guess."

"I know you think I should let this go, but even if I were willing to do that, Mitch wouldn't let this go. He's going to keep pushing and prodding and digging until he comes up with an answer he likes. Or maybe he'll just make one up. I don't know. But I can't keep playing defense. I have to go on offense."

She understood, but she had a feeling things were going to get a lot worse before they got better.

Her phone rang, and her heart jumped at the number. It wasn't Emma; it was Paul—again. She'd really hoped she'd heard the last from him. "It looks like neither one of us can escape our past," she muttered. She muted the phone, letting whatever Paul had to say go to voicemail. Then she played it back on speaker.

"They know you're in San Francisco, Maddie," Paul said. "I don't know how they know, but they sent me a photo of you walking in the city. They said if I didn't pay up, you were going to get hurt. Call me back. Tell me where you are. We need to figure this out." She sighed. "He has to be making it up."

"You said you felt like someone was watching you earlier."

"That was my imagination."

"Or not." He shot her a look. "Looks like we both have problems."

"Paul has made stuff up before. He's a liar."

"Text him. Ask him to send you the photo he saw."

"Okay, good idea." It took a minute for Paul to reply. "He says he doesn't have it. They showed it to him, but they didn't give him a copy."

"Ask him what was in the photo—if there were any landmarks."

Paul's answer was vague. "He doesn't remember. He was just shocked to see that they were following me. He remembers that I was wearing jeans." She looked over at Burke. "I pretty much live in jeans. He's just trying to scare me. He thinks I can get help from my parents or from friends." She put her phone into her bag as Burke drove into his parking garage.

Despite the fact that she thought Paul was just trying to rattle her, she was more than a little happy to have Burke's strong body next to hers as they made their way up to his apartment. She must have gotten a little too close, because Burke gave her a speculative look.

"You're scared, aren't you, Maddie?"

"A little. I'm worried that I might bring trouble to you, Burke, and you have enough on your plate. Maybe I should go to a motel."

"You're not going anywhere. And tomorrow we'll call Max and see if he can also look into your problem."

"We're going to be keeping Max busy."

"He won't mind."

As Burke opened the door to his apartment for her, she felt like she was coming home, and that worried her even more than the threat from Paul.

She couldn't let herself get too comfortable here. This wasn't home. She was just crashing here until she found somewhere else to live, and that was something she needed to start focusing on very soon.

"What time do you go to work?" she asked as she took off her coat.

"My shift runs seven a.m. tomorrow until seven a.m. Tuesday. You'll have the place to yourself."

"I really appreciate this, Burke."

He put up a hand. "You've already thanked me too many times, Maddie. Please stop."

"All right, but—"

"No 'buts'."

As they stared at each other, she was suddenly acutely aware of how alone they were. It was a Saturday night, almost ten-thirty, but a little too early to go to bed. What on earth were they going to do?

The ideas that ran through her head at that question were all bad.

Clearing her throat, she said, "Do you want to watch some TV or something?" She mentally kicked herself for adding *or something* because it brought up more bad ideas, all of which involved taking off her clothes and getting a lot closer to Burke.

"Yeah, we could watch a movie." He walked over to the couch and sat down, then picked up the remote. "I've got *On Demand*. Have you seen any of the new releases?"

"I haven't been to the movies in ages."

"Let's pick one." He patted the couch next to him.

She hesitated for a second, thinking the chair might be a better choice, but in the end she joined him on the couch. This was Burke—he wasn't going to do anything she didn't want him to do.

What if she did want him to do something...

No, she didn't want that. She didn't need to complicate her life any more than it already was. They were just friends. Burke was helping her out because he was a good guy. There was nothing else going on.

That reminder made it easier to sit next to him, and soon they were scrolling through the list of movie suggestions.

"What do you like?" he asked. "Romance, mystery, sci-fi..."

"Anything with a good story. What about you?"

"Same." He flung her a quick smile. "We actually have something in common. Who would have thought?"

"Certainly not me," she said, smiling back at him. "I saw some popcorn in your cupboard earlier. You pick the movie. I'll make us a snack."

"Sounds like a plan."

Fifteen minutes later, Maddie was sitting on the couch next to Burke, a blanket around her shoulders, a bowl of popcorn on the table, watching a World War II adventure and love story. She liked Burke's choice. The movie had enough suspense to be intriguing and enough romance to not be boring. She liked stories that came alive through characters and not just action/chase scenes.

She also liked sitting next to Burke. His body was so close to hers she was tempted to rest her head on his shoulder or cuddle into his arms, but she had to remind herself that this was not a date and they were not anything more than friends.

The movie was long and the battle scenes started to go on and on.

She found her eyes drifting closed. She heard Burke say her name but after that, nothing.

She felt warm, comfortable, safe, and it had been forever since she'd felt that way.

—▶▶◀◀◀—

He should wake Maddie up. He should go to bed and let her stretch out on the couch.

At the very least, he should move her away from him. But as Maddie had drifted off to sleep, she'd curled up next to him, resting her head on his shoulder and putting her arm across his waist. Her silky hair brushed his chin, and he could smell the faint scent of lavender clinging to her skin. Her breath came softly through her parted lips, lips so pink and sweet, he was dying to take a taste.

But this was Maddie.

She was in a vulnerable position. She was fragile and a little scared. He couldn't take advantage of those emotions.

Sighing, he rested his head against the back of the couch. He felt off his game, too.

Memories of the day flashed through his head. The horseback ride on the beach seemed like it had happened weeks ago instead of hours ago, but since they'd gotten back to the city, there had been one nasty surprise after another, both for him and for Maddie.

He closed his eyes, his head starting to throb from the

stress and puzzling, unanswered questions. The television hummed in the background. He told himself he'd get up in a minute…

———⟫⟪———

Maddie woke up feeling deliciously warm and content, as if everything was completely right with the world, but as her sleepy haze turned to awareness, other senses came into play. The steady beat of her heart was mirrored by another. The arms that held her were not her own but belonged to Burke. Her pillow was his chest, and her leg was not entangled in the blanket but wrapped around Burke's thigh.

Blinking her eyes open, she lifted her head and found herself staring straight into his intense blue eyes. His sleepy gaze and sexy morning scruff made her mouth water. But it was the gleam in his eyes that sent the butterflies dancing in her stomach.

He wanted her.

It seemed almost too surprising to be true.

But she knew what desire looked like…and what it felt like. And it felt like this.

She licked her lips, and the gesture only darkened his gaze. His arms tightened around her.

And slowly, so slowly, he pulled her closer.

Another long look…

A moment to escape…

She didn't want to run. She just wanted him.

There was so much electricity in the air, so much tension between them, it felt like the kiss started long before their lips came together.

She'd expected a tentative, wary kiss, because Burke didn't leap without looking. She, on the other hand, usually jumped right in. Their kiss started somewhere in the middle, but quickly escalated into a fiery, passionate encounter.

She'd wanted to kiss Burke so many times over the years she could hardly believe it was happening. A half dozen fantasies came true with each angled open-mouth kiss, each slide of their tongues, each intermingled breath of passion. Kissing Burke kicked off a desire that ran through every nerve ending.

She slid down on top of Burke, her soft breasts tingling with pleasure as they came into contact with his hard chest. She loved the feel of his body beneath hers. She also loved the way he held her to him with power and strength, as if she were his for the taking. Hell, maybe she was. All she could think about right now was removing the clothes between them. She fought her way to a sitting position and then pulled her sweater up over her head, tossing it onto the couch.

Burke's gaze turned even more appreciative as he took in her hot pink lacy bra with cups that barely covered her generous curves. He pulled her forward, running his mouth along the edge of her bra, driving her crazy with anticipation.

Finally, he flicked open the clasp and kissed one breast, then the other, swirling his tongue around her taut nipples.

She reached for the hem of his shirt, wanting to touch him more intimately.

He helped her get the shirt off, and she stared at his hard, ripped body with genuine amazement. "You're in great shape," she muttered.

He smiled, meeting her gaze. "I like your shape, too." He pulled her back in for another kiss. It had barely gotten started when the sharp peal of a phone alarm broke them apart.

"What's that?" she asked in bemusement.

"My phone." He picked up his phone from the table and shut off the alarm. "Damn, Maddie, I have to go to work."

"Right. Work." She pulled the sides of her bra back

together and grabbed her sweater off the couch, holding it in front of her as she slid away from Burke.

Now that she was really awake, now that she was fully aware of exactly what they were doing, she didn't know what to say, how to act. It had been a lot easier to pretend she was just living out a really good dream.

"I guess we fell asleep on the couch," she said, feeling stupid for stating the obvious.

"I meant to get up, but you were so comfortable with your head on my shoulder."

She groaned. "I fell asleep on you?"

"I didn't mind. I liked waking up with you even more."

She couldn't deny the past few minutes had been fairly spectacular. "Me, too."

His gaze darkened with her admission. "I wish I didn't have to leave, but we're shorthanded at work."

"I understand."

"Do you? Because I sure as hell want to blow off work and take this into the bedroom."

Her pulse raced at the image his words created. She licked her lips. "We both know that shouldn't happen. We don't want to do something we'll regret."

"You think you would regret it?" he asked, his question suddenly sharp.

"Me? No. But I'm a lot better at living in the moment than you are. You usually prefer to have a plan. Am I part of any plan?"

His hesitation gave her the answer.

"I didn't think so," she said, pulling her sweater back over her head.

He got to his feet. "I'm going to take a shower."

She was more than happy to send him on his way so she could pull herself together.

He moved toward the hallway, then paused. "Just for the record, Maddie..."

"What?" she asked when he left the sentence hanging.

"Taking you to bed has been featured in more than a few of my plans over the years."

Her jaw dropped at his provocative words, but before she could say anything, he was gone.

What? He'd thought about taking her to bed? She had never expected him to say that.

Her body tingled all over.

If he wanted to take her to bed, and she wanted to go to bed with him, there was a good chance they were going to end up there, but then what?

She'd told herself she was done with men. It was time to concentrate on a career, on getting her life together, and that's what she should do.

But sex with Burke sounded like a lot more fun...

No, she'd had fun. Maybe too much fun. It was time to be a responsible adult, wasn't it?

Ten

As Burke showered under a cold streaming spray, he couldn't help wondering if Maddie wouldn't surprise him in the shower. If she did, he was going to be really late to work. He'd always felt the sparks with her. She was crazy if she didn't think he'd ever dreamed about her, ever wondered what it would be like between them.

Over the years he'd fantasized many times about how she would kiss, but the reality had far surpassed the dreams. He'd expected passion, impulsiveness, generosity and he'd gotten all that, but he'd also gotten tender, deep and serious, as if the kiss was the start of something more.

That thought was unsettling. He didn't know if he was ready for another relationship, especially a relationship with someone like Maddie.

But damn she was beautiful. Those eyes of her seduced him at every turn. Her lips invited him in with every smile, and she had a really gorgeous pair of breasts. His body tightened at the memory of her soft flesh in his hands.

Damn! He had it bad.

Had he always wanted her? When had annoyance turned to attraction? Not that she probably wouldn't still annoy him, but it might be worth a little irritation to get closer to her. He'd spent the past decade of his life focused on building his career, being the firefighter his father and grandfather wanted him to be and the kind of firefighter he wanted himself to be.

Maybe that focus had caused the rift in his relationship with Leanne. Had he put too much of his energy into work and not enough into her? Is that why she'd cheated on him? She'd had to have felt something was missing from their relationship to go to Mitch. Would they have worked out their problems if she hadn't died? Would she have told him about the baby? Would she have really had the nerve to terminate a pregnancy?

He would never know the answers to any of those questions.

But knowing how much he'd missed in that relationship made him wary of getting involved with someone else, at least not until he knew what had happened three years ago.

He frowned. Now he was sounding like Mitch Warren, so obsessed with the past, he couldn't move forward.

Shivering in the cold water, he finally stepped out of the shower and dried off.

After getting dressed, he returned to the living room to find Maddie had whipped up pancakes for breakfast.

"I know you're probably in a hurry," she said, not quite meeting his eyes. "But maybe you can grab a quick bite before you go."

"You're spoiling me," he said, sitting down at the table. The stack of pancakes was too delicious to resist.

"It's nothing much. Cooking isn't work to me. It's a joy. Better than therapy, my mom used to say, although you probably think I could have used some actual therapy."

He was happy to hear the joking note in her voice. Maddie had a way of making whatever tense situation she was in feel less awkward. "I think you handle yourself really well. What are your plans today?"

"I'm meeting Emma and Nicole at the farmer's market. Then I'm going to practice some cooking techniques in preparation for my interview tomorrow. I should probably also go online and start looking for an apartment. So, lots to do."

Even though he knew she would move out soon, he didn't really like the idea. He'd been living on his own for a long time and had always thought he preferred it that way. But having Maddie around was nice, maybe a little too nice. He could almost imagine them living together, sleeping together, having breakfast together.

The intensity of that thought shocked him a little. He needed to get a grip.

He focused on the other part of Maddie's statement. "I didn't realize you had made plans with Emma and Nicole."

"Is it a problem?'

"No, but I'm sure they're both going to grill you about me."

"I'm sure. Anything in particular you want me to say?"

He shrugged. "Whatever you want, Maddie. I'll leave it up to you."

"Okay." She hesitated. "Burke, should we talk about what happened earlier?"

"I don't need to, do you?"

"I guess not," she said slowly. "We were both waking up and not thinking straight…"

"So you do want to talk about it?"

"No. I'm good."

He was happy with her response, because the last thing he wanted to do was discuss what had almost happened and what might be coming next. "I need to get to work. Thanks for breakfast. Call me if you need anything. Or if you get bored, you can always come by the firehouse. It's at the corner of Hobart and 27th." He paused. "If your ex calls you again, if you feel at all worried or concerned about him or anyone else, please let me know."

"I'll be fine, Burke."

"Are you going to call Paul back?" He really hated that idea. He didn't want her to have anything more to do with the guy.

"No, but I have a feeling I haven't heard the last of him."

"You should get a new phone."

"Maybe when I'm not so cash poor."

"I could lend you some money."

"Absolutely not," she said with a definitive shake of her head. "You've done enough."

"Fine, but you should tell Emma about Paul. I was going to contact Max this morning, but why don't you talk to Em about it? Perhaps Max can talk to the police in Las Vegas and find out who's threatening Paul and subsequently threatening you."

She groaned. "I know you're right, but I really hate to bring Emma and Nicole into this."

"I don't think you have a choice, Maddie. Paul is hounding you and raising the stakes with each call. He could go after your parents when they get back from their trip. You need to get help."

"All right. I'll talk to her."

"Good. You shouldn't underestimate the actions of a desperate person."

She stared back at him with her big green eyes. "I should give you the same advice, Burke. I worry about what Mitch is going to do next."

He both liked and hated the concern in her eyes.

Impulsively, he leaned down and gave her a quick kiss. "Don't worry. Everything is going to be fine."

As he left the apartment, he really hoped that was true.

———※※———

Maddie met Nicole and Emma at the Java Hut just before ten. After getting coffees and a pastry to share at the small café near the Ferry Building, they sat down at a table by the water. It was a beautiful San Francisco Sunday, plenty of sunshine and blue skies.

Maddie had barely taken her first sip of her soy latte when Emma said, "What's going on with you and Burke?"

"Why did I know that was going to be the first question?" she asked.

"Maybe because you got into his car last night," Emma returned.

Maddie glanced away from Emma's sharp gaze to see a thoughtful look in Nicole's eyes. "I suppose you're curious, too."

"I am," Nicole admitted. "I'm a little surprised that you didn't mention you and Burke had come to the party together. You did come together, didn't you?"

"Yes. We didn't want everyone to get the wrong idea, but I guess that's exactly what happened." She paused and sipped her coffee, then said. "Burke is letting me crash on his couch for a few days while I find a new apartment."

"How did that come about?" Emma asked.

"The sublet I had fell through, and Burke was around when I discovered that I had nowhere to live."

"How was Burke around?"

Maddie sighed, beginning to see why Emma was such a good investigator. She did not miss a detail. "You have a lot of questions."

"I do. You and Burke—it's an interesting combination, as I mentioned last night."

"And as I told you before, Burke and I are like oil and water. We can coexist, but we don't mix well." Although they had mixed it up earlier that day with a really great kiss.

"How are you so different?" Emma challenged.

"I'm spontaneous and free-spirited. I like to travel and try new things. Burke is organized and a planner. He doesn't do anything without considering the pros and cons, not that that is a bad thing. He's obviously doing better in his life than I am."

"It sounds to me like you complement each other, like you need each other."

"It sounds to me like you're matchmaking."

"Guilty," Emma admitted. "It's just nice to see Burke smile. When he was with you last night, he looked happier than he's been in a long time. Friday night, at Leanne's dinner, he was grim and weighed down. But somehow, in twenty-four hours that changed, and I think that's because of you." She glanced at Nicole. "Don't you think so, too?"

"I'm not sure," Nicole said a bit more cautiously. "I don't know if it's such a good idea for you and Burke to get involved."

She was a little surprised at Nicole's reaction. "Just out of curiosity—why?"

"Burke has been in a dark place for a while, and I wouldn't want you to get hurt."

"You think Burke could hurt me?"

Nicole met her gaze. "I think there have always been sparks between you two, even back in high school. But as you said, you're very different people. Burke is guarded and you're very open. After Leanne, I don't know how easy it will be for him to give his heart again, and I think sometimes you give your heart away too fast."

"It's funny how you still know me so well," she murmured.

"We were good friends. I wish we hadn't lost touch. I know I'm a lot to blame for that. After I had Brandon, and especially after he was diagnosed with autism, I've been completely caught up in his life, his problems. I've lost most of my friends."

"I'm sure you haven't lost anyone," she said. "I just wish I'd been a better friend to you."

"You didn't know what I was going through." Nicole sipped her coffee, then said, "I'd love for you and Burke to get together, if it's what you both want. Just make sure you're on the same page. I adore Burke. He's the best guy in the world, but a lot has happened in his life, and now it all seems to be happening again."

"Neither of you needs to worry about me and Burke. We're friends. And there's a better chance of driving each other crazy in the next few days than falling in love. It's probably more believable that we'll go from friends to enemies than friends to lovers."

"Love and hate—two sides of the same coin," Emma said.

She laughed. "Who told you that?"

"I don't remember, but I think it's true. I thought I hated Max in the beginning, but I quickly learned that I loved him."

"Max seems like a very good guy."

"He's amazing. But enough about Max and Burke—are you working at the Hanover Club full time, Maddie?"

"No, I only work Thursday and Friday nights for special events. It's a part-time gig. I'm interviewing for a chef's position tomorrow. I want to pick up some fresh produce and proteins at the farmer's market so I can practice a few dishes tonight. I'm not sure what they're going to have me make, but I want to dust off my techniques a little bit."

"Which restaurant?" Emma asked.

"311 Post."

Emma raised an eyebrow. "Posh. I've never been there, as it's out of my price range, but I've heard it's amazing. Don't they have a celebrity chef?"

"Wilder Harte is the owner. He has three Michelin stars. But he doesn't cook much anymore. He's too busy running his restaurants all over the world."

"Wait, is that his real name—Wilder Harte?"

Maddie laughed. "I know it sounds made up, but I think it's his real name. He's thirty-five years old, gorgeous, arrogant as hell from what I hear, but also brilliant in the kitchen. I'm applying for a job on the line, but his line cook is like any other restaurant's executive chef position. So I have to be on my toes and wow him and his executive chef tomorrow."

"Sounds stressful," Nicole said. "Are you sure that's the kind of place you want to work? It doesn't really sound like the free-spirited Maddie I grew up with, the one who liked to experiment by mixing pickles and peanut butter."

She laughed. "It was pickles and pretzels mixed into butterscotch cookies, and they were good."

"That sounds disgusting," Emma said.

"Actually, they were amazing," Nicole said. "I was shocked."

"Pickles and peanut butter is a good combination, too," Maddie added.

"Somehow I don't think they serve that at 311 Post," Nicole said.

"No, but right now it's my only interview, so I'm going to

go for it." 311 Post might be a little stuffy and rich for her taste, but beggars couldn't be choosers, and she would learn a lot. Wilder was a brilliant chef and restaurateur, and his menu was innovative and complex.

She finished her coffee and was about to suggest they head to the market when her phone rang. One look at the screen told her it was Paul, reminding her that she was supposed to talk to Emma about him.

"Something wrong?" Emma asked.

"You really don't miss a thing, do you?"

"I've gotten very good at reading body language. Are you avoiding someone?"

"My ex-boyfriend. He's turning out to be an even bigger problem than I thought."

Emma's gaze filled with concern. "Is he stalking you?"

"Yes and no. He doesn't want me back, but he does want me to help him pay off some loans. He's a gambler, and he's gotten into debt with the wrong people—people who have already threatened me in his name. That's why I left Vegas and came here. I was hoping to put the problem behind me, but apparently not."

"Did you go to the police?" Emma asked.

"I should have."

"You should have," Emma agreed. "Why don't you give me the particulars, and I'll ask Max to look into the situation?"

"Would you mind?"

"Of course not. I want you to be safe, Maddie."

"I don't know that I'm in danger, but Paul did tell me yesterday that the guys who are after him know I'm here in the city, that they showed him a photo of me."

"That's creepy," Nicole said.

Emma picked up her phone. "Tell me what you know

about the people involved in this bad loan deal. Names, places, anything you can remember. I will get Max on it as soon as I get home."

Maddie related everything she knew about Paul and his bookie friends while Emma jotted down the information on her phone.

"I feel so stupid for being such a sucker," she added.

"Some people are good at hiding their true selves," Emma said. "Don't blame yourself for not being able to see what they're hiding. I was the victim of a stalking and I had no idea who was doing it until he finally confronted me."

"You're going to have to tell me that story sometime."

"Sometime," Emma said. "But not today. Are you ready to go to the market?"

"More than ready."

As they headed to the nearby farmer's market, their conversation turned to old friends, shared memories. There were a lot of stories, a lot of laughs.

It was just like old times, Maddie thought, feeling amazingly happy to have reconnected with the Callaway women—and the Callaway men...

Eleven

After spending hours wandering through the farmer's market, Maddie returned to Burke's apartment and started to cook. With music playing through her ear buds and spices warming her senses, she felt happier than she had in a long while.

By midnight, the refrigerator was packed with the results of her efforts, and she was exhausted. After changing into her PJ's, she wandered down the hall into Burke's bedroom. She lay down on top of the bed for about two minutes, wondering if she should take him up on his offer to use his bed while he was at the firehouse.

It was very comfortable, but lying in Burke's bed felt almost too—intimate. She could smell his aftershave on the pillows. She could imagine him next to her, on top of her, their naked bodies moving in perfect sync.

That thought sent her to her feet.

She went back to the living room—to the couch—to the reminder that she was just a guest in Burke's home. They weren't involved. They weren't having a relationship. And in a few days, she'd be gone.

While she'd had a few short-term flings in her life, she

couldn't do that with Burke. If she slept with him and never saw him again, it would probably break her heart. Her emotions were too tangled when it came to him. They had too much history and too much baggage. She needed to keep things exactly where they were. No more making out, no more wild fantasies.

But as she closed her eyes, it was Burke's image that took her into sleep.

Monday morning she got up, took out her yoga mat and did some stretches and easy poses to help herself get focused and centered. She had a big day ahead of her, a chance to change her life for the better, and she wanted to be ready for the opportunity.

At half past one, she was on her way across town, arriving at 311 Post just before her two o'clock appointment.

The restaurant was only open for dinner, so she knocked on the front door. A manager let her in and escorted her through the spectacularly luxurious dining room to the equally amazing kitchen. He told her the executive chef would be with her shortly.

As she looked around the kitchen, she felt both excited and terrified. There was a sleek sterility that worried her, but that was ridiculous. How could she complain about a state-of-the-art cooking facility? Sure, it wasn't like the country kitchens in Italy that had been overflowing with home-grown produce and constantly smelled of garlic, oregano and rosemary, but this kitchen probably had the best equipment she'd ever seen in her life and some equipment she'd never seen before.

Wilder Harte liked to experiment with molecular cooking, which turned cooking into a science. It wasn't an area she knew much about, but it was steadily gaining in popularity among the foodie crowd, so she probably needed to learn more about it.

A tall, rail-thin man walked into the kitchen wearing a white chef's coat. He had a short, almost military haircut that matched the stern expression on his face. Somewhere in his early forties, he might have been somewhat attractive if he didn't look mean.

"Miss Heller," he said with a nod. "Chef Partaine."

He had a decidedly French accent, which didn't make her feel any better. She'd found the few French chefs she'd worked under to be very exacting and not a particularly good fit for her. They could cook, though, and she needed to be open to every possibility. "It's nice to meet you, Chef," she said, shaking his hand.

"Katherine Bates gave you a glowing recommendation. I hope you can live up to it."

Katherine was a chef she'd worked with in Las Vegas, and without her recommendation, Maddie doubted she would have gotten the interview. "I hope so, too."

"I'd like you to prepare two of our most popular dishes so I can see your technique." He handed her the menu. "The pistachio crusted rack of lamb with pancetta and the pigeon breast cooked sous vide with beet puree. I assume you're familiar with sous vide."

"Yes." Sous vide was a method of cooking food sealed in airtight plastic bags in a water bath, temperature-controlled steam environment. She didn't do it often, but at least she was familiar with the technique.

"You have exactly ninety minutes to complete your dishes. You'll find everything you need in the pantry."

"Okay," she said, already making up a mental to-do list. It was asking a lot to work in a new kitchen with recipes she had never tasted before and didn't know that much about, but she would give it her all and hope for the best. "Will Mr.

Harte be judging the dishes as well?"

"No. Mr. Harte was delayed. He won't be coming in today," Chef Partaine said, looking down his long nose at her. "If you have talent, we'll discuss options."

She let out a breath as the chef left her alone in the kitchen.

Ninety minutes to change her life—she hoped it was enough time.

An hour and a half later, she knew it wasn't nearly enough time. She wished she could have had another ten minutes to perfect her dishes, but she did manage to get two plates ready for Chef Partaine. They weren't as pretty as she would have liked. However, she was fairly certain her flavors were right. Time would tell.

He studied her plates in silence for a good five minutes, then he proceeded to taste each element separately. His expression revealed absolutely nothing. He didn't finish all the food on the plate, but he didn't spit anything out. That had to be a good thing.

She surreptitiously wiped some sweat off her brow as he finished his tasting. She hadn't felt such pressure while cooking in a very long time. Making food was a joy for her, but today it had felt very much like work. She hoped she'd been able to fake some of the pleasure she usually felt, because cooking with love, nurturing each element, was the way she usually came up with the best dishes.

Chef Partaine finally set down his fork. "Competent, adequate, the flavors worked well for the most part. I thought the lamb was undercooked, and there was a slightly bitter quality to the beet puree. Otherwise, it was acceptable."

She didn't think *adequate* and *acceptable* were adjectives that would get her hired.

"We're interviewing two other chefs this week," he

continued. "We'll be in touch if we decide to have you back for a second interview."

"Okay, thank you. It was a privilege to cook in this beautiful kitchen."

"It is a privilege. We hire only the best of the best."

"Is there anything else I can tell you about my background?"

"I know all I need to know. Thank you for coming in."

She nodded. "Shall I clean up?"

"We have staff for that."

"All right." She took off her chef's coat and set it on the counter, then followed the chef out of the kitchen.

Chef Partaine engaged a server in conversation as they entered the dining room, so she made her way out of the restaurant on her own. The prep was already beginning for dinner service, and she could feel the tension in the staff members as they reported for duty. It was almost a relief to step outside.

When she hit the sidewalk, she took a deep breath of fresh air. It was four o'clock and the sun was starting to go down. The sky was a beautiful mix of pink, purple and orange, a refreshing view after the sleek gray steel environment she had just stepped out of. Heading down the street, she caught the bus back to Burke's apartment.

Fifteen minutes later, she flopped down on the couch, happy to be done with the pressure of the interview. She was not at all certain she would be asked back for a second interview unless the other two chefs they were speaking to managed to do something lower than adequate and acceptable. But she had learned something about herself today and also last night. Cooking was what she wanted to do with her life. If it didn't happen at 311 Post, then she'd simply have to find another opportunity. But she did not want to be a waitress anymore, and she didn't want to be stuck making salads or sauces; she wanted a job where she could showcase her talents.

It was her own fault for having jumped around so much, sometimes throwing away opportunities because of personal relationships or because it was time to move on to the next big thing. That wasn't going to happen anymore. She needed to put her career on the front burner.

Getting up from the couch, she walked into the kitchen to grab a diet cola out of the fridge. When she saw the stacked dishes, an idea took form in her mind. There was no way she could eat all this food, and she doubted Burke could work his way through it even if she froze a few items for later in the week. She needed to find a few people to share it with, and what better place than a firehouse without a good cook?

Burke had told her to call or come by after her interview. She hadn't wanted to bother him at work, but what the heck…she'd come bearing food. That should make her welcome.

She grabbed some canvas tote bags out of the closet and packed up the food, then called a cab on her way out the door. She'd bus it on the way home when her load was lighter.

--➤◆◄--

Burke leaned back in his office chair as he glanced at his watch. It was almost five. Maddie had to be done with her interview by now. He was very curious as to how it had gone. He could call her. It would be the polite thing to do.

Only he wouldn't be doing it out of politeness.

The truth was he hadn't been able to stop thinking about her since he'd left his apartment the previous morning. He'd picked up the phone to call her a half dozen times, but somehow he had found a way to stop himself.

So he'd call her now. He had good reasons to make contact. He wanted to hear about her interview. He wanted to make sure that Paul wasn't hassling her or that Mitch hadn't shown up at his apartment again. But those reasons didn't take into account the fact that he just wanted to hear her voice.

Damn! He drew in a breath and slowly let it out. He hadn't felt so tied up in knots over a woman in—forever. Not even with Leanne had he felt such a push-pull.

With Leanne, it had been easy. They had the same values. They both liked to work. He'd thought they were very compatible. They'd never really argued until they'd gotten engaged, until all hell had broken loose, for reasons he still didn't understand, but those reasons obviously had something to do with Mitch.

The thought of Mitch brought a frown to his face. He'd already received a call from his father, acting in his official capacity as Deputy Chief of Operations. Jack Callaway wanted him to come by tomorrow morning after his shift and talk about what had happened between him and Mitch at Leanne's party. It was not a conversation he wanted to have. He'd managed to avoid talking to his father about it at Nicole's party, but apparently his dad was not going to be put off indefinitely.

On the other hand, he probably needed to talk to his father, because he was concerned that Mitch was running a firehouse and that his erratic behavior and obsession with Leanne's death would somehow play a factor in his competency as a firefighter, as a captain, as a man who had the power to send his brother Colton into a dangerous situation. He'd like to think Mitch could separate his professional life from his personal life, but from what he'd seen over the weekend, he wasn't sure that was true anymore.

A knock came at his half-open door, and he looked up to see Shelby in the doorway.

She gave him a tentative smile. "How's it going? We haven't had any time to talk this shift."

"I know; it's been busy."

"Have you heard from Mitch again?" she asked, taking a seat in the chair in front of his desk.

"He showed up at my building on Saturday. He's hired an investigator to look into Leanne's death."

"Again? I thought he already did that."

"He's starting over."

"Has the investigator found anything new?"

He hesitated. Shelby had been a good friend to him since Leanne died, but he didn't want to tell anyone about the pregnancy, at least not right now. "I don't think so, but Mitch is still convinced that he will."

"The accident was three years ago. What could anyone find out now?"

"That's what I said."

"Is there anything I can do to help, Burke? Do you want me to speak to Mitch? I haven't talked to him much since Leanne died, but I could approach him, see if he would talk to me. We were all pretty friendly at one time."

His gaze narrowed at her answer. "What do you mean—you were all pretty friendly?"

Confusion entered her eyes. "I don't understand."

Of course she didn't understand, because she didn't know what he knew, and he wasn't sure he should bring her into the loop. But Shelby had been close to Leanne in the weeks before her death. Shelby's aunt was a wedding planner in Los Angeles, and because Shelby had worked for her aunt while she was in college, she'd offered to help Leanne plan the wedding.

"Burke?" Shelby prodded. "What aren't you telling me?"

"Did you ever think that Leanne and Mitch were more than friends?"

Her eyes widened at the question. "Are you saying that you think Leanne cheated on you?"

"Mitch has suggested that to me."

"Oh, I don't know, Burke. Can you really believe anything Mitch has to say?"

"I'd prefer not to."

"Mitch was always jealous of you. He definitely had a thing for Leanne, but I never saw her return his feelings."

He felt relieved to hear that. Or at least relieved that Shelby had never noticed anything that he might have missed. "Leanne was stressed in the weeks before she died. I thought it was just the wedding, but now I wonder if there was something else. Did she ever confide in you, Shelby?"

"She told me she was overwhelmed with all the details. She wanted to keep both you and her mother happy, and you both wanted different things. I told her that she should really only worry about you, because you were the one she was marrying, not her mother. She said that was good advice." Shelby paused. "Leanne was a lovely woman. Her death was tragic. But I hope you don't allow Mitch to pull you back into that dark place, Burke. It has been so nice to see you smiling again. I don't want that to change."

"Thanks, Shelby."

She got to her feet, then paused. "So how long is your friend going to stay at your place?"

"I'm not sure. Maddie is looking for somewhere else to live, but I don't know how long it will take her to find the right situation."

"You know her from high school, you said?"

"Yes. Her parents hired me to tutor her in algebra. She

and my sister Nicole were friends, so I also saw her around the house. Maddie was a wild child back then with pink and purple streaks in her hair."

"She doesn't sound at all like the kind of girl you would date."

"Definitely not. At least not then," he heard himself add, then felt like kicking himself after he saw the interest in Shelby's eyes. Like his sisters, the women he worked with at the firehouse were always looking to set him up.

Speaking of women, he was surprised to find Rachel now in his doorway. She had a curious gleam in her eyes. "Chief, there's someone here to see you."

"Who's that?"

"A very attractive blonde with really pretty green eyes, which would have made the guys swarm around her on any day, but she also brought food—lots and lots of food."

He was on his feet before Rachel finished speaking. Maddie was here?

His pulse sped up as he walked out of his office, barely aware of Rachel and Shelby following close behind. When he got to the kitchen he found Maddie surrounded by his coworkers, and the men were all suddenly eager to help with dinner.

His cousin Dylan gave him a grin. "Our prayers were answered, Burke."

"Like you've been to church in the last decade," he muttered, his gaze seeking Maddie's.

She gave him a bright, somewhat uncertain smile, as if she wasn't quite sure of her welcome. "Hi, Burke. I made food."

"I can see that."

"I was practicing for my interview, and I got a little carried away." She stepped around the counter and crossed the room, leaving the men to unwrap the casserole dishes. "Hi, Shelby."

"It's nice to see you again, Maddie. Thanks for bringing food. It's been slim pickings around here the last few months." She paused. "My break is over. I have to get back to dispatch. If you need anything, Burke..."

"I know where to find you."

As Shelby left, he turned his gaze back to Maddie, feeling like his heart was about to explode with happiness at the sight of her. What the hell was wrong with him?

"I hope it's all right that I brought food," Maddie said. "I didn't want it to go to waste, and I remembered what you said about losing your cook."

"It's more than all right; it's great."

"Should I heat things up?"

"I think the guys can handle that. Why don't you come into my office for a minute?"

"Okay." As they walked out of the room and down the hall, she said, "I've never been to a firehouse before. Is there an actual pole you slide down when the alarm goes off?"

"Nope. One-story building."

"Right," she said with a little laugh. "I should have figured that out."

He grinned as he led her into his office.

"This is all yours?"

He moved behind the desk. "Yes, it is. My job has turned into a lot of paperwork."

"It's very impressive—all that you've accomplished."

He shrugged and urged her to take a seat. "How did the interview go?"

She sat down and said, "Not horrible, not great. The executive chef said I did an adequate job. Not exactly a stellar review. He's interviewing other people, too. I don't think I'm going to get it."

"Sorry," he said, hating to see the disappointment in her eyes.

"It might be a good thing. I'm not sure that restaurant is the right place for me. I wouldn't have any opportunity to be creative. I could tell it's very rigid and regimented, and I don't have a long attention span. I'm afraid I'd get bored cooking up the same dishes day after day."

"Isn't that what happens in a restaurant?"

"Yes, that's why I need my own restaurant, then I can change things up."

"You'll get there, Maddie. You have a strong will."

"My will has taken a few hits in the last year, but I'll bounce back; I always do."

"Have you heard from your ex?"

"I got a call yesterday but I didn't answer it. Nothing today. I don't know if that's a good thing or a bad thing. I did talk to Emma about it. Max is going to look into the situation."

"Good."

"What about you? Any more word from Mitch?"

"No. But I wouldn't expect him to show up here. What happened Friday night has already gotten back to the top brass, and while they don't usually intervene in personnel problems—"

"You're a Callaway and your dad is going to want to know what's going on," she finished.

"That and the fact that Mitch assaulted me. That goes a little beyond just a personnel issue. I'm more concerned for my brother Colton; he has to work with Mitch, and that can't be fun."

"The sins of the brother, not the father, in this case."

"Exactly. I don't want Colton to pay for Mitch's intense

dislike of me, especially considering the work we do."

"Then maybe it's good your father is getting involved."

"It's rarely good when my father gets involved in my business," he said dryly. "But this might be the exception." He paused. "Did you sleep in my bed last night?"

His question turned her cheeks pink, and there was a brighter gleam in her eyes when she looked back at him. "No, I took the couch. Your bed is waiting for you."

"I want you to be comfortable, Maddie. It's really fine."

"And I was really fine on the couch."

Her words brought back the fact that they'd both slept on that couch Saturday night, and it had been very comfortable.

Dylan interrupted their conversation. "Hey, Burke, I just wanted to let you know that the food is going fast, so if you want some…"

"I do," he said, getting to his feet. "I'm starving."

As they walked out of his office, Dylan fell into step with Maddie. "I've never had fried ravioli before," he said. "It was fantastic. Did you cook everything you brought?"

"Yes, I was practicing my skills for an interview I had earlier today for a chef's job."

"Did you get it?" Dylan asked.

"I don't think so."

"Their loss. I'm sure you'll get snapped up." He stopped abruptly. "Wait a second. Have you ever thought about doing a food truck?"

"Sure, but I don't have the capital to invest in something like that," she said.

"I have an idea for you. My sister Kate has a friend who has a food truck, but he just broke his arm in a motorcycle accident. He can't cook with his cast, and he's losing business. He needs a temporary chef. I wonder if you could help him out for a few weeks while he's recovering and you're in between jobs. I'll give you my sister's number if you're interested. She can hook the two of you up."

"I'd really like that," Maddie said with excitement in her voice. "Thanks."

"No problem. Someone who cooks like you should definitely be cooking for the public. I'll call Kate and find out when you two can meet. Burke, can you be the go-between?"

"Sure." While Burke appreciated the way Dylan's words had made Maddie's eyes light up, he was thinking just the opposite, that he wouldn't mind keeping Maddie's cooking just for himself. Maybe he'd keep Maddie to himself, too.

"I'm so glad I came down here," Maddie said as they walked back into the lounge.

"A lot of people are happy about that," he said, waving his hand toward the table where his fellow firefighters were happily cleaning their plates.

"That's what dinner is supposed to look like. When I was at the restaurant earlier, I couldn't help thinking that I didn't feel very happy when I was cooking, and when I'm happy the food tastes better. Yesterday, when I was making all these dishes, I felt great. Maybe a food truck would be a better place for me."

"It probably doesn't pay as well. I doubt there are benefits. In fact, I'm not sure Kate's friend will be able to pay you anything." He hated to dampen her enthusiasm, but one of them had to be practical.

"You're right," Maddie agreed. "But it could be fun. Maybe that's worth more than security."

And just like that, he was reminded that he and Maddie had very different outlooks on life.

"I know you wouldn't think that," she added.

"I don't think fun is worth more than security, but it's worth something. It's good to love what you do—otherwise, why do it?"

She nodded, a hint of surprise in her gaze. "I agree."

"But it's nice when fun and security meet up. I'm not sure that's in a food truck run by my cousin's friend."

"Only one way to find out."

"True. I'm going to grab some food." He'd barely started toward the counter when the alarm went off. "Dammit. I have to go."

"I'll wrap up the food and put it in the fridge," Maddie said. "You can have it when you come back."

"You're an angel."

"I never thought I'd hear you call me that," she said with a laugh.

He grinned back at her. "I'm a little surprised, too."

"I guess food really is the way to a man's heart."

He didn't bother to answer, but it wasn't her food that had his heart beating faster. It was her beautiful green eyes, her enticing smile and those inviting lips...

The fire inside of him was burning just as hot as the one he was about to put out.

Twelve

⏤⇒≫⇐≪⇐⏤

After three hours spent working a warehouse fire, Burke got in five hours of sleep before his shift ended at seven Tuesday morning. He wanted to go directly home. He wanted to see Maddie again. He hadn't felt so eager to leave the firehouse in a long time. Work had been his salvation the last few years. But getting home would have to wait. First, he had to meet his father. If his dad hadn't asked him to come to the office, he might have tried to put him off, but when he went to headquarters, Jack Callaway was Deputy Chief of Operations and he was a Battalion Chief. He didn't ignore a direct call from his Deputy Chief. He just hoped he could limit the conversation to Mitch's behavior. He didn't want to get into a discussion with his father about Leanne.

When he got to his dad's office, he was surprised to see Colton standing in the hallway, texting someone on his phone. His youngest brother wore jeans and a T-shirt under a gray jacket. Like Burke, Colton was working the same shift out of another firehouse, a firehouse run by Captain Mitch Warren.

"Colton," he said.

Colton looked up and gave him a nod. "One second. I

have to send this to Olivia."

"How is Olivia?" Colton's girlfriend was in the process of relocating her life from New York to San Francisco and had been going back and forth the past few months.

"She's good," Colton said with a happy smile. "Liv will be officially living here starting next Monday. I can't wait. So Dad called you in, too?"

"Yes. I'm assuming this is about Mitch. How was your shift?"

"It was great. Mitch called in sick, so I didn't have to deal with him." Colton paused. "From the first day I started working with him, I knew there was tension between you, but Friday night he was out of his mind. He hates your guts. I know it has something to do with Leanne and that you're probably not going to tell me what it is, but I'm going to tell you that Mitch is not someone you should ignore—not anymore. Something tripped a switch in his brain. He's not just annoyed and grieving; he is fired up, and you're his target."

"I know. I'm handling it."

"I hope you can handle it. But the last time the two of you were together, Mitch ended up getting in the first and only punch."

"I chose not to hit back."

"Was that when you were on your ass tangled up with a pretty blonde?" Colton joked. "The same woman who happened to show up at Nicole's party with you?"

"Maddie is staying with me for a few days," he admitted. "And she did throw me off my stride last Friday night, but I also didn't want to get into a fight with Mitch and ruin the Parkers' memorial celebration." He thought about telling Colton that he'd gotten in a shot on Mitch on Saturday but decided it wasn't important to share that right now. It would just bring more questions.

His father's office door opened, and Jack Callaway beckoned them inside.

The office was comprised of a large oak desk in front of a big bay window with floor-to-ceiling bookcases on one wall and a large scheduling board on the opposite wall. Two straight chairs were placed in front of the desk. Burke and Colton slid into them while Jack sat back in his large leather chair and gave them both a contemplative look.

"We've got a problem," Jack said.

"The problem is mine," Burke cut in. "Colton doesn't need to be here for this."

"Hey, I work with the guy; you don't," Colton said. "So I'm in this, too."

"Colton is right. He's in a difficult position, caught between his brother and his boss." Jack paused. "I've called Captain Warren, but he hasn't returned my calls. I've told him that if he doesn't get back to me by five o'clock today, he'll be placed on temporary leave until we can speak to each other."

"That's a good decision," Colton said with an approving nod. "The last two weeks, Mitch has been acting erratically, blowing up at everyone for little to no reason, and he's been drinking a lot after work. He's not in a good mental place to lead. I don't know what changed, but something happened."

"I agree," Jack said. "I've spoken to some of the other firefighters at your house, Colton, and their opinions are the same as yours. I'd like to get Captain Warren a psychological evaluation to see if we can get to the root of his problems."

Burke knew what the root of Mitch's problem was—Leanne.

"Can you shed any light on the situation, Burke?" Jack asked.

"Mitch and Leanne were friends. He's been unable to

accept the fact that no one has been made accountable for Leanne's accident. He believes in some twisted way that I'm responsible for her death."

"You were working the night she died," Colton said quietly.

"He thinks I orchestrated the hit-and-run."

"That's absurd," Jack said, his gaze turning hard. "Why the hell would he think that?"

"You're going to have to ask him."

"Why don't you tell me why he thinks that?" Jack countered.

He hesitated. But if he couldn't trust his father and his brother, who could he trust? "Mitch told me that he and Leanne had an affair, that she was pregnant when she died, and he thinks I knew that she was having his baby, and that's why I wanted to kill her, or at least get rid of the baby."

Colton's jaw dropped and even his father looked taken aback by his words. For a long minute, there was nothing but silence in the room.

Jack was the first to recover. "I'm sorry, Burke. Did you know that—"

"They slept together? No. And I have only Mitch's word on that."

"You can't believe anything he says," Colton put in.

"I don't know that I believe him. I don't know that I believe any of it. I'm still trying to figure it all out. Apparently, the new investigator he hired discovered Leanne's medical records. And now he's looking into the accident again. Mitch is fired up, thinking he's going to finally know the truth."

"I wondered what had happened to knock him off the edge he was on," Colton said.

"Now you know."

"How can we help?" Jack asked.

"There's nothing you can do to help," he said, getting to his feet. "I'll work this out on my own, and I expect what I just said to stay between the three of us."

"You never need to say that," Jack returned. "We're family."

"Thanks. I'm glad you're pulling Mitch off the job. I think that's a good decision."

"I agree. Be careful, son."

"I will be."

He and Colton left the office together. They didn't speak until they left the building and were out on the busy streets of San Francisco.

"I want to help you, Burke," Colton said. "What can I do?"

"Nothing, Colton."

"I could reach out to Mitch's family. His sister came to the firehouse a few weeks ago. I'm sure I could get her number, see if she knows anything."

"I appreciate the offer, but I don't want you getting involved in this. Mitch could turn on you just as easily as he's turned on me."

"I'm not worried about that. I've been dealing with his bad attitude the past few months, and it hasn't been fun, but I've managed."

"Just stay out of it, Colton."

Colton sighed, shaking his head in disgust. "I know you still think of me as your bratty little brother, but I'm a grown man. I can help you out."

He smiled. "You were a brat, but I don't think of you that way anymore. You've proved yourself to be a good firefighter and an even better man. But I still don't want you involved in this. However, if you want to get Mitch's sister's phone number, I wouldn't say no."

"Consider it done. I'll text it to you as soon as I have it." Colton paused. "Don't believe the worst until you know for sure what the truth is."

Colton was talking about Leanne's infidelity, warning him against jumping to conclusions. The problem was—deep down—he knew it was true. *Why* was something he wasn't ever sure he'd find out unless he could get one of Leanne's friends or her parents to tell him something he didn't know.

But those concerns were for later. He wanted to get home. He wanted to see Maddie. And at the moment, that was all he really cared about.

———⋘⋙———

Tuesday morning, Maddie woke up to the sound of the front door opening. She jolted to a sitting position as Burke walked through the apartment door.

He gave her an apologetic smile. "Sorry, did I wake you?"

"What time is it?"

"Almost nine."

"That late?" She ran a hand through her tangled hair, wishing she'd woken up before he got home so she would have had a chance to shower and get dressed. She wrapped the blanket around her shoulders as he set a coffee down on the table in front of her.

"I wasn't sure what you liked, so I went with hazelnut latte."

"That's perfect. I can make us some breakfast."

"You've done enough cooking for me. Why don't I take you out for breakfast? There's a great little diner not too far from here."

"That sounds good. Can I take a quick shower?"

"Of course."

She got up from the couch, acutely conscious of her skimpy boxer shorts and clingy tank top. She grabbed the first clothes she could find from her open suitcase on the floor and dashed down the hall to the bathroom.

As she showered, she became fully awake and very aware that things were about to get more complicated. It had been one thing to stay at Burke's apartment while he was gone, but he was home now, and what that meant, where that would lead, she had no idea.

There was an attraction between them. She'd been trying to deny it for days, but it was real. She just had to decide what to do about it, and she didn't want to do anything for the wrong reasons. She was a little lost, drifting on a sea of uncertainty, and Burke was an anchor. But she didn't want to grab on to him because she was close to drowning. If there was going to be something between them, they had to come together as equals.

Too many people leaned on Burke. She didn't want to be one more. And he would let her lean on him, because that's the kind of man he was. He rescued people. He solved problems. He was a fixer. And she was probably in desperate need of fixing. But that wasn't the kind of relationship she wanted.

Not that she even wanted a relationship, she thought with a sigh. She was still trying to get rid of the tangled ties of her last affair. This wasn't the time to start another.

On the other hand, love wasn't something that necessarily waited for the right time, and she didn't want to miss out on something because she was afraid.

But she and Burke weren't in love, she told herself firmly. There was just some chemistry going on—probably because they were sharing a small space. Once she moved out, they'd probably never see each other again.

Turning off the shower, she toweled off, dried her hair and got dressed. Looking in the mirror, she felt a lot more ready to face the day.

When she returned to the living room, Burke was sitting on the couch and he was on the phone. She hesitated, not sure if he wanted some privacy, but he motioned her forward. She sat down in the chair next to the couch as he finished his call.

"Thanks, Max," he said. "Yeah, I'll let her know, and we both appreciate your help."

"What did Max find out?" she asked.

"A couple of things. It appears that your ex-boyfriend is in debt to a loan shark named Harry Barker. He's a well-known Vegas bookie who doesn't tolerate unpaid debts. He has a lot of muscle working for him, and to date he's been very good at avoiding arrest. Max said that your boyfriend should go to the police and see if he can work with them to get Harry Barker's operation shut down. They can protect him if he helps them build a case."

"I can't imagine he'd agree to that. It's a good idea, but Paul isn't..." She wasn't sure how to finish that sentence. "I don't think he's very brave. Since all this happened, he just seems to get weaker and weaker, like a scared little boy. I don't even recognize him anymore. Maybe he was always like that, and I just didn't see it."

"Well, if he calls you back, which he probably will, you might want to suggest this as an alternative to running away and trying to get other people to lend him money."

"I will."

"Max also said to keep your eyes open. While Barker operates mainly out of Vegas, he's been known to have ties in California. Depending on the size of the debt Paul is under,

Barker may be willing to send his men to San Francisco to find you and use you as leverage."

"But I don't have any more money."

"They could still use you to flush Paul out."

"Like bait?"

"Yeah," he said grimly.

"I don't think Paul would come to my rescue."

"They might not know that; you were engaged, after all."

"I barely remember that now. Did Max have any news for you about Mitch?"

"He's identified who Mitch is using as a private investigator, but he hasn't had a chance to contact him yet. We're hoping the investigator might be more objective and reasonable. We need to find a way for us to work together."

"Excellent idea. I know that in light of what Mitch told you about his relationship with Leanne that working with him is an abominable idea, but working against him isn't great, either. Mitch needs to know what you know and vice versa. Maybe you should set up a meeting with some neutral third parties present like Max and this investigator. They can stop things from getting ugly, and you and Mitch can hash it all out."

Burke gave her an incredulous look. "You think Mitch and I can just talk ourselves to a resolution?"

"I don't know, but you both have questions. You both know a piece of the story. It's time to compare notes."

"I don't want to talk to him, Maddie. I don't want to see his face. I don't want to hear him tell me how much Leanne loved him."

"It would be really uncomfortable," she agreed. "But you have to play the cards you're dealt, and you're not going to rest now until you know the truth. That truth can probably only be found if you, Mitch, Leanne's parents and friends sit down and talk."

"I'll think about it. I'm going to let Max talk to the investigator first." He got to his feet. "Let's get some breakfast."

"Great."

"By the way, I called my cousin Kate and her friend wants to talk to you about the food truck. She said she'd call me back and we can set up a time to meet this afternoon or tomorrow."

"That would be great," she said, excited about the possibility. "You've done so much for me, Burke. I don't know how I'm going to pay you back."

He smiled. "I'll think of something."

A little shiver ran down her spine. She wondered if what he was thinking was the same thing she was thinking...

→→➤➤◄◄◄←

Molly's Diner was a small restaurant a few blocks from Burke's apartment building. It was run by a rather large, middle-aged woman named Norma who gave Burke a very friendly smile and quickly ushered them to what she claimed was the best seat in the house. After a quick perusal of the menu, Maddie ordered up blueberry waffles while Burke settled on the French toast.

"You're very popular here," she told Burke as she drank her coffee.

"I gave Norma some suggestions a few months back on how to bring up her wiring to fire code. I'm now one of her favorite customers."

"Do you come here a lot?"

"A fair amount, when I don't have beautiful blondes cooking me breakfast."

She smiled. "I'm always more beautiful when I'm cooking. It's funny how that works out."

He grinned. "Not the first time you've heard that compliment?"

"Definitely not the first, but I still enjoy it." She paused. "When I left the firehouse yesterday, you were going to a fire. Was it a bad one?"

"It was a warehouse with a lot of potential combustible materials. We managed to contain the fire and prevent it from reaching the worst chemicals and spreading to other buildings."

"That sounds dangerous."

"No one was hurt, so it was all good."

"Have you ever been hurt on the job?" she asked curiously.

He waited for the server to set down their plates and ask if they needed anything else. Then he said, "I've had a concussion, a broken hand and suffered smoke inhalation, nothing too serious."

"That all sounds serious."

"They were minor issues. They didn't keep me off the job long."

"You don't like anyone to feel sorry for you, do you?"

"Nothing to feel sorry about, Maddie. I survived. And injuries can be part of the job, but I love what I do. These days my life is rarely in danger. I worry more about keeping everyone else safe, especially the young guys. They get overeager and impatient. A fire is a living, breathing thing. You have to respect it. You have to be ready for it to change at any moment. And you can never underestimate it."

"There's a reverence in your voice," she commented.

"I don't revere fire, but I respect it. I have to. It's my job to not only make sure I put the fire out, but that the men I send into a building are going to come out safe and healthy."

"Have you ever lost a fellow firefighter?"

His lips tightened. "Two good friends a couple years back. It was rough. I still think of them a lot. They were great men."

"I'm sure. I was thinking when I was at the firehouse that Shelby and Rachel are surrounded by some good-looking men. Have there been any hookups?"

"Not at our house. Rachel was dating a firefighter from another house for a while, but I think that ended. Shelby dates outside of work. If there has been anything going on at the house, they've kept it away from me."

"Would it bother you?"

"I wouldn't be a big fan of such a relationship. It can complicate things and when you're on a fire, you can't have emotions or friendships or relationships playing any kind of role." He paused. "Have you dated at work?"

"Yes. I went out with the owner of a restaurant in Italy for almost a year. When we broke up, I also lost my job."

"Did you learn your lesson?" he asked with a teasing smile.

"Not entirely," she conceded. "I did date another sous chef while I was in New York. That ended more amicably, but it was still awkward to work there afterwards. Since then I've kept my romantic life away from my job."

"How many romances have there been?"

"Uh, I don't know," she said vaguely. "A few."

"Serious ones?"

"A few," she repeated, not really wanting to get into actual numbers. Thankfully, her phone rang, and even more thankfully it was her mother's number on the screen. "It's my mom. Do you mind?"

"Go ahead."

"Hi, Mom, how was your trip?"

"It was lovely, very relaxing," her mother said. "And we were thrilled to find the remodel done when we arrived home last night. I was a little worried we might end up in a hotel for a few days."

"I can't wait to see it."

"Which is why I'm calling. We'd love for you to come down today if you can."

"Today?" She'd thought her mom would have wanted time to catch up on her sleep and get over her jet lag.

"If you're free. We want to talk to you about something that's worrying us."

"What's that?" she asked warily.

"Paul left us some rather disturbing messages. What's going on? I thought we'd seen the last of him."

"I can't believe he called you. I didn't think he had your number. It's really nothing you need to worry about."

"Well, we're concerned, and we'd feel better if we could sit down with you." Her mother paused. "I just remembered you don't have a car anymore. Do you want us to come to your apartment?"

Since the last thing she wanted was to tell her parents about her living situation, she immediately dismissed that suggestion. "No, I'll find a way down there. I'll text you when I'm going to come, but it will be sometime this afternoon."

"Can't wait to see you, honey. Try and make it for lunch. Your father is going to grill some steaks."

"I'll try."

Burke gave her a questioning look as she ended the call. "Paul called your parents?"

"Yes. They're worried, and they want to see me today. I just have to figure a way to get down there. Maybe I could get a zip car."

"I'll drive you down."

"I couldn't ask you to do that."

"You're not asking me, I'm offering."

"I'm sure that's the last thing you want to do on your day off."

"Actually, it would be nice to get out of the city. I wouldn't mind the drive. Just say yes. We don't need to do this dance every time I offer to do something for you or you offer to do something for me."

"So far all I've done for you is cook you a few meals."

"And they were great. I'm happy to help, and to be honest it takes my mind off the whole Mitch/Leanne situation. So in a way I'm doing this for myself as much as for you."

"Then yes."

"Good. I always liked your parents. It will be nice to see them again."

"They liked you, too. They were so impressed with your academic focus, especially my father. He was always big on grades, and Dani was much better at bringing the good grades home than I was. I tended to get distracted during class— butterflies flying outside the window, the kids passing notes to each other, people walking by the open door."

"There was apparently a lot going on in your classes," he teased.

"I just tended to be more interested in those things than in what the teacher was actually talking about. How did you keep your focus?"

"I wanted the good grade more than I wanted to stare at the butterflies."

She nodded. "That's the difference between us. I liked the butterflies."

"What time do you need to get down there?"

"Any time that works for you. I said I'd text when I knew

for sure."

"Let's go back to my place and we can figure it out. Are you done?"

"Yes," she said popping the last bite into her mouth. "That was really good."

Burke called for the check, then laid down a twenty-dollar bill and told Norma to keep the change.

Maddie liked that he was a generous man. Having worked in restaurants for a long time, she appreciated someone who respected and rewarded the service they'd been given.

As they walked down the street, she said, "By the way, I have an appointment to see an apartment tonight around eight-thirty. It's a roommate situation. The woman looks fairly normal on social media, so I'm going to check it out."

"Do you really want a roommate?"

"It wouldn't be my first choice, but I do need to find a place to live."

"Just make sure it's the right place," he said. "There's no rush."

She didn't know why Burke was so easygoing about letting her stay on his couch. It didn't really fit his personality. He'd always seemed like someone who liked his own space, but he didn't seem to mind at all that her clothes and things were all over his living room. Maybe it would bother him more if he was around, but he'd been gone for two days. She'd see how the next two days went when they were living in each other's pocket.

She stepped off the sidewalk to cross the street when a car suddenly came out of nowhere. She froze.

"Maddie," Burke yelled, grabbing her around the waist and pulling her back to the curb as the car hurtled past them. "What the hell was that?"

"Didn't they have a stop sign?" she asked in confusion.

"Yes, but they obviously didn't see it. Are you all right?"

Her heart was beating in triple time, but she was still alive, so she counted that as all right. "Yes, I'm fine. Thanks for the save."

Burke looked down the street. "I wish I'd gotten a better look at the car. Did you see it? Did you see who was driving?"

"No. I just saw silver glinting in the sunlight. Why?" She saw the answer in his eyes. "That wasn't deliberate. They weren't trying to run us down. Were they?"

"I hope not."

Thirteen

—➤➤➤◄◄◄◄—

Burke felt restless on the drive down to Portola Valley, still dwelling on the fact that a car had almost run Maddie down. Where had it come from? He hadn't seen it until it was inches away from her. Thank God he'd been able to yank her back to the sidewalk in time.

Maddie hadn't said much since the near miss, which was unusual for her. She was usually happy to fill quiet spaces with conversation, but she'd fallen into some type of reverie that also made him worry.

"Are you all right?" he asked, glancing over at her.

She was staring out the window, lost in thought.

"Maddie," he said again.

She turned, blinking dazedly as if he'd once again pulled her back to reality. "Sorry, what?"

"You're quiet."

She stared back at him, concern darkening her green eyes. "That car. I keep trying to remember what I saw. Did I notice who was driving? Was it a man or a woman? Did I see a license plate?" She gave a helpless shake of her head. "It's all just a blur."

"I know. I've been running it through my head, too. I

know I saw the car, because that's what made me reach for you. But I can't remember any details."

"Should we have tried to ask someone else what they saw? Were there other people on the street?"

"No one near us. At least I don't think so." He'd been more interested in making sure she wasn't hurt and getting her back to his place than he had been in chasing down witnesses. It probably would have been smarter to do that.

"Am I making this too personal, Burke?"

He wanted to say yes, but he couldn't. "I don't know, Maddie. If Paul hadn't told you that a loan shark had taken pictures of you and was threatening you, would we have chalked it up to an inattentive driver?"

"Maybe. I've seen people on their cell phones blow through intersections without even realizing they'd done it. Maybe that's all it was."

"It's definitely possible."

"I've just felt on edge ever since Paul told me about the photograph of me. I wish I knew if he was lying. Should I call him? See if I can get him to be honest with me?"

"Would that work?" he countered. "Or would he just use the opportunity to make you feel sorry for him or to scare you into asking your parents for money? If you tell him someone almost ran you over, he's going to suggest you help him. He'll use it as leverage." Perhaps he was wrong not to want her to talk to Paul again. But it seemed important to keep her away from him.

"You're right. I just keep thinking that the good I once saw in him is still in there somewhere, that he could be rational or kind or honest."

"You've always liked to see the good, but sometimes it's just not there. I've seen a lot of people in bad situations during my years in firefighting, and I know without a doubt that there is evil in the world. Some people can't be saved, not even from themselves."

"I don't think Paul is evil, just weak."

"I can't believe you'd defend him after everything he did to you."

"I'm not defending him; I'm just explaining." She blew out a breath. "All right, I'm done. I'm going to stop stewing over what almost happened and just be grateful that it didn't—thanks to you and your incredibly good reflexes. I need to be more aware of my surroundings. I don't always pay as much attention as I should."

"It's a good lesson, especially while walking around the city." He paused. "And I'm not sure that near miss was about you or about Paul."

She shot him a quick look. "Mitch?"

"Running me over would be his vision for the perfect kind of payback—an eye for an eye."

Concern filled her eyes. "I hadn't considered that. But you weren't in the intersection; I was."

"Two seconds later, I would have been. His timing could have been off."

"I guess. I have to say this theory doesn't make me feel much better. What happened with your dad? Didn't you see him this morning?"

"I did. Colton was there, too. Mitch has been calling in sick from work. In light of his erratic behavior, my father is suspending him until he comes in and talks to him, which so far has not happened. I'm happy that he's not on the job, though."

"It's certainly better for your brother."

"Yes." He took a moment to change lanes, then said. "Let's leave all the crap behind us for a few hours. It's a beautiful day. There's no traffic. And you'll be seeing your parents in a little while."

"I am eager to see them again."

"When did your parents move to Portola Valley?"

"About ten years ago. They actually moved into my grandmother's house after she passed away. Even though I've never really lived there with them, it still feels very much like home because I spent so much time there when I was growing up. Dani's first year of treatment was handled almost exclusively at Stanford, so we pretty much moved down there that first summer. After that, it was every other weekend. Dani really loved it down there. The house sits on two acres. There's a creek, some great climbing trees, a barn and a riding ring."

"No horses?"

"Not anymore." She gave him a smile. "You liked riding better than you thought you would, didn't you?"

"Guilty." He also liked her more than he'd ever thought he would. "Flying down that beach was something else. I'd like to do it again."

"You should."

"Or we should," he said.

She gave him a smile. "Whenever you want. You should let yourself relax more often. You work hard. You should leave time for play."

"I'll put that on my to-do list."

"Play should never be on a to-do list; that defeats the purpose."

"Baby steps, Maddie."

She laughed. "You're right. That's a good first step for someone like you."

"Thank you. But do you want to explain what you mean by 'someone like me'?"

"I really don't. Let's just enjoy the drive."

He was happy to follow that suggestion, because every mile that took them away from San Francisco and away from his past made him feel less stressed. His problems would be waiting when he got back to town, but for now he was going to let them all go and enjoy not just the drive, but also the beautiful woman next to him.

Maddie sat up straighter as Burke drove down the long, winding one-lane road to the house that had been in her family for three generations. She hadn't thought she was homesick until the familiar two-story home came into view with its wide, welcoming front porch, cozy wicker chairs and love-seat swing, and the beautiful flower boxes bringing color to every window.

"It's beautiful," Burke murmured. "There's a lot of land."

"My grandmother was originally born in Iowa on a farm. When her parents moved to California, they bought this land. It wasn't a farm, but it was big enough for horses and chickens and there was also room to garden. My grandmother used to grow the most amazing vegetables: tomatoes, squash, zucchini, cucumber and all kinds of lettuces. She'd make them into the most perfect summer salad you've ever had."

"She was a cook like you."

"Yes. She was very good in the kitchen. She didn't care much for meat, but she could spice up her vegetables like no one I'd ever seen." Her heart filled with love as she saw her mom and dad come out onto the porch. Her mom reminded her so much of Dani. They'd shared the same oval-shaped face, same light green eyes, same smile.

Her eyes blurred with unexpected moisture, and it wasn't just seeing Dani in her mother; it was also seeing her father's familiar loving gaze, his tall, lean body, his confident stance. She hadn't just missed home; she'd missed her parents, maybe more because of everything she'd gone through in the last couple of months.

She'd been running fast and furiously for a long time, jumping from adventure to adventure and never stopping long enough to pause, to take a look at her life, remember where she came from, what was really important—who was important.

She jumped out of the car and walked quickly up the steps hugging first her mom, then her dad. She'd seen them four months ago, but it felt like it had been much longer than that. But then a lot had happened since they'd visited her in Las Vegas.

"You both look so tan," she said. "Hawaii must have been wonderful."

"It was beautiful and very relaxing," her mother replied.

"Also very hot," her father put in. His gaze moved past Maddie to Burke. "Who's your friend?"

She turned, seeing Burke hovering by the car. She waved him forward. "This is Burke Callaway. I don't know if you remember him—"

"Your tutor, of course," her mom said, reaching for Burke's hand. "It's been a very long time, Burke."

"You look just the same, Mrs. Heller."

"Oh, please, call me Louise."

"And you can call me Scott," her dad added, shaking Burke's hand. "I didn't realize you two were friends."

"We ran into each other a few days ago, and Burke was nice enough to give me a ride," she explained.

"Well come on in," her mother said. "Let's get you something to drink. I thought we'd have lunch in a bit, too."

"Sounds great. I'm eager to see the remodel."

"It's really just the two bathrooms and our master bedroom closet. But it makes a huge difference."

Maddie fell into step with her mother while Burke and her dad followed them into the house. After touring the newly remodeled rooms, they went out to the deck off the kitchen and sat down at a table under a colorful umbrella. Her mother served them lemonade while her dad started the barbecue.

"You really don't have to go to all this trouble," Maddie said.

"It's no trouble. It's been a long time since we were together." Her mother smiled across the table at Burke. "How are your parents? I always enjoyed your mom. She wrote me a very sweet note after Danielle died. And before that she used to organize the other mothers in the neighborhood to bring us food. It was very kind."

"That's my mother. She's doing well," Burke said.

"And your father? Is he still a firefighter?"

"Yes. He's Deputy Chief of Operations for the Fire Department now."

"I thought he might have retired by now."

"He loves to work. They'll probably have to force him out."

"Well, work is good. And you're a firefighter, too, isn't that right?"

He nodded. "I followed in the family tradition along with two of my brothers and a sister."

"How lovely. I'm sure you've made your father proud, Burke. I always knew you were going to do great things. You were such a smart kid when you were young. You got our Maddie through algebra."

"Kicking and screaming," he joked.

"I wasn't that bad," Maddie protested.

"Oh, yes, you were," Burke said. "If your parents hadn't

paid so well, I would have dropped you in a second."

She made a face at him. "Maybe you weren't such a great teacher."

"No, you were the problem," he said without a doubt in his voice. "But once you decided you actually wanted to pass the class, you picked things up pretty quickly."

"Maddie was always good at whatever she set her mind to," her mom put in. "School just usually wasn't where she wanted to put her energy. And she was stubborn. Once she made her mind up, it was impossible to change it."

"That was apparent the first day we met," Burke said.

"Hey, I'm right here," she protested, thinking Burke and her mom were getting a little chummy when it came to her bad habits. "And believe me, Mom, Burke is just as stubborn as I am, if not more so."

"But I'm stubborn in the right direction," he said.

"I'm sure you think any direction you're going in is the right direction," she countered.

"Because it usually is."

Her mother laughed. "I think I heard this same conversation when you were tutoring Maddie. I'm going to make the salad."

"Can I help, Mom?" she offered.

"No, you just relax. Let me take care of you for a change."

"What about you, Dad? Need any help?" Maddie asked as her father fiddled with the grill.

"I'm good."

"It looks like we have a little time before lunch," she said to Burke. "Want to explore?"

"Lead the way."

"We'll be back, Dad. I'm going to show Burke around."

"Take your time. Lunch won't be ready for a while.

Afterwards, we'll have a chat."

She saw the pointed gleam in his eyes and knew this day would not end without a discussion about Paul and what was going on with her life. But for the moment, she was going to take a trip into the more distant past.

She took Burke through the backyard, pointing out the now somewhat modest vegetable garden on their way to the creek. "My mom tries to carry on my grandmother's traditions, but she doesn't have the same desire or flare to keep the garden in its former glory," she said. "Plus, she and my dad like to travel. So they have to depend on a neighbor to keep it going while they're gone."

"So you got your wandering instincts from your parents?"

She thought for a moment. "I don't really know where I got them from. My parents like to go to resorts with buffets and drinks and organized activities. When I travel, I like to get out of the tourist districts and live like a local. That's the best way to experience another culture."

"Were there any cultures you didn't care for?" he asked as they moved away from the garden and took a dirt path through a patch of trees.

"Some of the countries that had restrictions on women's dress and rights were challenging. You know I don't really like to be confined, not even by a head scarf."

"And your blonde hair would have shone like a beacon in some of those places."

"Exactly, but I wasn't always blonde."

He laughed. "You always did like to change things up. I remember being fascinated by a purple streak in your hair when I was tutoring you one day. You were actually concentrating on the assignment, but I couldn't seem to take my eyes off your purple hair."

"I had no idea I actually distracted you. Interesting."

A spark flashed in his eyes. "You distracted me a lot. More than I liked."

"Good."

"Why good?"

"You get a little too focused sometimes, Burke. You have to stop and look around once in a while."

He accepted the criticism with a thoughtful nod. "I didn't realize that back in high school."

"Well, I didn't realize a lot of things back in high school," she said with a self-deprecating laugh. "We both had some growing up to do."

As they got further into the woods, she could hear the trickle of water hitting the rocks, and a moment later, they were at the creek.

There had been a fair amount of rain the past month, so the water was a foot deep and flowing fairly quickly downhill. The creek was about six feet across with several large rocks that were barely seen above the water.

"This was one of my favorite places growing up. Dani and I used to come down here all the time. Those were our stepping stones into a magical world." She pointed to the rocks. "We used to make up all kinds of stories. We were either going back in time and using the rocks as a portal to another era or we were crossing into a land of mystical creatures. We were far enough away from the house that we could be anywhere."

He smiled at her words. "Who had the bigger imagination? You or your sister?"

"It was probably me, but we were twins, so Dani had some great ideas, too, especially after she got sick. She became very spiritual and philosophical. She talked about heaven a lot. I wanted to believe in everything she said, particularly the part where we would see each other again." She paused, reflecting on how many years had passed since those childhood days. "I've now lived without her longer than I lived with her. That was a weird point to cross. I still miss her, too. Sometimes I wish her voice in my head was louder. It seems to get fainter every year."

"You'll never forget her, Maddie. She's part of you."

"For a long time I asked myself why she got sick and I didn't. We were twins. We shared so much, but somehow I dodged that bullet. They said it was a mutation of genes, not familial, not inherited, just exceptionally bad luck. It was so unfair." She drew in a deep breath, trying not to let the old anger take hold. "But Dani handled it with a lot of grace and fight. She was really amazing. I wish you'd known her."

"Me, too."

She glanced over at him. "Sorry. I didn't mean to take this day down."

"You didn't," he said quietly.

"Good, because I love being here. See that?" She pointed toward a beautiful yellow-winged monarch dancing from leaf to leaf on the bush across from them. "We used to try to catch butterflies here, too. My grandfather made a net for us, and we'd chase them all over the property."

"Did you catch any?"

"A few, but we always let them go. They're pretty to look at, but butterflies are meant to fly, right?"

He nodded. "Yes. It sounds like you had a lot of great times down here."

"The summers were the best. Did the Callaways ever get away? Did you have a favorite place growing up?"

"We didn't take many vacations. Eight kids made traveling both expensive and a huge headache. We did go up to the Russian River a few summers. My dad's uncle had a big house up there, and when he wasn't renting it out, we'd get to go. We used to canoe down the river, watch old movies in the park on hot nights and eat a lot of ice cream."

"That sounds nice," she said, happy to hear about some of Burke's memories.

"The first six of us were really close in age, so there was always someone to play with, but as I said, there wasn't as much money when I was really young. Dad was probably working every extra shift he could find to keep the ship afloat. Lynda used to work part-time, too, whenever she could squeeze in a few hours somewhere."

"I didn't realize money was an issue. You lived in a beautiful house."

"My mother's parents had money. The house was a wedding gift to my mom and dad. After my mom died, they insisted we stay there. They wanted their grandchildren to grow up in that house. I think they helped my dad out from time to time, although he's a proud man, so who knows if he was willing to take that help. And he did a good job providing for everyone. We never lacked for anything we needed, but I always knew that I was going to need to take care of myself as quickly as possible. There were a lot of kids behind me to put through school and get to adulthood."

"No wonder you were responsible so early."

He shrugged. "It wasn't difficult to see that my parents had their hands full. The twins, Shayla and Colton, had a lot more one-on-one time with Jack and Lynda. By the time they were in their early teens, the older kids had moved out. There was more room, more time, more money. Sometimes we tease them that they grew up in a different family from the rest of us."

"Are they close? Do they have the twin bond?"

"I think so. They definitely watch out for each other, but

they're very different people. Shayla is a little more like me—intense, driven, ambitious, likes to be the best. Colton has a lot of drive, but he's much more easygoing, friendly, one of the guys."

"You're one of the guys, too, Burke. I saw how you were at the firehouse. You're their leader, but you're also their friend, and that's not always an easy combination to achieve."

"I try. What else are we going to see today? Or is this it?"

"Definitely not it. We haven't been to the barn yet. Come with me." She impulsively extended her hand, happy when Burke took it.

It felt right to hold his hand as she led him down a flowery path to a dark red barn about fifty yards from the main house. They paused by the empty riding ring.

"This is where I learned to ride," she said. "I think I was about four when my grandpa first put me up on a horse. Back then they had two horses in the barn, Lily and Rose. My grandmother liked to name her horses after her favorite flowers."

"I thought there was a Lulu."

"Lulu arrived when we were about ten. We were better riders by then, and my grandpa used to take us riding in the valley. There's a path over there that leads through some open land. You can take it all the way out to the ocean, but it's several miles away, and we never made it that far."

"No horses anymore," Burke commented as they entered the empty barn.

"There haven't been since my parents moved in. My mother was never enamored with riding. She had a scary experience as a kid. She got pushed into a stall when one of the horses was acting up, and she almost got kicked. After that, she pretty much avoided the barn. Every couple of years, my parents talk about demolishing this place or taking it down to the foundation and rebuilding it as a guest house, which I'm sure would be more practical and increase the value of the property, but I'd miss this old barn."

"Why?" he asked, doubt in his voice. "It's really not much to look at."

"Not down here, no. But you haven't seen the best part." She let go of his hand to pull down a ladder on a nearby wall. "Ever been in a hayloft?"

He smiled back at her. "No, this would be a first."

"Good. I love to be the first to show you something new."

"That actually seems to happen a lot when you're around," he said dryly.

She climbed up the ladder, and Burke quickly followed.

The loft wasn't very high, so Burke had to stoop as they walked toward the large window that overlooked the valley behind the property. She cranked open the window, letting a cool breeze into the stuffy loft, then she sat down on one of the three bales of hay that had probably been in the barn for at least a decade.

Burke squeezed onto the bale next to her, his powerful legs brushing against hers.

Maybe this hadn't been such a good idea, she thought, as a tingle ran down her spine.

"Great view," he said. "I didn't realize the house was on such a hill until now."

"The property dips down into the valley pretty quickly."

"Was this another spot you and Dani used to come to?"

"Yes, but as she got sicker, she couldn't make it up the ladder, so that pretty much ended that. I used to sneak down here at night, give Lulu a carrot, then come up here and look out at the stars." She didn't add that she'd spent a lot of those nights praying that her sister would get better. "It was a special place for me."

Burke put his hand on her thigh. She turned her head and looked into his eyes, seeing something in his gaze that she couldn't quite define.

"What?" she asked.

"Did you ever bring a boy up here?"

"No. This was my grandparents' house. I didn't know any boys around this neighborhood."

"So you never kissed anyone in this hayloft?"

She shook her head, her nerves jumping in anticipation at the playful, sexy gleam in his eyes. "I did not."

"Interesting. You're a hayloft virgin."

"Is there such a thing?"

"I'm pretty sure. Now let's see. What firsts have you introduced me to: First detention—"

"You're never going to forget that are you?"

"First time I ever ate pink mashed potatoes."

"You didn't even taste the pink and it was Valentine's Day."

"First horseback ride on the beach."

"Which was a first for both of us."

His gaze darkened. "True. It was a first for both of us, and today could be another first."

Her heart leapt into her throat and blood rushed through her veins at the purposeful look in his eyes. When Burke Callaway wanted something, he went after it, and he usually got it.

"Show me what you've got," she said lightly.

"Happy to." He put an arm around her shoulders, leaned in and covered her mouth with his. It was a kiss that started out slow…savoring, exploring, the heat rising as their breaths mingled and their tongues slid against each other in a deep, passionate kiss that quickly took on a life of its own.

It wasn't just his taste, his touch, his scent that undid her, it was the way he made her head spin, made her heart ache, made her need another kiss as much as she needed to breathe.

She felt surrounded, enveloped, overwhelmed and happy, happier than she'd ever been. Her rational brain suggested she fight the tempting feelings, that she protect her heart because it had already taken too many hits, but the other part of her brain wanted nothing more than complete and utter surrender. Making love with Burke would be amazing, wonderful, beyond any other adjectives she could think of. She knew that with a certainty. But afterwards... what would this man want from her?

She told herself not to go there. She didn't need to think about the future. She was the woman who lived in the moment. And what a moment it was...

Burke finally lifted his head, his breath coming fast, the pulse in his neck jumping to a wild beat. "Oh, Maddie," he murmured. "I don't know what to do about you. I've never known."

She'd never known, either. He'd always been that guy just out of her reach, someone she could want, but how much of herself would she have to give up to get him? It had always seemed like a lot, but not so much anymore.

"You're beautiful, smart. You kiss like a dream. Why didn't we do this before?" he asked.

"I don't know. We were both scared, I think. Maybe *still* a little scared."

He ran his hand down her cheek, brushing off a bit of hay. "Maybe," he agreed.

Before she could say anything else, her mother's voice drifted through the open window.

"Maddie, are you up there?"

Burke groaned. "I forgot about your parents."

She smiled. "It's been a long time since we had to worry about parents catching us in a make-out session." She moved off the hay and stuck her head out the window. "We're up here, Mom."

"Your dad says the steak is the absolute perfect temperature. Are you ready for lunch?"

"We'll be right down." She turned back to Burke. "Time for lunch. No decisions to make today," she added lightly.

He smiled. "Guess not. You might want to fix your hair a little. Or your parents might think you were rolling around in the hay."

She patted down her hair, tucking the strands behind her ears. "I'm sure they already think that. And I'm also certain they're very curious as to why you came with me, but they won't ask. They gave up trying to talk me in or out of a romantic relationship a long time ago. I'm not very good at taking their advice," she added, moving down the ladder. "I probably should get better."

"You like to make your own decisions, nothing wrong with that," he said, as they walked out of the barn.

"Unfortunately, some of those decisions have been bad."

"Live and learn."

"You're very philosophical today."

"I am," he said with an agreeable smile. "You bring out a lot of different sides of me, Maddie Heller."

"I like seeing your different sides. When you were younger, I didn't think you had any other side but intense."

"I was focused on what I needed to do."

"Are you still that focused?"

"I was, but since you showed back up in my life, I've been thinking about making some changes."

"Really? I've inspired a new thought?"

"More than one," he said dryly.

She felt the heat run through her cheeks at the look in his eyes. "I wasn't talking about *those* kinds of thoughts."

"I know. You've inspired me because of all you've done. You've been all over the world. You've met an amazing number of people. You've challenged yourself and tried new things. I've lived in San Francisco my entire life."

"You can still travel, Burke. There's time."

"Only if I make the time."

"Well, that's true. It's all up to you."

He gave her a thoughtful look as they walked up the path. "Are you going to stay in San Francisco, Maddie?"

"I'm thinking about it."

"Do you believe a free spirit like yourself could ever be happy settling in one place? You've always reminded me of the butterfly you showed me earlier, always flitting from one place to the next, never finding home, never resting too long."

His words were very true. Up until she'd said "yes" to Paul's impulsive proposal, she'd never been ready to call anyplace home. During the two months in which they were engaged, she'd tried to see Las Vegas as home. It was where Paul's life was, and it could be her life, too. At least that's what she'd told herself. But that life had ended. Now she was back in San Francisco—where it had all begun.

Had she come home? Or was she just resting in between flights?

"I don't know," she said, finally answering his question. "I guess one day I'll find out."

Fourteen

Burke bit into Scott Heller's flank steak with real enjoyment. Maddie's father definitely knew how to grill meat. Cooking was a talent that obviously ran in the family, because Louise had contributed not only a salad but also a variety of grilled asparagus, squash and green beans. "This is excellent good," he said. "I've eaten really well since Maddie came back into my life."

Louise smiled. "Maddie was always a better cook than I was. She loved making food from the time she was a toddler. Whenever I started dinner, she was always by my side, so curious, so excited to taste everything." Louise gave her daughter a loving smile. "We had a lot of fun in the kitchen."

"We did, Mom," Maddie said. "Cooking dinner with you was my favorite time of the day."

"Since you're a firefighter, you must know how to cook," Scott interjected. "Do you take turns at the firehouse?"

"We do, although we try to pawn that duty off on the rookie of the moment. Our last rookie was a fantastic cook, but he got transferred a few months ago. Since then, we're back to the basics—spaghetti, chili, pizza, nothing too adventurous. But the guys got a treat yesterday. Maddie dropped off some food for everyone. She was a big hit. My crew is hoping she'll be a frequent visitor."

"Didn't you have an interview yesterday?" Scott asked his daughter.

Maddie nodded. "Yes. I had actually prepared some food earlier in the day so I could practice some recipes and hone my rusty techniques. That's why I had extra food on my hands and decided to share it with Burke's crew."

"Well, tell us how the interview went," Louise said.

"It was all right. The restaurant is very high-class. The executive chef didn't seem overly impressed with me. He said he'd be in touch if they wanted me to come in for a second interview, but I'm not holding my breath."

Louise looked disappointed at Maddie's news. "I'm sorry. I was hoping for better."

"Me, too, but Chef Partaine did not seem to like me much."

"Then he's an idiot," her mother declared. "Who couldn't love you? You're delightful."

"Thanks, Mom, but I think you're prejudiced."

"No, she's right," Burke said. Maddie was the kind of person who could charm a stranger in five seconds. He'd seen it at the stables, at Nicole's party and at the firehouse. She had a natural, warm charm that drew people to her, and not just the men but the women, too.

"Well, we'll see what happens," Maddie said. "I'm still looking into other opportunities. Burke's cousin has a friend who might need someone to run his food truck for a while. We're going to try to talk to them later today maybe."

"A food truck?" Scott asked, his brows pulling together in a frown. "Is that safe?"

"Sure, of course. They're very popular," Maddie answered.

"But it's not like working in a restaurant," Louise said. "Why would you want to cook in a truck? They're small, cramped, and I can't imagine you can be as creative as you'd like."

"Sometimes you can be more creative, because you have more freedom."

"Yes, but a restaurant will look better for the long term," Louise argued. "It has more prestige, and the hours would be longer, the customer base would be more stable."

"Exactly," Scott said, following up on his wife's words. "Food trucks are risky. You can face potential lawsuits if health standards aren't met. And you're out on the street. You run the risk of getting robbed."

"Well, it's just an idea," Maddie said. "I haven't decided anything."

Burke was beginning to see that while Maddie's parents adored her, they also tried very hard to get their opinions heard. He didn't know if they'd always been like that or if recent events, like their daughter getting all her money stolen, had pushed them into taking a more proactive role in her life.

But Maddie was going to do whatever she wanted. He knew her well enough to know that.

"We want you to be happy, Maddie," her mother continued. "But we'd also love to see you settle into something more permanent in San Francisco. Then you'll be close enough to visit more often. We've missed you, honey."

Maddie's expression softened at her mom's words. "I've missed you both, too. But we're together now. And you don't need to worry about me. I'm like a cat; I always land on my feet."

"Not always," her father said, clearing his throat. He set down his fork and clasped his hands together. "We need to talk about Paul."

"I know," Maddie said.

Scott glanced over at him. "I wonder if you would give us some privacy, Burke. If you're finished."

"Sure."

"No, you don't have to go," Maddie told him, waving him back into his seat. "Burke knows everything. I told him about Paul, the money, the loan shark and the threats. You can speak freely in front of him."

"All right," Scott said. "Paul left several disturbing messages on your mother's phone saying you were both in trouble and that you needed money. He indicated that you didn't realize how much danger you were in."

"You didn't call him back, did you?" Maddie asked.

"No, we wanted to talk to you first, honey," Louise said. "What kind of danger are you in? What is Paul talking about?"

"He thinks that the people he owes money to will try to use me for leverage. He wants to scare me into getting him more money. I told him I was broke, thanks to him. So he asked me to talk to you. I told him I wouldn't. I don't know how he got your phone number."

"How much does he need?" Scott asked.

"It doesn't matter," Maddie said. "I'm not going to let you give him money."

"We don't want you to be in danger," Louise said, a worried look in her eyes. "If it's not that much—"

"It is too much," Maddie said, cutting her off. "And I doubt that whatever we gave him would be enough. He'd keep coming back for more."

Burke was happy to see how realistic Maddie was about Paul's need for money. She might have been blinded by love for a while, but she was seeing clearly now.

"I thought you would be safe in San Francisco," Louise

said, exchanging a quick look with her husband. "Maybe you should come home for a while. You don't have a job yet. You don't need to be in the city."

"I do need to be in the city so I can get a job."

"I think you should talk to the police, Maddie," her father said.

"I am talking to the police now. Burke's brother-in-law is a detective with the SFPD. He's looking into the situation for me."

"Good," Scott said with an approving nod. "I thought you were going to argue with us about that. You're always so stubbornly independent, but sometimes you have to let people help you."

"I'm going to be okay. Just don't talk to Paul and delete his messages if he calls either of you again."

"I'm watching out for her, too," Burke put in.

Her father looked really happy to hear that. "Thank you, Burke."

"I can take care of myself," Maddie protested, shooting him an annoyed look.

He ignored her, as did her parents. Instead, he said to Louise. "Do you still have the voicemail Paul left earlier?"

"Of course. It's on my phone," she replied.

"If you could get it and play it for me, I can record it and talk to my brother-in-law about it."

"I'll get my phone." Louise stood up. "Can I get you anything else to eat or drink while I'm in the house?"

"Not for me," he said. "I'm stuffed."

"Well, there's still dessert, so I hope you left a little room. Scott, do you want to get the pie while I look for my phone?" Louise asked her husband.

"Sure. We'll be back."

"I hate that they're getting involved in this," Maddie said

as her parents left them alone.

"Paul made that happen, not you."

"I'm going to call him back and tell him to stay the hell away from my family."

"I'm not against that idea, but you should make the call with Max listening in."

"I really don't think your brother-in-law wants to make my problems his full-time job."

"It's only going to take a few minutes. We'll touch base with Max when we get back to the city." He paused. "By the way, I like your parents."

Her tension eased. "They're great, aren't they?"

"It must have been hard for them to lose a child."

"They did everything they could to save Dani's life, and when they knew that wasn't going to happen, they made sure she was happy, comfortable, surrounded by love."

"How was it after Dani died? Did they cling to you, Maddie?"

She hesitated. "We all grieved in different ways. I don't know that I remember what they did. I know they tried to be there for me, but you have to understand I'd been left on my own a lot while Dani was sick. It wasn't their fault. They couldn't be there for me when she needed so much more than I did. I think some of my independence sprang from those years when I had to look out for myself. Then I just kept doing it."

"That makes sense."

"Good. I finally make sense," she said lightly.

He smiled. "Your parents must have missed you when you started traveling the world."

"We missed each other. But they loved hearing my stories. And when I got a little lonely, I knew they were only a phone call away. I don't want you to get the wrong idea.

We're a close family. We're just not always geographically close." She paused. "By the way, my parents like you as well, maybe a little too much."

"How can it be too much?"

"They're going to start building a relationship between us in their heads, and they'll be disappointed when it doesn't happen."

"Who's to say it won't happen?"

Her eyes widened. "Well, me, for one, and you, for two."

He laughed. "Speak for yourself, Maddie."

"Come on, Burke. It wasn't an hour ago that you said I was a butterfly. Do you really want to spend time chasing a butterfly?"

It was a good question. It wasn't the chase he minded, but having to let that butterfly go—that would be a lot more difficult. Fortunately, Maddie's parents returned to the table, saving him from having to come up with an answer.

⇀⇉⇇↼

They left Portola Valley to return to the city around three o'clock in the afternoon. Maddie was a little sorry to leave the beautiful property that had truly felt like an escape from reality. But she was also eager to move forward with her life. She was hoping to talk to Burke's cousin, and then she had an apartment to see and a possible roommate to meet later in the day. She supposed at some point she'd also talk to Max, but she didn't want to spend much more time dwelling on Paul. She really wanted to put him behind her.

"What are you thinking about?" Burke asked, as they drove down the beautiful highway by Crystal Springs Reservoir.

"Whenever someone asks me that question, I can never

remember what I was just thinking, but then things tend to pop in and out of my brain rather quickly."

"That doesn't surprise me."

She'd actually been thinking a lot about their kiss in the hayloft, the easy way Burke had fit in at her parents' house, how much she liked talking to him, being with him. She also kept hearing his challenging words in her head about having a relationship—*who's to say it won't happen?*

The idea that Burke would consider a relationship with her was both exciting and terrifying and she didn't really know what to make of it. Had he just been teasing, joking, playing along with her parents' obvious approval? She really didn't know. She couldn't read Burke that well. He was good at keeping his private thoughts private.

And a relationship...well, that was a mind-boggling thought. It didn't feel like the right time—for either of them. She had Paul and his problems to deal with. Burke was caught up in a three-year-old mystery. They both had a lot of baggage still to unpack.

What would happen when they finally emptied all those bags?

A shiver ran down her spine. Maybe they could finish one of the really excellent kisses they'd started.

She jolted as Burke's cell phone suddenly rang through the car's speakers.

"It's my cousin," he said. He pushed the button to answer. "Hi, Kate."

"Hi Burke. Dylan told me that you have a friend who is an amazing cook and might want to help Joel out in his food truck, so I'm calling to tell you that Joel loves the idea and really wants to meet your friend. Can we set something up?"

"Absolutely," he said, shooting Maddie a quick look. "What's good for you?"

"How about today—around four? I know it's short notice, but that works best for us."

Maddie gave a nod, excited about seeing the truck and maybe having a chance to work in it.

"That will work," Burke said. "Where shall we meet you?"

"Go to my parents' house. Joel's truck is temporarily parked across the street."

"Okay, see you at four." He ended the call and smiled at Maddie. "Looks like you're going to get a shot at working in a food truck."

"We'll see. I'd love to know what kind of food he serves."

"I should have asked."

"I'll find out soon enough."

"Are you at all concerned about committing to help out on the truck and then possibly getting a second interview at the restaurant?"

Trust Burke to be always thinking two steps ahead of her. "I don't think I'm going to get that second interview."

"But you might."

"Then I'll figure it out. One step at a time. I don't like to get too far ahead of myself." She gave Burke a thoughtful look, suspecting he had reservations about the food truck just as her parents had. "Do you think I'm making a mistake? Should I be focused more on a restaurant job?"

"It depends on what you want, Maddie."

"I want a career as a chef, the opportunity to make enough money to live comfortably, and I want to be able to cook dishes that inspire me."

He laughed. "And here I thought you weren't that clear on what you wanted."

"I think losing everything, including my apartment, has really given me a new perspective on my life."

"A restaurant would offer security, benefits, maybe more money. I'm not sure how much cash a food truck brings in. Working for yourself would allow you the freedom you want, and I can certainly see you creating amazing dishes if you were free to do so. That might be in a truck or in a restaurant with a great boss. You have to weigh out all the pros and cons and decide what your priorities are."

"Well, I didn't think this would ever happen," she said, somewhat surprised to find they were on the same page.

"What?"

"That we would agree one hundred percent with each other."

"You agree with me?" he asked with doubt in his voice.

"I do. Everything you said echoes my own thinking. I know that there's often a trade-off for freedom of expression, and that trade-off is usually less money. But as I rebuild my life and look toward the future, I know that I don't just want to work a job anymore. I've done that a dozen times. I've taken on whatever work I could just so I could live somewhere or travel someplace. But those part-time days are over. I need a career. I know I still have to pay some dues, because I'm in a new city, and my job history has been spotty, but I'm good at what I do. I just need someone else to see that, too."

"You'll make that happen, Maddie. It's not like one path is right and one is wrong. They both have advantages and disadvantages. Only you can decide what's right for you."

She liked that he wasn't telling her what to do. She'd always thought of Burke as someone with very strong opinions, and for the most part he liked to share those opinions, but at the moment he was giving her a chance to think for herself, to find her own way, and she appreciated that. Unfortunately, she now had one more reason to like him.

"Did I meet Kate at Nicole's party?" Maddie asked a half hour later when Burke exited the freeway.

"No. My Uncle Tim and Aunt Sharon were there as well as my cousin Ian, but I don't think anyone else from that family was there."

"Tim is your father's brother?"

Burke nodded. "He's two years younger than my dad. He was a firefighter for twenty-five years but retired about six years ago. My aunt is a nurse. They have six kids."

"The Callaways definitely like to procreate."

"That they do."

"Where is Kate in the line-up?"

"She's at the bottom. Dylan is the oldest. He's two years younger than me. Then it goes Ian, Hunter, Annie, and the twins Mia and Kate."

"More twins?"

"Yes, they seem to come at the end of each family line-up."

She laughed. "Or maybe having twins just puts an end to the desire for more children. My parents didn't get past Dani and me. Are Kate and Mia identical?"

"Fraternal twins. They don't look alike, and they're very different in personality, too. Mia is a studious, intellectual girl pursuing advanced degrees in art history or something like that. She's been fascinated with art and museums since she was a child. Kate is a kick-ass tomboy who recently applied for the FBI. She wants to be a special agent."

"That sounds fun and dangerous and very Callaway," she said. "How old is Kate?"

He thought for a moment. "I think she's around twenty-five."

"How many cousins do you have?"

"You're really testing my memory and my math skills, Maddie."

"Somehow I think you're up to the challenge."

"Let's see. Uncle Kevin and Aunt Monica have five kids. Aunt Ellen and her husband Greg Coulter have six kids. So that makes seventeen cousins."

"Do they all live in San Francisco?"

"No, the Coulter clan lives in Chicago, although I heard my cousin Wyatt might be moving out to San Francisco when he gets out of the Marine Corps, which is apparently very soon."

"Another dangerous job," she commented.

"My grandparents instilled a strong sense of duty into all their offspring."

"Are any of the Coulters firefighters?"

"One. My cousin Jason is a firefighter in Chicago."

"When was the last time the entire Callaway clan got together?"

"We haven't done it in a few years. Usually, a wedding will pull in most of the group. I know my mom is trying to plan a big family reunion in Lake Tahoe next summer. She's been working on it for a year. Hopefully, we'll get everyone there, or at least as many people as we can. My generation is starting to spread out, get married, have kids…so we'll see who shows up. Do you have any extended family?"

"Three cousins in the Denver area. We hardly ever see them. So, not a big family."

"But I bet you have friends all over the world."

"I do. It makes traveling easier. There's usually someone willing to put out the welcome mat." She paused. "I've lost track of a lot of the kids I grew up with, though. I'd love to reconnect with some of them now that I'm back in San Francisco."

"You should. I'm sure they'd love to see you."

"I'd just like to have a little better story to tell before I reconnect and have to answer questions like 'where do you live' and 'what do you do for living'."

"I suspect that will happen very soon."

"Let's hope so."

"Here we are," Burke said a few minutes later. He drove down a street that paralleled the ocean and the Great Highway.

"They must have a view," she commented.

"It's great when it's not foggy. Dylan and Ian grew up surfing every morning before breakfast."

"Did you ever join them?"

He shook his head. "I went a few times, but I didn't enjoy surfing."

"You didn't like challenging the waves? I'm surprised."

"That part was fun, but there was too much waiting around for my taste." He pointed across the street. "I think that's your truck."

"Not my truck yet." She laughed at the name scrawled in green paint across the side of the truck. "*Holy Meatballs.* I like it. And I'm really good at making meatballs."

"It's a far cry from the fancy restaurant you just interviewed at."

"I was expecting that."

Burke parked just behind the truck. They got out and walked around it, but everything was locked up tight.

"It looks in good shape from the outside," she murmured.

"Let's go find Kate."

They walked across the street to a two-story home that shared common walls with the houses on both sides. "Did your aunt and uncle raise six kids in this house? It doesn't seem that big."

"The Callaway kids are used to sharing rooms. Aiden and I shared until I was fifteen. Then my father finally allowed me to move into the unit over the garage. My siblings were incredibly jealous, and that room was constantly being fought over."

"But you got it first."

"The perks of being the oldest. Colton told me that he never got a chance to live there. By the time he was old enough, some of the older kids had moved home and back over the garage."

"I always loved your parents' house. It was so warm and happy, lots of people around, lots of laughter. And the Callaways ran all the street games in the summer."

"It was a good place to grow up, but this house by the beach isn't bad either," he said as he rang the bell.

A moment later a blue-eyed attractive redhead in her mid twenties opened the door. She wore workout clothes, and her hair was pulled back in a ponytail, giving her an athletic look.

"Burke," she said with delight, giving him a hug.

"Nice to see you, Kate. This is Maddie Heller. Kate Callaway."

"Hi Maddie. My friend Joel is so excited that you're interested in helping him out."

"Is he here?" Burke asked. "We'd love to see the inside of the truck."

"He's on his way. He had to wait for a ride. He broke his right arm and fractured some fingers on his left hand in a motorcycle accident two weeks ago. That's why he's out of commission, and he's starting to run out of money. There's a big food truck festival at Crissy Field in two weeks that he really doesn't want to miss out on, but I'll let him give you the details. Come in and say hello to Mom. She said she hasn't seen you in a few months."

Maddie smiled as the effervescent Kate grabbed Burke's hand and drew him into the house. Kate definitely had the outgoing Callaway personality. Maddie sometimes wondered who Burke took after—maybe his biological mother. He definitely seemed to be the most serious of the bunch.

Sharon Callaway was an older version of her daughter with blue eyes and darker red hair. She was sitting at the table looking at a digital e-reader while a large pot of water boiled on the stove. She immediately got to her feet to greet them. She was still wearing blue scrubs with a dark blue sweater, so she'd obviously just come from work.

"My favorite nephew," Sharon said.

"I bet you say that to everyone, Aunt Sharon." Burke gave her a hug. "This is Maddie Heller. I don't know if you met at Nicole's party the other night."

"I think I saw you in the distance. It's nice to meet you, Maddie. Can I get you something to drink? I'm making spaghetti if you want to stay for dinner."

"Sorry, but we have some things to do later," Burke replied.

"Well, sit down, make yourselves comfortable," Sharon said, resuming her seat at the table.

"I'm going to call Joel, make sure he's on his way," Kate said, leaving the room.

"How's work going?" Burke asked his aunt.

"Keeping me busy, but I love it. I'm on the maternity floor now, so it's a happy place. Those brand new babies just melt my heart. Makes me long for grandchildren."

"I'm sure you'll get there."

"I don't know. My children seem to be stubbornly single. By the way, I'm so happy for Nicole. I know she was afraid to take another chance after Brandon's issues, but I'm glad she did. Hopefully, she'll have an easier time of it with this baby."

"Even if she doesn't, she'll be a great mother," Burke said.

"So true. I've always been in awe of the way she fights to help Brandon. She's amazing. Not every woman is cut out to be a mother, but Nicole was made for it." Sharon paused. "How are you doing, Burke? I heard about the incident at Leanne's memorial dinner. Dylan said that one of the other firefighters is trying to prove Leanne's death was not an accident. I don't understand that."

Burke stiffened. "I sometimes forget what a good network our family has."

"We all worry about each other. You know that. So what's the story?"

"I don't know. I don't really want to talk about the past anymore. I just want to move forward."

"That's understandable. I'm sorry I brought it up, Burke."

"Don't worry about it. Tell me what's going on with Ian. Dylan said he just got a research grant."

"To study something that I cannot begin to understand." She smiled at Maddie "My second oldest son is a scientist."

"You have very accomplished children from what I hear."

"Two firefighters, a scientist, an art historian, a graphic designer and a wanna-be FBI special agent," Sharon said. "Sometimes I can't quite believe all the different directions my kids are going in, not that they are kids anymore. Time moves very quickly, especially when you get older. It's a good idea not to waste it."

Maddie thought that was excellent advice. Listening to Sharon talk about her children's accomplishments had only reminded her that she would have been a lot farther along by now if she'd set some goals, made some plans. But she couldn't change the past. She could only affect the future.

Kate came back into the room. "Joel is outside. Are you guys ready to see the truck?"

"We are," Maddie said, quickly getting to her feet. She was eager to move on to the next phase of her life. She didn't know if banking her life on meatballs was the best idea she'd ever had, but it couldn't possibly be the worst.

Fifteen

—➤➤◀◀◄—

Joel Edwards was a skinny guy in his late twenties wearing a T-shirt and low-riding jeans. His brown hair was long enough to be pulled back in a ponytail, revealing tattoos down the side of his neck. His right arm was in a cast up to his elbow and the two middle fingers of his left hand were also splinted.

After exchanging introductions, Joel said, "I'm really hoping you can help me out, Maddie. I'm losing so much money not being able to work." He opened the door to the truck. "Let me show you around."

As she stepped inside the truck, she was impressed by the cleanliness of the small kitchen. It was set up very efficiently with oven, burners, microwave, sink, cooking space and paper supplies. The window that opened to the street had a nice wide counter and again was in excellent condition.

"I serve meatballs, as you might have guessed," Joel said. "I have twenty different kinds on the menu ranging from Italian to Spanish to Mediterranean. I also serve up three pastas, rice, and a grilled meatball sandwich smothered in cheese and onions, one of the most popular dishes I offer. Sometimes I run a special if I get a discount on a particular protein. The meatballs are a mix of beef, pork, turkey and chicken. I also have a vegan ball. I aim to be as creative and innovative as possible, so if you have ideas, you're welcome to try them out."

"I like the sound of that."

"Where have you been cooking? Kate told me you were an experienced chef but in between jobs."

She nodded. "Yes, I've been cooking my entire life. I took classes in both France and Italy and worked in restaurants in both countries as well as some restaurants here in the States."

"You've gotten around."

"I have. What about you? Where did you learn to cook?"

"My grandfather's Italian restaurant right here in San Francisco. He taught me everything I know."

"What does he think of this truck?"

"Sadly, he passed away three years ago, so he didn't get to see it, but I think he would have liked it. He always told me it's not where you cook, it's what you cook."

"Very true," she agreed. "What happened to his restaurant?"

"My uncle runs it now," Joel explained. "He and I don't see eye to eye when it comes to food, so when I had the chance to get this truck, I grabbed it. I can do 70-30 on the net proceeds with you. You get the 70 percent. I take 30."

"How long do you think you'll need help?"

"At least four weeks. I usually set up for lunch at Civic Center Plaza from eleven to two Monday through Friday. On the weekends, I'm on the Embarcadero from eleven to five. I also attend some special events. There's a truck festival at Crissy Field in two weeks that is attended by thousands; it's a huge moneymaker."

"How busy are your weekday lunches?"

"They've been getting better every week. I'm not sure

how it will be since I've been out of commission for two weeks, but hopefully we'll get the regulars back."

"What about permits?" Burke interrupted. "Has the truck been inspected?"

"Everything is in order. I can show you the paperwork." Joel paused. "Why don't you and Burke take a minute to look around and discuss things? I'll wait outside with Kate."

As Joel stepped out of the truck, she gave Burke a questioning look, eager to hear his opinion. "What do you think?"

"It looks better than I thought," he admitted. "The propane tanks are securely placed, so there shouldn't be any danger of a fire."

She hadn't even considered that possibility. "I'm glad you were here to check that."

He smiled. "I don't bring much expertise to this project, but I can tell you that much."

She looked around, imagining herself cooking in the truck, serving hungry customers. "I like it. The menu is creative, fun and right up my alley. Joel seems like a good guy."

"You've only known him about three minutes."

"Well, he made a good first impression. I know you think I'm too impulsive, and maybe I am, but this feels right."

"It's your call."

She ran her hand along the counter and then walked out of the truck to speak to Joel.

He gave her an expectant and hopeful look. "What do you think?"

"I'd like to do it. I am interviewing for other restaurant jobs, but I'll commit to four weeks and then we'll see where we're at."

"It's a deal." Joel gave her a big grin. "Welcome to *Holy*

Meatballs."

"Thanks. What's next?"

"I'll give you some of the recipes to try. Why don't you cook some up at home, then we'll meet tomorrow and talk about all the details? I'd love to get back out there on Friday. It's always a good day for lunch sales at the Civic Center."

"Let's aim for that."

"Great. I'm really happy you're going to help me out."

"You haven't tasted my meatballs yet."

"I have a good feeling about you."

It was funny that he'd just repeated what she'd said to Burke about him. "Likewise."

She gave him Burke's address, and they agreed to meet the following day to hash out more of the details. Then she and Burke got back into the car and headed down the street.

Burke didn't have anything to say, which she thought was a telling sign. He'd told her it was her decision in the truck, but she had a feeling that he had a few comments he was having a hard time holding back.

"Just say it, Burke. You think I'm moving too fast."

"You obviously like to move fast."

"When opportunity knocks, you open the door."

"And then you ask questions, like how much can you expect to make in a week after expenses? Who's going to buy all the food, stock the truck, do the cleanup? Will that be part of your responsibilities? What about promotion or advertising? I think food trucks often have social media followings, but someone has to be promoting your appearances at various locations across town. Who's doing that—you? Joel gave you a percentage split, but do you have any idea what the costs are in turning out those meatballs?"

She had somewhat of an idea from having worked in a restaurant, but she didn't know it to the dime. "Can I retract my invitation for you to share your thoughts with me?" she asked with a little sigh.

"You did ask."

"And you've made some good points. I will go over all of those questions when I meet with Joel tomorrow." She opened the recipe folder Joel had given her. "Maybe I'll whip up some meatballs for you later, and then you'll be totally on board."

"It doesn't matter if I'm on board, Maddie. This is your thing. If you're happy, that's all that matters."

She was glad he saw it that way. "Thanks," she said, meeting his gaze. "I'm sure that wasn't easy for you to say. You don't like to stand by and do nothing when you think someone is making a bad decision."

"I don't, but I've begun to realize that I should spend a little more time trying to fix my own life instead of worrying about everyone else. So, what's next? We have a few hours before you need to go see that apartment, right?"

"Yes. I don't have to be there until eight-thirty."

"Want to get a drink, maybe some food?"

"Sure." She'd rather be out with Burke than in the quiet of his apartment where all kinds of bad ideas could come into play. "Where do you like to go?"

"I usually go to Brady's, but we don't have to go there. It is a firefighters' bar."

"Sounds perfect. I'd love to meet more of your friends."

⟶⟫⟪⟵

Brady's Bar and Grill was a large open restaurant with brick walls, an open grill and a long bar. A line of booths ran along one wall with tables taking up the center space. Flat screen televisions hung in the four corners of the room, each playing a different game. Team banners, professional jerseys, and trophies from local sports teams were displayed in cases and on the walls. There was also a wall dedicated to the firefighters of San Francisco, with numerous historic photographs as well as more current pictures.

As Burke walked Maddie through the room, she thought it had a great vibe. It was warm, friendly, a neighborhood kind of place. The people were dressed casually, and there were more than a few good looking guys in jeans and T-shirts, some with the SFFD insignia on them.

Everyone seemed to know Burke, and it was clear that he wasn't just well-liked by the men but also by the ladies. He was the kind of guy men wanted to be friends with and women wanted to sleep with. In other words—the perfect kind of guy.

She couldn't help but feel a little pride being at his side, even though a few of the other women in the room shot her looks that were not all that welcoming. Burke had been the lonely, grieving bachelor for the last three years, and no doubt there was more than one single woman in the bar who'd hoped he would turn to her when he was ready to get back in the game.

Burke grabbed her hand, pulling her out of the way of a waiter carrying a heavy tray of burgers and salads. "Careful," he said.

"Thanks again," she said, giving him a smile. "I really need to watch where I'm going. You're more alert than I am."

"Probably because while you're looking at everyone else, I'm looking at you."

The admission startled her as well as the intense look in his eyes. She didn't quite know what to say. Then they were interrupted by the two women she'd met at his firehouse: Rachel, the paramedic, and Shelby from dispatch.

"You came, Burke," Rachel said with delight, clapping her hands together. "This is great. And you brought Maddie, even better. We're about to start a mixed doubles pool tournament in the back room, and we need another woman. What do you say, Maddie?"

"I haven't played in a long time," she replied.

"That's fine. You can play with Dylan. He's the best, and he needs a handicap."

"Hey, what about me? I'm not bad," Burke protested, squeezing Maddie's fingers as she let go of his hand.

"You're not bad, but you're not Dylan," Rachel said candidly. "You may outrank your cousin, but when it comes to pool, he towers over you."

"I don't think that's true," Shelby interrupted. "You can be my partner, Burke. You're just as good as Dylan. And we are undefeated."

"We've only played once together," he said.

"And we won," she returned with a gleaming smile. "We're a good team."

"I'm game. Maddie?"

"I'd love to play."

"Great," Rachel said. "Come on." She led them through the crowded bar into the backroom of Brady's where three billiard tables were spread across a spacious room that also boasted pinball machines and dart games.

Dylan and Colton were already playing at one of the tables.

"I found a partner for you, Dylan," Rachel said.

Dylan finished his shot, which neatly swept two balls into the corner holes, then lifted his gaze to the group. "Which one of you lovely ladies is going to be on my team?"

"Maddie claims she hasn't played in a while, so she's all yours," Rachel said.

Maddie gave Dylan an apologetic shrug. "Sorry, it looks like you're stuck with me."

He grinned. "Don't worry. Anyone who cooks like you do can be on my team."

"If only this were a cooking competition," she said with a laugh. "I'm going to be a handicap."

"I'm not concerned. I'm pretty good."

"So I hear. Modest, too," she teased.

Dylan Callaway reminded her a lot of Aiden, the brother Burke was closest to in age. Like Aiden, Dylan had that happy-go-lucky, easygoing manner. He seemed like the kind of guy who didn't get worked up too easily. But he did have a good share of the Callaway cockiness, and why not? The men in that family had it all going on—including the other man at the table, Colton Callaway.

Colton came around the table to say hello. Colton was also attractive. His hair was a lighter brown than Burke's, and his demeanor was less intense than his older brother's but not quite as relaxed as Dylan. He was somewhere in the middle.

"Nice to see you again, Maddie," Colton said. "So who's going to be my partner? Shelby? Rachel?"

"I'm with you," Rachel said. "Shelby and Burke will play the winner. We'll see which Callaway ends up with bragging rights."

—⋙⋘—

While Maddie and Dylan started their game against Colton and Rachel, Shelby pulled Burke a few feet away from the table and gave him a concerned look.

"I'm glad we have a chance to talk for a second," she said. "I spoke to Mitch today."

His gut tightened. "How did that happen?"

"He showed up at my apartment. I was shocked, to say

the least."

"What did he want?"

She licked her lips, her gaze sweeping the room, as if she wanted to make sure that Mitch wasn't there. Then she looked back at him. "He said something quite shocking."

He had a feeling he knew what she was about to say. "What's that?"

"He told me that he thinks you had something to do with Leanne's hit-and-run. Of course, I said he was crazy. I actually think he's having some kind of breakdown. How he could think you would do anything to hurt Leanne is beyond me." She paused. "He also wanted me to pull the dispatch transcripts from the night Leanne was killed."

His stomach turned over. How far was Mitch going to go? "There's nothing in those transcripts. The police investigated the accident. They didn't leave any stone unturned. I made sure of that."

"Mitch doesn't agree."

"I know. What did you tell him about the transcripts?"

"That he'd have to talk to someone higher up than me. He wasn't too happy about it. He claimed I was trying to cover for you."

"You should stay away from him, Shelby."

"Trust me, I don't plan on talking to him again. You should stay away, too. I don't want you to get hurt."

"I can take care of myself."

"Mitch might not go after you. He might be smart enough to know he can't take you down and turn his attention to someone else." She tipped her head toward Maddie. "I don't think Mitch is going to like you replacing Leanne with another woman, not in the mood he's in these days."

She had a point, and her words reminded him of the car that had almost run Maddie down earlier in the day. He'd thought it was just an accident, or if it was deliberate, it was tied to her ex-fiancé. But maybe it was tied to Mitch.

"You know I hate to give advice," Shelby added.

He smiled. "You love to give advice."

"Okay, I do," she admitted. "And while you usually hate to take my advice, you should consider my suggestion carefully."

"What's your suggestion?"

"Put your dating life on hold for a few weeks. Don't put Maddie in the crosshairs of Mitch's anger."

He should take her advice, but he really didn't want to. He couldn't imagine not seeing Maddie. He usually needed to have his own time, but with Maddie, he hadn't felt that need for space. His need had more to do with getting closer than getting farther away.

When he didn't say anything, Shelby tilted her head, giving him a speculative look. "You really like her, don't you? She's not just an old friend. She's more than that, isn't she?"

"I think it's our turn to play," he said as Maddie and Dylan gave each other high-fives.

"You didn't answer my question, Burke."

"Yes," he said shortly. "She's more than an old friend." How much more was still to be determined.

Sixteen

Burke couldn't believe how good Maddie was at pool, how well she mixed in with his friends, or how she got prettier every time she smiled at him. He wasn't the only one drawn to her flame. Every single firefighter in the bar had his eye on Maddie. She had a natural charisma that drew people to her. She was having so much fun that it was impossible not to have fun with her.

After the pool tournament, they shared appetizers and beers at a long table and talked about everything under the sun. Dylan and Colton regaled Maddie with tales from Burke's youth, most of which were highly embellished. Rachel and Shelby contributed with tales from the firehouse, including one particularly grateful survivor who'd brought him casseroles for a week after he'd pulled her out of a burning car.

While he didn't usually like his life being put on display, he did like Maddie's interest in hearing every story. And she was happy to throw in a few of her own stories from their high school days. All in all, it was a great evening, and he was sorry when it ended, but Maddie had an appointment to look at an apartment.

After saying their goodbyes, they made their way out of the restaurant.

"Are you starting to feel like my cab driver?" Maddie joked as they got back into his car and buckled up.

"It's been a while since I had to drive anyone around."

"Nicole said you got off sibling driving duty as soon as she got her license."

He laughed. "Very true. I did pawn a lot of those trips off on her."

"You did. We always had to stop what we were doing to go pick up one of your brothers or sisters."

"Nicole was much nicer than I was. But getting back to your original point. I'm happy to help you, Maddie."

"Well, hopefully I won't be a burden much longer."

"What's the story on this apartment?"

"It's a one-bedroom. I'd be renting the living room."

"Wait? Seriously? Why wouldn't you just put two beds in the bedroom?"

"Because I'm in my thirties and my potential roommate is twenty-nine. We're a little past the stage of wanting to share a room."

"You won't have privacy in a living room."

"Carla said she works most nights, so the living room would be private because she wouldn't be there. The apartment is in lower Nob Hill, and apparently there's a bus stop right in front of the building, so it's easy to get around."

He needed to be supportive and happy for her, but there was nothing about what she'd just said that he liked. "Do you really want to live with a stranger?"

"Strangers are just people who aren't friends yet."

"Do you really believe that?"

"I've had strangers for roommates before. Sometimes it's great."

She was working really hard to put a positive spin on things. He admired that, but he was kind of hoping that the apartment wouldn't work out, that she'd have to stay with him for a few more days—a few more weeks.

But that wasn't realistic. She would get tired of sleeping on the couch, and he would get tired of fighting the urge to swoop her off that couch and carry her into his bed.

"I think it's the gray building," Maddie said a moment later, pointing to a four-story building near the corner.

"Let me drive around the block. This street is crowded."

"I can always run in while you double park."

"I want to take a look at it with you. I want to meet Carla."

It wasn't that he didn't trust her, but he also didn't want to see her make a bad decision because she was desperate.

A moment later, he found a parking space on the next block and they walked down the street to the apartment together. He found the neighborhood a little run-down for his taste. It wasn't bad, but it wasn't great, either.

The security lock on the front door was broken, which he didn't like, but maybe that was in the process of getting fixed. They went up the stairs to the second floor and knocked on 2B.

A woman opened the door. She had dark eyes, jet black hair that hung down to her waist and she wore tight black leather pants and a tank top that barely covered her extremely large rack. Her face was pretty but heavily made up, making him wonder what she really looked like. He also couldn't help wondering exactly where she worked that kept her out most nights.

"Hi, are you Carla?" Maddie asked, giving the woman a warm smile. "I'm Maddie Heller."

"Come on in," Carla said.

His first impression when he stepped into the apartment was that it was dark and smelled like cigarette smoke. The green carpet had definitely seen better days, and the paint on the walls was peeling in a few places. The kitchenette was very, very small, and the only window in the living room looked out over an alley.

While Maddie talked to Carla, he poked his head into the bedroom, which was only big enough to hold a double bed. There were clothes strewn all over the bed, and on the nightstand were several pill bottles and an empty wine glass. What the hell was Maddie getting herself into?

When he returned to the living room, he could hear them both trying to make a possible living situation sound great. Carla assured Maddie that she would have lots of privacy and that the couch was a comfortable pullout bed. Maddie commented on the great location and that she liked having roommates.

He thought Maddie was out of her mind to consider living here.

She was a butterfly. She needed light, space, air, and this place struck out on all three. She also needed a kitchen to cook in, a real bed to sleep in and a roommate who didn't look like she was on her way to work a street corner.

"I can give you a hundred-dollar discount off the rent this month if you agree to rent the place tonight," Carla told Maddie.

"What is the rent?" he asked.

"Nine hundred a month," Carla returned. "It's a great deal."

"Seriously?" He shouldn't be surprised. Rents were exorbitantly high in San Francisco, but a couch in someone's living room was hardly worth nine hundred bucks a month.

"You can't get a studio for less than fifteen hundred,"

Carla put in. "And you can't share a one-bedroom for less than twelve hundred."

"She's right," Maddie murmured, giving him a helpless shrug.

"You've only been looking for a day or two," he said.

"I looked before when I got into the bad sublet," she reminded him.

"You need to think about it, Maddie."

"I've got other people coming in tonight," Carla said.

"She'll take that chance," he told Carla. He strode to the door and opened it, giving Maddie a pointed look. "Come on."

Annoyance flashed in Maddie's eyes, but she did tell Carla that she'd have to call her later with her answer.

"Don't take too long," Carla warned her. "This place will be gone by tomorrow."

He seriously doubted that, but he kept his mouth shut, not wanting to drive Maddie into making a bad deal just to show she was making the decision, not him.

"That wasn't your call, Burke," she said, as they walked out of the building.

He paused when they reached the sidewalk. "She had pill bottles next to her bed."

"They could have been prescriptions for a cold or something."

"Or something. She was washing them down with wine."

"You're making a big deal out of nothing."

"I'm not. Look around you, Maddie. Look at this neighborhood. Is this where you want to call home?"

"It's not that bad. Carla was nice. She was friendly."

"I think she's a hooker."

"No, she's a dancer and a waitress."

He rolled his eyes. "You're so naïve."

"I am not naïve. But I also don't judge people in two seconds like you do."

"Don't you? It seems to me you found her delightful in the same amount of time that I came to the conclusion that she was not."

"That wasn't the conclusion you came to. You decided she was a drug addict and a hooker because of a pill bottle and a sexy outfit."

"I might be judgmental, but I'm right."

She blew out a frustrated breath. "You're not always right, Burke."

"I am this time. You know that wasn't the right place for you to be. You need to stop rushing into the next part of your life, stop trusting strangers who have a nice smile. Things might turn out better if you think before you act."

She stared back at him, not just anger in her eyes but also hurt. "Well, at least you're not silently judging me anymore. It's all out on the table. You think I'm an idiot."

"I didn't say that. You can be impulsive. You know that. You said so yourself when you told me about Paul and your whirlwind engagement."

"This isn't the same thing. She's just a roommate. I'm not going to marry her."

"I hope you're not going to live with her, either."

"It's the best option I have, Burke. I can't do the food truck from Portola Valley. It's too far away and I don't have a car, so moving in with my parents doesn't work for me. I barely have enough money to cover what Carla was asking for rent. It's not like there are dozens of people dying to rent me a room."

"She was charging you nine hundred dollars to basically sleep on her couch. You can sleep on mine for free."

"For how long?" she challenged.

"However long you need," he replied.

She let out a breath. "I like to pay my own way."

"We'll work something out. You can cook for me, maybe bring some more meals to the firehouse." As he waited for her decision, he felt his stomach twisting into a knot. It suddenly seemed very, very important for her to say yes, to agree to stay with him, at least temporarily.

"I think I should take your advice and consider all my options," she said.

Now she wanted to take his advice...

"Fine. We can hash out all the pros and cons at home. If you decide in the end to move in with Carla, then I won't say another word."

"Somehow I doubt that. I used to think you were the tall, silent type, but you seem to have a lot to say, especially when it comes to other people's lives."

Not other people's lives, just hers, but he wasn't going to tell her that.

On the way back to Burke's place, Maddie pondered her options. Despite what she'd said to Burke, she hadn't been in love with the apartment. It was gloomy and the smell was bad. Nor had she found Carla to be someone she wanted to be roommates with.

But what choice did she really have? She had to go somewhere, and she had to go soon. Staying with Burke was like playing with fire. She was starting to like him too much. He could hurt her if she let him. So she couldn't let him. Which meant she really needed to move on, before she started to believe that she and Burke might be able to have a relationship together.

He'd asked her at her parents' house why they couldn't have a relationship, and there were a million reasons why, weren't there?

They had different approaches to life, they both had a lot of personal baggage, and Burke didn't respect her. He might be attracted to her, but he didn't hold her decisions in very high regard; she'd just seen evidence of that. She couldn't be with someone who didn't value her opinion.

But she did value *his* opinion. She thought he was amazing, smart, generous, sexy as hell—which was exactly why he could hurt her.

A little sigh escaped her lips...

She'd never been afraid of risk. After losing her sister as a teenager, she'd always felt like the worst had already happened, that there was nothing left to be afraid of. For the most part, that had been true. As long as she didn't put her heart on the line, she could do anything she wanted. And not putting her heart on the line had been easy. Most men didn't want her heart.

But Burke would be different. He didn't do anything halfway. He had always been all or nothing. If he committed to anything, he went all in. He'd want everything from a woman.

And she'd never given a man *everything*.

She told herself Burke wasn't asking for everything. He wasn't really asking for anything at the moment except that she take more time to make decisions. Well, she could do that.

She straightened in her seat as they stopped at a light. "Can you drop me off at the market?" she asked.

"It's almost nine."

"It's still open," she said, pointing to the lighted building. "I need to pick up some ingredients so I can try out some of

Joel's meatball recipes."

"Tonight?"

"I like to cook when I'm thinking. It brings me clarity. And you told me to think, remember?"

"Okay, the market it is—as long as I get to be your taste tester."

"That works for me."

As Burke pulled into the parking lot, his phone rang. "Why don't you go ahead?" he said. "I need to get this."

"I'll be quick."

"Take your time."

As Maddie closed the car door, he answered his phone. "Hello, Max."

"Burke, how's it going?"

"You tell me. What have you found out?"

"Maddie's ex-fiancé was arrested in Las Vegas yesterday for embezzling money from his employer. Maddie wasn't the only one he stole money from to finance his gambling addiction. I spoke to my friend at the LVPD, and he said that they've convinced Paul to work with them to put Harry Barker out of business. They've been trying to shut down his operation for years. If Paul helps them out, he should get an easier sentence, but he probably will serve time."

Burke felt as if a weight had just fallen off his shoulders. If Paul was in Vegas and now under the watch of the Las Vegas Police Department, Maddie would be safe. At least, he hoped so. "Paul told Maddie yesterday that Barker's collection group was after her, that they could possibly use her to leverage Paul. He said they had photos of her here in San Francisco. I don't want Maddie to get caught in the middle of this sting operation."

"I don't know anything about photos. I'll run that by the detective out there, see if he can get the truth from Paul."

"Maddie thought Paul might have made it up to scare her into helping him."

"Let's find out."

Max was always very pragmatic, never too optimistic or too pessimistic. He focused on facts. It sometimes amazed him that Max had gotten together with Emma, who was fiery and emotional and always put her heart on the line. But somehow the two of them worked.

"Thanks for your help, Max. I am happy to know that Paul has been arrested."

"I think Maddie is probably safe here, but until Barker's operation is shut down, I'd still keep an eye out. I'm also tracking down the man who illegally sublet his apartment to her. She's definitely run across some great guys in the last year," he added dryly.

"She trusts a little too easily."

"Emma says she's sleeping on your couch. How's that going?"

"It's all right," he said, hearing the question in Max's voice.

"It's not getting a little too crowded in your apartment?"

"Surprisingly not."

"Interesting."

"What about Mitch's private investigator? Have you been able to reach him?"

"I've got a name but haven't made contact yet. Have you heard from Mitch again?"

"Not since he showed up at my apartment on Saturday. But one of the fire dispatchers told me that Mitch wanted her to give him the transcripts of the call that went out the night

Leanne was killed. He's not done."

"It doesn't sound like it."

"Keep me posted, Max, and thanks. I owe you."

"I'll put it on Emma's bill," Max said with a laugh. "I prefer the way she pays me back."

"I'll bet."

As he put his phone down, he saw Maddie coming out of the store with two grocery bags in her arms. He got out of the car to help her put them in the trunk. "Did you find everything you needed?"

"I did. We're going to be eating a lot of meatballs."

"I can't wait."

"Was that call important?" she asked as she got into the car.

"Yes. Max said Paul was arrested in Vegas for embezzling from his company."

Her eyes widened. "I always wondered if he'd tried to take money from them."

"He did. He's now being forced to cooperate with the cops in order to bring down his bookie's operation."

"What does that mean exactly?"

"It means you're not going to have to worry about him anymore."

"That would be a huge relief. I'm almost afraid to believe it's true."

"Max is going to check on the alleged photos that Paul told you about. He'll let us know if there's anything else to be concerned about."

"Okay, good. I guess I know why Paul stopped calling."

"It's possible you can levy some charges against Paul yourself."

"I just want to be done with him."

As much as he wanted Maddie to be finished with Paul,

too, he hated the idea that the guy was going to get away with what he'd done to her. "You should make him pay for what he did."

"It sounds like he's going to be punished."

"For what he did to his company, not you." Anger rose within him. "He took everything from you, Maddie."

"But he didn't take me," she said, meeting his gaze. "I'm going to be okay. And I don't want to waste energy on him. I want to move forward. That's all you can really do in life. You fall down. You get up." She paused. "I know you want me to hold him accountable, and I'm probably letting you down again, but—"

"You're not letting me down," he interrupted. "Actually, your philosophy is probably a much healthier one than mine. You don't hold grudges, do you?"

"I try not to. Anger tends to hurt the person who's angry more than anyone else. Thanks for suggesting I get your brother-in-law involved, though. It is a relief to know that Paul is talking to the police and that I don't have to worry about his loan collectors coming after me." She blew out a breath and gave him a happy smile. "Let's go home."

"You got it," he said, thinking that he liked the idea of her calling his apartment home. He liked it quite a bit.

Seventeen

Despite the late hour, Maddie decided she didn't want to wait until the next day to try out some of Joel's recipes. While she headed into the kitchen to whip up some meatballs, Burke settled on the couch. He flipped on the Warriors game, relieved to see his team leading the Lakers by ten. Then he grabbed his laptop off the coffee table and logged onto his banking website.

It didn't take him long to push a couple of payments through, which was too bad because he'd been hoping that concentrating on his bills would do something to quiet the reckless urges coursing through his body, those urges getting a little stronger every time he caught a glimpse of Maddie.

She'd put some ear buds in and was listening to music as she cooked. He could see her add a little dance move every now and then. She was happy, he thought, sometimes humming with the music, sometimes muttering under her breath about ingredients and measurements. She was definitely caught up in what she was doing. He doubted she'd spared even a momentary thought to him since they'd come back to the apartment.

He wasn't used to coming in second to a meatball, he

thought with a smile.

Judging by the delicious aroma drifting out of his kitchen, it was probably going to be a damn good meatball.

He watched the Warriors play for another half hour. Then he got up from the couch to see what was going on in the kitchen. He was a little stunned at how much Maddie was doing at once. She had every burner on the stove going, with a variety of frying pans and saucepans in use. She was also chopping onions faster than anyone he'd ever seen.

When she saw him, she gave him a cheerful smile, her green eyes bright, her cheeks flushed from the heat.

"What are you making?" he asked.

She pulled the ear buds out of her ears. "Bacon jalapeño poppers with ground turkey meatballs and chicken parmesan meatballs."

"Sounds interesting."

"The jalapeño popper is going to be hot. Do you like it spicy?"

He grinned. "The hotter the better, and I'm not just talking about meatballs."

She raised an eyebrow. "Really. I thought you might be more vanilla than spice."

"Those are fighting words, Maddie."

She laughed. "Am I wrong? You're a rule follower. You don't like to combine things that don't obviously go together. You think everything through before you do it."

"But when I do it, I do it really, really well," he said, moving close enough to her to see the tiny beads of sweat on her brow.

A darker gleam entered her eyes. "You're very confident. I will say that."

"I can back it up."

"Let's see if you can."

He thought for a second she was going to kiss him, but her quick move took her around him. She picked up a toothpick and stabbed one of the meatballs cooling in a bowl. She brought it back to him, holding her hand under the meatball to catch any drips.

"Ready?" she asked.

He saw the dare in her eyes. He was going to eat that meatball and enjoy it, no matter what it actually tasted like. He leaned forward and sucked the meatball into his mouth.

It was actually incredibly flavorful, the bacon and jalapeño mixing together extremely well. "That's really good," he said as he swallowed.

She laughed. "You sound surprised."

"I don't know why I am. You're an excellent cook."

"It's just a meatball, and not even my recipe," she said with a modest shrug.

"I suspect you made that recipe your own."

"Well, maybe a couple of tiny changes, but nothing significant."

"What are you working on next?"

"The chicken parmesan meatballs. That will do it for tonight. I'll do some other ones tomorrow." She paused, tilting her head to the right. "You could help me if you want."

He wanted to do pretty much anything with her that she wanted to do with him. "I'm not very good in the kitchen."

"Where's that confidence now?"

"I know my strengths."

"Why don't you help me roll the meat into tiny balls? It's ready to go."

"All right. Do I need a special spoon or something?"

"No, just wash your hands and then dig in. I'll show you."

He turned on the sink, washed his hands with soap and

water, then dried them off on a paper towel. Maddie stood next to him at the counter as he put his hands into the spicy ground chicken mixture. It felt wet and gooey, and he wasn't all that excited to be mucking around in it.

"Don't be afraid to put some elbow action in it," she encouraged, as he grabbed a chunk and started to roll it in hands.

"It feels kind of disgusting."

"Just imagine how good it's going to taste at the end."

"If you say so. I hope I don't mess these up for you."

"You can't really do it wrong at this point." She pulled out a tray. "Just put them on here when you're done."

While he felt rather clumsy on the first few meatballs, he quickly got the hang of it and soon had two trays ready to go into the oven. While Maddie took over, he washed his hands and the bowl, then helped her straighten up the kitchen while the batch of meatballs turned to a golden brown.

Twenty minutes later, she pulled the trays out of the oven and said, "Look at your work. Not bad, right?"

He nodded, somewhat impressed with his own efforts. "You're a good teacher."

"Well, it was nice to turn the tables on you for a change. And you weren't a bad student, probably better than I was back in our tutoring days."

"Definitely better than you were."

"I think this is going to work out," Maddie said.

For a moment, he had the crazy idea she was talking about the two of them working out, but then she tipped her head toward the meatballs.

"I like making meatballs, and Joel's are particularly good," she continued. "I don't think he was bragging about how successful his truck is. These are perfect for lunch or dinner, especially if we add in rice or pasta."

"Or turn them into a meatball sandwich." He liked how caught up she was in her new venture. There was definitely a part of him that thought she was making a mistake by not taking a job in an established restaurant, but there was another part of him that really admired her nerve and willingness to take risks.

He risked his life every day on the job, but those were calculated risks backed by training and experience. He wasn't as good as Maddie was at trying new things. But that had started to change since she'd come back into his life. No one had ever pushed him the way she did. Actually, she didn't push him, she just offered, and whatever she was offering, he always wanted to accept.

She covered the trays of meatballs and slid them into the refrigerator. "I guess that's it for tonight."

"It is almost midnight."

"I didn't realize it was so late. I lose all track of time when I'm cooking."

"You were having fun."

"I think you enjoyed it, too."

"I did," he admitted. "You always bring the fun, Maddie."

"That's what life is supposed to be about." She paused. "At least, that's what I've always thought. But your goals have probably been more serious."

"They have been, but you've reminded me that there's another side to life."

"A wild side?" she teased.

"Wild, spicy, sexy, fun." He moved a little closer to her with each word. Then he placed his hands on her waist, loving the way her eyes turned a shadowy green at his touch. Her gaze was so expressive. He could read her emotions in her eyes, and right now those emotions were all over the map.

He saw desire but also restraint, eagerness warring with caution.

"We can fight or we can surrender," he said.

"Are those our only choices?" she asked, meeting his gaze.

He slowly nodded. "I think so."

She licked her lips. "I don't know what to say. You scare me a little."

"I thought you were fearless."

"There's always been something about you, Burke. A line I was afraid to cross."

"Why?"

"I don't know why," she said helplessly. "Maybe because I think you'd ask for more than I want to give. You expect a lot from people."

"All I expect from you is—you. I don't want to change you, Maddie. I don't want you to be anyone other than who you are, because who you are is who I want."

She stared back at him with those luminescent green eyes, and he felt more nervous than he had in a very long time.

"I want you, too," she said softly. "I've wanted you since I was fourteen years old, but if you look at the pros and cons—"

He cut her off with a shake of his head. "I know you're not looking at the pros and cons, and neither am I. Not tonight anyway."

"You really think you can live in the moment?"

"You underestimate me, Maddie." He lowered his head and kissed her on the mouth, pulling back just as she parted her lips. He leaned in and pulled her hair away from her ear long enough to whisper, "And by the way, I don't like vanilla. So if that's what you want…"

"It's not," she said a little breathlessly.

"Then let's see what we can cook up together."

"I like the sound of that." She wrapped her arms around his neck and pulled him back in for another kiss. "I could do this all night," she murmured against his lips.

"I'm counting on that."

Maddie didn't know how they got from the kitchen to the bedroom. She couldn't remember how their clothes came off. But when the back of her knees hit Burke's bed and she fell into the soft mattress with Burke coming down on top of her, she felt like she was living out every fantasy she had ever had.

Burke enveloped her with his kiss, his touch, his overwhelming desire—a desire that was matched only by her own.

She quickly realized that Burke's thoughtful, deliberate plan of attack worked really well in the bedroom. He wasn't impatient or self-centered. He didn't want to get anything over with; he wanted to get it all right—so right.

She sighed as his mouth trailed down her cheek and into the corner of her neck, shivered as his tongue slid lower, tracing her collarbone, traveling around the peak of her breast, teasing and tasting and driving her a little bit mad.

She ran her hands up and down his bare back, loving the play of his muscles under her fingers. He was strong and powerful. He took the lead like the natural leader that he was. And she let him. She wanted to be at his mercy, because so far he was showing her that he knew exactly what to do.

His hands, his lips, his breath—were everywhere. Each touch lit up her nerve endings. She had to fight against her own impatient tendencies as Burke showed her that not only could he live in the moment, he could make every minute last as long as possible.

It was one peak after the next. He drove her crazy. Fight or surrender, he'd said, and she knew now that surrender was the only option. What a beautiful surrender it was.

And then she found a way to turn the tables on him. Now it was his turn to take the pleasure she was giving, to suffer the delicious torment of her mouth exploring his body.

When they finally came together in a rush of pent-up need, she felt like she shattered into a thousand pieces. The years they were apart slid away. The pains of the past were crushed by amazing pleasure.

She hadn't felt trapped, but when the guard walls around her heart came down, she realized that Burke had just set her free in a way she'd never expected.

Afterwards, she rolled onto her side, her head on his chest, his arm around her shoulders, their hearts pounding down to a steadier beat.

She ran her fingers through the wiry strands of hair on his chest, loving how solid Burke felt beneath her.

"You okay?" Burke asked.

"I feel wonderful. That was better than the fantasy."

"You fantasized about me?"

"For a long time." She lifted her head and gazed into his eyes. He looked happy, satisfied and content. "That was amazing."

"No, that was good. Amazing is still to come."

"Really? You think you can do better?"

He grinned. "I set high goals, Maddie. I usually reach them."

"I know that. But you've already driven me crazy, what's left?"

"Why don't we find out?"

There was a challenge to his words, an invitation she couldn't refuse. She was just a little afraid that the only thing left was love.

Still, how could she say no? She was fearless Maddie, after all.

"Why don't we?" She slid up his body and kissed him again, feeling the sparks of the fire kick back into flames. "It's a good thing I have a firefighter in my bed," she said with a laugh.

He laughed with her. "I don't want to put your fire out— at least not yet."

"We'll play a little first," she suggested.

"Yes, we will."

A second later, he flipped her onto her back and showed her that he could do playful as well as he could do serious.

Maddie took up most of the bed, Burke thought with tender amusement, watching her in the early morning light. Her cheeks were a beautiful pink, and her blonde hair fell in soft waves around her bare shoulders. He liked the dusting of freckles on those shoulders. He wanted to trace a path from one to the other. Maybe later…

He also liked that she had a hand on his waist and one of her legs was thrown over his, as if she didn't want him to leave, didn't want to be away from him. Or maybe she just wanted more room in the bed, he thought pragmatically. Either way, he was just happy to finally be in bed with her.

She'd been everything he imagined and more, making love with total abandon, no rules, no worries, a lot of smiles, a few laughs, and a tremendous amount of passion. When

Maddie was fully engaged in something, she went after it with all of her heart and soul. He'd never thought she'd put her heart and soul into him.

He was the luckiest man in the world. But how long would his luck hold out?

Would Maddie even stay in San Francisco?

She didn't have a history of sticking around. While she was excited about the food truck, that was a one-month job. Then what? Would she get an unexpected offer from a friend in some other city? Would she blow out of town with the next big wind?

He hated to think she would disappear from his life again, but it was impossible not to consider that that might happen.

She murmured something unintelligible in her sleep, a smile crossing her lips. Whatever she was dreaming about made her happy.

Maybe she was dreaming about him…

She might not stay forever, but she was with him now, and she'd challenged him to live in the moment for a change, so he was going to do that for as long as he could. Reality would intrude soon enough.

Eighteen

Maddie slid out of bed just before eight, a little surprised to see Burke still fast asleep. He seemed like the type to be up early, ready to face the day. On the other hand, they hadn't gotten a lot of sleep the night before. She gave a happy sigh at the memories. Her muscles felt deliciously achy, and her body still tingled from Burke's touch. Whatever came next, she was not going to be sorry about last night.

She slipped into the bathroom, put on her yoga wear and went out to the living room. She unrolled the mat she'd put next to the couch, put in her ear buds and played some soothing meditation music to get her morning ritual started. She needed the extra stretches this morning. She also needed to focus, because there were things she had to get done today. And those things probably wouldn't get done if she allowed herself to go back into the bedroom and snuggle up next to Burke.

She was almost done with her routine when Burke walked into the living room wearing jeans and a T-shirt, his hair damp from a shower.

Her stomach turned over and a rush of desire immediately ran through her. Why did the man have to be so damn attractive?

He gave her a slow-burning smile and she was so distracted, she fell out of her pose, having to touch the nearby coffee table to get her balance back.

"Sorry, did I startle you?" he asked, coming over to her.

"A little," she said, as he took her hand and pulled her back into a standing position. He didn't let go even after she was on her feet.

"Good morning," he said, his voice husky, his gaze intimate.

"Morning," she murmured. She saw a tiny droplet of water by the corner of his mouth. She really wanted to lick it up.

His gaze darkened. He pulled her up against his chest and gave her a hard, possessive kiss that left no doubt that whatever they'd started the night before was still going on.

"Let's go back to bed," he said.

"Uh," she hesitated, wanting to say yes, but knowing she probably shouldn't.

He gave her a thoughtful look. "What are you thinking, Maddie?"

"I'm not really sure, which isn't unusual for me. I've never been as clear-minded as you, Burke."

"You're not having regrets are you?"

She immediately shook her head. "No, I try to never have regrets. It seems pointless."

"Then what's the problem?"

"I find myself worrying about something I never worry about."

"Which is what?"

"What's next?"

"I thought we were living in the moment."

"We were—we are," she amended, wishing she'd never

taken the conversation in this direction. "Forget what I said."

He put his hands on her shoulders and kneaded the suddenly tight muscles in her neck. "I don't know what's next, Maddie, but I'd like us to find out together."

"Me, too. Last night was fun. You surprised me a little."

His lips curved into a smile. "Likewise."

"It only took us eighteen years to make that happen."

"A lot of wasted time."

"Not wasted," she said with a shake of her head. "We grew up. We lived. We learned. We loved. I wouldn't trade any of it."

"I might trade some of it," he said practically. "But I get your point."

"The past has made us who we are now, so we can't wish any of it away. It would be like wishing a part of ourselves away."

"Did they teach you that in yoga?"

"As a matter of fact, yes. Yoga is about awareness, being mindful of your body, your breath, centering yourself, accepting your weaknesses and also your strengths. We should do it together sometime."

"I can think of other things I'd rather do," he said.

"There's a time for everything. I'm going to get dressed."

"What happened to going back to bed?"

"I have meatballs to make."

He laughed. "First time I've ever heard that excuse. You're one of a kind, Maddie Heller."

"Don't you forget it." She gave him a quick kiss on her way to take a long, cold shower.

———⋙⋘———

After Maddie left the room, Burke picked up his phone,

scrolling through the contacts. He needed to call Leanne's mom. He'd been putting off speaking to the Parkers, but he wanted to get in touch with them today. He had no idea where Mitch's investigation was going to take him, but he didn't want the Parkers to be caught off guard. Besides that, he also needed to find a way to ask Leanne's mother if she'd known her daughter was pregnant. How he was going to do that he had no idea.

However, before he got to the Parkers' phone number, a name popped out at him—Kelly Hamilton. Kelly had been one of Leanne's best friends and was to have been a bridesmaid in their wedding. Maybe Leanne had confided in Kelly.

He was going to shock the hell out of her by calling after all these years, but what choice did he have? And it was highly possible Mitch had already been in touch with her.

"Hello?" she said, her voice tentative.

"Hi, Kelly. It's Burke Callaway."

There was a surprised gasp on the other end of the line. "Burke, I must say I didn't expect to hear from you. How are you?"

"I'm all right. And you?"

"Good." She took another breath. "It's been a long time since we spoke. I was thinking about Leanne the other day—that I can't believe it's been three years since she died. Anyway, what can I do for you?"

"I was wondering if I could come by and talk to you for a few minutes."

"About what?"

"It's not something I want to discuss on the phone. Ten minutes is all I need. Are you still in San Francisco?"

"No, I'm living in Hillsborough now. I got married last year."

"Congratulations." An odd feeling ran through him at her words. Kelly had been single without a man in her life when Leanne died. In fact, Kelly had jokingly told Leanne more than once that she was hoping to find a single guy, maybe a firefighter, at their wedding. But Kelly was married now. Time had moved on for her as well as for him. "I'm off today if you have some time this morning or this afternoon. I'll come to you."

"I'm here until one. If you can make it down this morning, I'd be happy to see you."

"Great. I'll be there in an hour." He made a note of her address, then set down the phone and headed into the kitchen to start the coffee maker. Maddie might be able to begin her day with yoga, but he was going to need caffeine.

He opened the refrigerator door and saw the casseroles of meatballs from the night before. On impulse, he took one of the dishes out, spooned a couple of meatballs into a bowl and put it in the microwave. The meatballs were steaming when he took them out.

He bit into one and was once again smacked in the face with a burst of flavor.

The meatball reminded him of Maddie. She knocked him over in so many ways: her cooking, her laughter, the way she made love…

She'd come back into his life, and nothing was ever going to be the same again.

"Meatballs for breakfast?" Maddie asked, coming into the kitchen dressed in jeans and a soft sweater, her hair falling loose around her shoulders, the way he liked it.

"They're good."

"You tried the chicken parmesan meatballs?"

"Yes," he said, swallowing the last bite.

"Do you like them better than the bacon jalapeño

poppers?"

"Tough call." He thought for a moment. "I can't pick a winner. Both are great."

"Well, let's hope the rest of them turn out as well. Do you want me to make you anything else for breakfast?"

"No, I'm going to run out for a while. I called one of Leanne's friends. She's agreed to see me."

Maddie's expression turned serious. "Okay. Are you going to ask her if Leanne was pregnant?"

"I know I need to do that. It's going to be awkward and uncomfortable, but maybe she can tell me something that makes sense."

"I hope so. You're handling the whole thing really well, Burke. I know it can't be easy to think that your fiancée cheated on you, especially with someone like Mitch."

"Anyone would have been bad."

She gave him a thoughtful look. "You do believe that she slept with Mitch, don't you? You don't think he was making it up?"

He let out a sigh. "I don't want to believe it, but the fact that she kept the baby news from me leads me to believe she was worried about who the father was. Why else wouldn't she just tell me?"

"I can't think of a reason. Talking to Leanne's friend is probably a good idea."

"Or a bad one. I just don't know what else to do. There aren't that many people I can talk to. If Kelly can't help me, I'll have to try Leanne's parents."

"I guess I know what you're doing today," she said lightly.

"Making meatballs sounds like more fun."

"If you want me to go with you—"

"No," he said quickly. He couldn't take another woman to

Kelly's house, not a woman he'd just slept with. It didn't feel right. "But thanks for offering." He paused. "What are you going to do about the apartment, Maddie? Because I really don't want you to move in with Carla."

"I can't stay on your couch indefinitely."

"I don't want you on my couch. I think you know that."

"I do know that, but I'm not really sure what we're doing."

He gave her a quick kiss. "Still living in the moment. I'll see you later."

"Good luck, Burke. I hope you get the answer you want."

He hoped so, too. He just wasn't really sure what answer he wanted.

Kelly Hamilton lived in a large, three-story house in the upscale neighborhood of Hillsborough, located about thirty minutes south of San Francisco. As Burke drove through iron gates and down a large circular drive to Kelly's massively large front door, he couldn't help but compare Kelly's current house with the small, cluttered two-bedroom apartment she'd shared with three other women when he'd first started dating Leanne.

While Leanne had been friends with Kelly and her roommates, she'd always liked having her own space. Unlike Maddie, who thought strangers were just friends she hadn't met yet, Leanne had been more protective of her privacy, of her personal space. Leanne had been more like him. He'd thought that was a good thing. Now, he wasn't so sure.

When Kelly opened her door to him, he got another surprise. An attractive redhead with a love of shopping and fashion, Kelly had always been a stylishly dressed woman, but she'd traded in her chic clothes for a maternity dress, and she was at least five or six months pregnant.

She smiled and patted her stomach. "Yes, it's true. I'm having a baby."

"Congratulations," he said, as she gave him a quick hug.

"Thanks. Vince and I are so excited. We're having a boy."

"That's fantastic news."

"Come in, Burke." She stepped back so he could enter the house.

Her home was just as impressive on the inside as it was on the outside. Kelly ushered him into a large designer-decorated living room that was a mix of white furniture, sparkling glass tables and expensive accent pieces, some of which were crystal.

"I know what you're thinking," Kelly said as they sat down on the couch. "We're going to have to do a lot of baby-proofing in here, and you're right. We have all new family-friendly furniture being delivered next week."

"Are you still working at the Museum of Modern Art?"

"I cut back to part-time after I got married. When I go on maternity leave, that will probably be it. Vince travels a great deal for his job, and I want to be free to join him and also to spend time with the baby. We're interviewing nannies right now, but it's not that easy to find a good one."

"A lot of changes for you," he muttered.

"All good." Her expression turned uncomfortable as she twisted her large diamond ring on her finger. "I'm sorry I missed Leanne's memorial dinner last week. I wasn't feeling well that day. I was going to try to make it."

"You don't have to apologize to me. It's the Parkers' thing."

"I think about Leanne all the time. I wish she could have been at my wedding. I wish she could have seen me pregnant.

She would have found it so funny, because I used to tell her that I wasn't sure I wanted kids. They're a lot of work, and I've always wanted to have the big job and travel."

"What changed your mind?"

"Falling in love with Vince. He made me see that I could have it all. I'm so lucky I found him. I must have done something right."

"It definitely looks like you've got it all."

"So what did you want to talk to me about?"

He drew in a breath, not sure where to start. "Mitch Warren."

"Oh, I had a feeling. He's been calling me the past few days, but we haven't connected yet. He was making bizarre comments about Leanne being murdered, which sounded insane. I played one of his messages for my husband, and he told me not to talk to Mitch. I had a feeling when you called this morning that it was going to be about him. What's going on?"

"Mitch told me that he and Leanne had an affair while she and I were engaged. I want to know if it's true."

Kelly's face paled at his words. Her inability to give him a quick *no* made his gut clench.

"Kelly?" he prodded.

"I don't know what to say, Burke."

"Leanne is gone. You can't hurt her with the truth. But you can help me."

"The truth is—I'm not sure. Leanne got really secretive right before she died. She seemed to be talking to Mitch a lot. He'd text her when we were out shopping for bridesmaids dresses. I did think at the time that it was annoying, and I wasn't sure how you'd feel about your fiancée texting another man all the time."

That matched what Shelby had told him.

"Did she tell you she was involved with him romantically?"

"No, she didn't say anything like that. I teased her about it once, and she jumped down my throat. She said it wasn't funny, and she actually accused me of being jealous and trying to ruin things for her. It was a really big over-reaction, and I was angry at first, but Leanne was stressed out, so I let it go."

"She was jumping on me for odd things, too. Did she ever tell you she wasn't sure she wanted to get married at all?"

"She did say that she worried you were too alike, that maybe you didn't push each other enough. But all brides get nervous. I thought she was just jittery until she canceled her dress fitting. That was weird. She wouldn't say why. I asked her about it, and she was really vague. That's when I started to wonder if she was really having doubts. But I didn't know what to do. She wasn't willing to confide in me."

He met Kelly's gaze. "Is it possible she didn't want to try on her dress because she was pregnant?"

Her eyes widened with surprise. "What? Leanne was pregnant?"

Kelly seemed genuinely taken aback by his statement.

"I was recently given that information."

"Who told you?"

"Mitch."

"Oh." She gave a sudden nod as if it had all become clear. "That's why you asked me if they were having an affair." She paused for a moment. "Now that you're telling me she was pregnant, other things make sense. She threw up a few times when we were out. She kept saying she had a virus, and that's why she was so tired all the time. But she was pregnant. Wow! Why wouldn't she tell you?"

"You know why. She wasn't sure I was the father," he said, feeling little to no emotion anymore. The shock had worn off, and the anger had burned itself out.

"I guess that would be a reason not to tell you," Kelly said slowly. "I can't believe Leanne really slept with Mitch. She had you. She was getting married. Why wasn't that enough?"

Her question echoed one that had been running around in his head ever since Mitch's big revelation. "I don't know. Is there anyone else you think Leanne might have confided in?"

"I was the closest to her of all the bridesmaids. Her mom might have known something. Have you talked to Marjorie?"

"I was saving her for last. I don't want to talk to her about it, but Mitch is on the warpath. He thinks I found out Leanne cheated and was having his baby, and that I had her run off the road."

"That's ludicrous. You loved Leanne." Kelly gave him a compassionate look. "I think she loved you, too, Burke. I don't know why she would have cheated on you, although Leanne could be a little selfish. She wasn't perfect. She wasn't a saint. I know we're not supposed to say bad things about people who die tragically, but we both know that she had her faults."

He didn't really know where Kelly was going with her statements. "Leanne definitely wasn't perfect."

"Sometimes I got a little frustrated with her when she acted if planning a wedding was the worst thing in the world, when it was all so great." She blew out a breath. "I'm sorry. I don't know where all that came from."

He didn't know, either. Maybe Kelly and Leanne had not been as close as he'd thought.

"Anyway," she continued. "If Leanne cheated on you, then it had to have been an impulsive thing. I guess the only person who would really know how that came to be is Mitch."

"He won't tell me the truth. Anyway, thanks for your help, Kelly."

"I wish you'd come for another reason, but it was good to see you. I hope Mitch leaves you alone—leaves us all alone. I really don't need this problem in my life. I finally have things exactly the way I want them."

"I hear you."

He got to his feet and Kelly walked him to the front door. "Have you picked out a name yet?" he asked.

"We're thinking about Eli—it was Vince's grandfather's name. He was very close to him."

"I wish you all the best, Kelly."

"You, too, Burke. You deserve to be happy. Leanne would want that."

He used to think he'd known exactly what Leanne wanted; now he wasn't so sure.

As he got into the car, he took out his phone and called Leanne's mother. He might as well make one more stop before he went home.

Nineteen

"What do you think?" Maddie asked as Joel popped one of the vegan meatballs into his mouth.

Joel and Kate had arrived fifteen minutes earlier and were working their way through her samples. Kate said she didn't know anything about cooking, but she knew a lot about eating. They'd given a thumbs-up to all the meatballs so far, but the vegan ball, which was a mix of nuts, rice and chickpea flour, was going to be the real test.

"Perfect," Joel said.

"I agree," Kate said. "Can I have another one?"

Maddie passed her the plate. "Of course. I was a little worried about that one. I'm so glad you like it."

"What did you add?" Joel asked.

"A little curry powder to give it a kick. But I can take that out next time around."

"No, it was an excellent idea. I think you and I are a match made in heaven, Maddie."

She laughed. "I do like your meatballs."

"All the girls do."

Kate groaned. "Please, Joel, I have heard way too many meatball jokes."

He laughed. "Well, you won't be hearing any for a few months, so you don't have to worry."

"Are you going somewhere?" Maddie asked.

"I'm going to Quantico," Kate said, a happy sparkle in her eyes. "I start training to be an FBI special agent next Monday. I'm so excited. It's a twenty-one-week program. Hopefully, I'll make it through. It will be really humiliating if I get kicked out. Callaways never fail."

Maddie smiled, realizing that the Callaway traditions obviously extended beyond Burke's family to his cousins.

"You'll do great," Joel said. "You're smart, tough, and you don't quit. The FBI will love you."

"I hope so. I am going to miss the meatballs. But I'm happy I'm leaving you in such good hands."

"I am, too," Joe said with a grin. "Maddie is going to be my savior."

"I don't know about savior, but I will be your cook."

Kate gave her a sly look. "And what will you be for Burke?" she asked. "I know it's none of my business, and he'd kill me for asking, but everyone in the family is really curious. Burke has been single a long time, and he never brings a woman around. And I am talking way too much."

Maddie laughed. She liked Kate a lot. In some ways, Kate reminded her of her younger self. "Burke and I are friends."

"Oh, please, not the friends thing," Kate said dismissively. "I'm not buying it."

"It's not your business," Joel put in.

"Burke is my cousin. He's family."

"And he's great," Maddie finished. "I like him. He likes me. Neither of us has any idea what's coming next."

"Now that's really interesting, because Burke is the one guy in the family who has always known what's coming next.

I think you're good for him."

"He's good for me, too," she admitted. "Anyway, back to the meatballs…"

"I've got us set up for Friday at eleven at the Civic Center," Joel said. "I'll meet you there."

"What about shopping? Do you need help with the food?"

"A buddy is going to help me with that. He's going to get the truck stocked up and parked at the Civic Center. Then you'll take over the cooking, and I'll be there to help with the customers."

"Okay, I'm excited. I can't wait to see how it all works."

"I think you're going to have fun," Joel said as he stood up.

"I wish I could be there to see it, but I'll be on a plane to Virginia," Kate said.

"What made you want to go into the FBI? Was it a lifelong dream?" she asked.

"It was something I had in mind for a long time," Kate replied, a shadow now in her eyes. "I just didn't know if I could really do it. I still don't, but I can't wait to find out. I'm just really glad you're able to help Joel. I hated to leave knowing he was in such a bind."

"Are you two a couple?" Maddie ventured, a little curious about their relationship.

"God, no," Kate said.

"Absolutely not," Joel agreed.

"We've been friends since we were five," Kate added, "but never romantically inclined."

Maddie couldn't help wondering if someday that would change.

She opened the door to let them out and was surprised to find a bouquet of flowers on the floor in the hallway. Her name was written in red ink across a white piece of paper.

"What's this?" she muttered. She leaned over to pick up the flowers, then realized they were composed of dead roses. She quickly straightened. "Oh, my God."

Kate and Joel crowded into the doorway to see what she was looking at.

"Someone sent me dead flowers," she said in bewilderment. "Who would do that?"

Kate grabbed the piece of paper, turned it over, then handed it to Maddie. "It's blank," she said. "Just your name. Someone doesn't like you. Do you have an ex-boyfriend?"

Had it been a message from one of the guys who were after Paul?

"We can throw those away for you," Joel said, concern in his gaze.

"No, I need to show them to Burke."

"I agree. Don't throw them away," Kate said. "You should call the police. Do you want us to wait with you?"

"No, thanks, I'll talk to Max. He's been helping me with something. I'm sure they're related to that. It's nothing to worry about. It's just a sick joke."

"Sick jokes should always be worried about," Kate said. "Promise me you will talk to Max, or I'm not leaving you alone. In fact, maybe I should call Burke."

"I'm going to call him. You guys have things to do. It will be okay. I promise," she added, seeing the doubt in their eyes. The last thing she wanted was for Joel to think he'd be risking something by hiring her.

"Okay," Joel said with a frown. "But let me know if there's a problem."

"I will, but I think with Burke, Max and the Callaways behind me, I'll be fine." She forced herself to scoop up the dead flowers and take them into the apartment. She locked the door behind Kate and Joel, then called Burke.

His phone rang a couple of times, then went to voicemail. She tried to keep the fear out of her voice when she said, "Give me a call when you get a chance." She didn't want to worry him.

She'd be fine, wouldn't she?

→➽◄←

"What's wrong? Is this about Mitch?" Marjorie Parker asked Burke as they sat down together in her living room.

"In a way. It's mostly about Leanne," he said, noticing the numerous photographs of Leanne that were displayed all around the room, including a large portrait that had been taken on her eighteenth birthday. The young girl that Leanne had once been stared back at him in a somewhat accusatory way, as if she couldn't believe it was taking him so long to figure things out.

"What is it, Burke?" Marjorie asked, drawing his attention back to her.

He hesitated, not sure how to begin. Marjorie had been so distraught after Leanne's death; he felt terrible bringing it all up again. But if he didn't, Mitch would—if he hadn't already. "Has Mitch spoken to you since the dinner Friday night?"

She nodded, her gaze troubled. "He's called a few times, but to be honest I didn't really understand what he was trying to say. I'm quite worried about him. Can you tell me what's going on?"

"That's what I'm trying to figure out. Did you talk to Leanne much in the weeks before her accident?"

"We spoke almost every day. You know we were close." She paused as the phone rang. "I have to get that. I'm expecting a call from my sister."

"No problem." After she left the room, he got up and walked over to the mantel, taking another look at the family photographs. The most recent one of Leanne and her mother had been taken during a mother-daughter trip to the Sonoma wine country. They stood with their arms around each other in front of the bed and breakfast where they'd stayed, a beautiful inn with colorful flowers dotting the path next to them.

But while Leanne looked happy, there was a strain in her eyes.

It was a strain he'd seen, too, but he hadn't paid attention to it. Leanne often worked long hours at her job. He'd suggested she cut back, but she liked to work; it was something they had in common.

"Sorry about that," Marjorie said, returning to the room.

He returned to the couch. "No problem. I was just remembering that you and Leanne went to Sonoma a few weeks before she was killed."

"The last trip we had together. It was very emotional."

"Why?" he asked, her word choice a little odd.

"Well, you two were going to be married soon. I thought it was probably the last time I'd have her all to myself."

"Is that why Chuck didn't go with you on the trip?"

"Yes, that was why."

The same strain that was in Leanne's eyes in the photograph was now in Marjorie's eyes. He had a feeling he knew what had caused her new tension. "When you were in Sonoma, did Leanne tell you she was pregnant?"

Her jaw dropped, then she licked her lips. "What?"

"You heard me. Did she tell you she was pregnant?"

"I don't want to talk about this, Burke. This is wrong."

"You have to talk about it. I'm sorry, but I need to know.

Was Leanne pregnant?" He drew in a deep breath as he forced himself to get the next sentence out. "And was it my baby or was Mitch the father?"

Marjorie put a shaky hand to her lips. "Leanne made me promise not to say anything."

"About the baby? About her affair? About both?" The questions flew out of his mouth. Marjorie shrank back in her seat. He knew he was pressing her beyond belief, but he was so close to finally knowing the truth, he had to make her answer. "Marjorie, please."

"Oh, Burke, I don't know what to say."

"Just tell me what Leanne told you. That's all. It's really pretty simple."

Her hands shook as she pressed them together, as she thought about his demands. Finally, she let out a sigh, and said, "Yes, Leanne was pregnant. She had wanted to get away that weekend so she could talk to me about it."

"And the father?"

Marjorie's face paled. "Leanne said she didn't know who the father was."

He finally had confirmation of what he'd known since the first second he'd seen that medical report and learned that Leanne was pregnant. He'd tried to fight against it. He hadn't wanted to believe that Leanne had cheated on him, that she'd kept two such huge secrets from the man she was supposed to love and was going to marry. But there it was. It didn't feel satisfying. It didn't even make him feel angry. He was just— sad.

"Leanne made a terrible mistake, Burke. She said she didn't know how it happened."

"How is that possible? She was a smart woman."

"No, you don't understand." Marjorie sat up straighter, no longer defeated, but wanting to fight for her daughter.

"Leanne said she was at a party. It was some firefighter pub crawl or something. She said you were supposed to be there, but you got stuck at work, some odd problem with the truck or something."

He frowned. "We had some vandalism at the firehouse. They stole parts from the truck. I had to stay past my shift to get that issue resolved. Is that what you're talking about?"

"I think so. She felt uncomfortable at the pub crawl, but you had been telling her that you wanted her to get to know your friends, and Shelby had also said it was really important to you that Leanne fit in with your work family. So she stayed. And she drank. She drank a lot. She told me that she felt better when Mitch got there, because she knew him better than anyone else. They went to the next bar together. That was the last thing she remembered until she woke up the next morning in Mitch's house."

"In his bed," Burke said harshly, not quite able to believe that Marjorie was trying to put Leanne's actions on him, on the fact that he'd left her alone at a pub crawl.

"Yes," Marjorie admitted. "But she didn't know how she got there. She believed someone spiked her drink at one of the bars. She couldn't remember anything. And you know she wasn't a girl to drink in excess, Burke. That wasn't her. For her to have a complete blackout of a night terrified her."

"I'm sure Mitch told her what happened."

Marjorie's brows drew together in a frown. "Mitch said she seemed unusually happy, but he didn't notice anything wrong with her. He told her that she was a willing participant, that she'd admitted she was in love with him and that she wanted to break off her wedding and be with him."

Were those more of Mitch's delusions, Burke wondered. Or had he been telling the truth?

"Leanne didn't know what to do," Marjorie continued.

"She didn't know if she should confess to you or just make sure it never happened again."

"She obviously didn't confess."

"She was torn. She loved you. She didn't want to lose you."

"She might have been afraid she was going to lose me, but I don't think she loved me, not if she did what she did."

"I think she was drugged, Burke. I do. Her behavior was so out of character."

He stared back at Marjorie, seeing the plea in her eyes. She wanted to believe the best of her daughter, but he couldn't go there with her. "If she thought someone had drugged her, then her first suspect should have been Mitch. But according to the people I've spoken to who spent a lot of time with her in the weeks before her death, Leanne and Mitch were in constant contact."

"Because she was trying to understand what had happened and also trying to make sure Mitch didn't tell you about the affair. Finally, she got him to promise he wouldn't say anything to you. She told him if he loved her as he said he did that he would let her go, that he would let her be happy with you." She paused. "That weekend in Sonoma, she said she thought she'd convinced him."

He thought about what she'd said. One thing that was odd was that Mitch hadn't told him about his hookup with Leanne until a few days ago. During the past three years when Mitch had come to talk to him—to ask him about the accident, to grill him about why Leanne had left him a cryptic, upsetting message—Mitch had never once said that he'd slept with Leanne. What did that mean? Why hadn't he played that card?

Had Mitch been keeping his promise to Leanne? Had he been so in love with her that he couldn't betray her, not even after she died?

He was beginning to think that Leanne had played Mitch, too.

"What was she going to do about the baby?" he asked. "Was she just going to pretend it was mine, hope that Mitch wouldn't add dates together and come up with another conclusion? Because that doesn't seem like a very good plan."

"She didn't know what to do. She was confused. I was terrified that she might get an abortion just so she could start her marriage with you on a clean slate."

"You think getting rid of a child who might have been mine, would make the slate clean?"

"I didn't think that. And Leanne didn't think that, either. Not really. She was just trying to figure things out. She wouldn't have gone through with it. She loved children. I told her she needed to slow down, take her time, not let her emotions get the best of her, but we both knew she was going to have to make some quick decisions. Your wedding date was rapidly approaching, and she was starting to feel the beginning weight of pregnancy. She wasn't sure she could fit into her dress."

Which reminded him of what Kelly had said about Leanne skipping her fitting.

"The day before the accident," Marjorie continued, "we spoke briefly. She said that the two of you weren't getting along that well, and that it was her fault. The guilt was eating her up. She was going to tell you everything before the wedding, and if you wanted to call things off, then she'd accept it, because she couldn't live a lie. I think she actually felt good about her decision." Marjorie's chest heaved with her next breath. "I was hoping for the best, and then the next night I got the worst call a mother can get."

For a moment there was nothing but silence in the room as they both reflected on that night.

"Why didn't you tell me after she died?" he asked a few moments later.

"I thought about it, but I didn't want to cause you any more pain. And I was hoping you'd never find out. It wasn't on the medical examiner's report. I didn't believe that Leanne had told Mitch. I thought I was the only one who knew her secret. I decided to keep it for her. It would only cause you pain, and Mitch, too."

"You really care about Mitch's pain, after what he did?"

"I don't know what he did. I don't believe he was the one who drugged Leanne, and she didn't think that, either. She thought it was someone at the bar. Maybe her drink got mixed up with someone else's. But Mitch had always been there for Leanne. He was a good friend. He loved her in a way she didn't love him, but he wouldn't have pushed himself on her."

"I don't know that I believe that. I didn't see him like a saint the way you and Leanne saw him."

"Well, you wouldn't. You probably always knew that he wanted Leanne. And he always knew that you were going to be the one to stop him from getting her." Marjorie paused. "But the real reason I didn't tell you or Mitch about the baby was because I didn't want to tarnish my daughter's memory. She was a good girl who made one bad mistake. I didn't want that error to outlive her. I'm sorry if you can't understand that."

He wished he didn't understand her motivation, but he did. "You were protecting your daughter as any parent would. But it would have been nice if you'd come forward a few days ago when you realized Mitch was going off the rails. You had to know that there was a chance he was going to discover Leanne's secret."

"I've been terrified ever since he hit you the other night. I could see that something had happened, but he didn't tell me until yesterday that his private investigator had discovered Leanne was pregnant. He asked me to confirm it, to tell him that he was the father, just as you're doing now. I told him I didn't know anything about an affair or a baby."

"So you lied to Mitch."

"Chuck said we should stay out of it." She paused, giving him a tortured, sad smile. "But I couldn't lie to you, Burke."

"So Chuck knew?"

"Not until after Leanne died. And I never told him that she was considering a termination of the pregnancy. That would have devastated him. You can't tell him that."

"I have no interest in hurting Chuck. But I can't say the same for Mitch. He believes his baby was killed that night, along with the woman he loved, and he's determined to find out who did it. He thinks it was me."

"I know he does. But we all know that you had nothing to do with it. It was just an accident. Leanne was on her way to yoga."

"Was she?" he couldn't help asking. "I think she was coming to see me, maybe to tell me about the baby, maybe to call off the wedding, I don't know. But we had been fighting, and I had asked her if she really wanted to marry me. She hadn't come up with an answer. I thought she was going to give me one that night, but she didn't make it to the firehouse."

Marjorie gave a helpless shrug. "I didn't talk to Leanne that day. I really don't know what she was thinking or why she was in the car that night. I know she left that cryptic message for Mitch about needing to talk to him about you and the wedding, but what she was actually going to say is a mystery to me. And I certainly don't know who was driving the car that ran her off the road that night. I have to believe that was an accident, because I can't imagine who would want to hurt Leanne. She didn't have enemies. She was a wonderful person." Marjorie took a breath. "I hate to think that you're going to remember her in a bad way now. She did love you, Burke. I know she did."

It didn't really matter anymore.

"I need to talk to Mitch," he said heavily.

"I think that's the last person you should talk to, Burke. I don't know what is in his head right now."

"He's going crazy because he can't get to the truth, and strangely enough I have a little more compassion now than I did before."

"I thought you'd hate him for what he did with Leanne."

"I hate him for a lot of reasons, but I need to end this. I need to be able to move on with my life, and he keeps dragging me back. That has to stop." He got to his feet, suspecting that this was probably the last time he and Marjorie would really talk to each other.

"Do you hate me, too, Burke?" she asked softly, sadness in her eyes. "Should I have told you Leanne's secret? Should I have broken my promise to my daughter?"

"I don't know. The person to blame for all this is probably Leanne."

"She didn't deserve to die."

"She didn't die because of what she did with Mitch. That was..." His voice trailed away as he realized the word accident was starting to sound a little false to him, too. Had Leanne died because of what she'd done with Mitch? Or did his former fiancée have other secrets he knew nothing about?

When he got into his car, he took out his phone and saw he had two missed calls and a voicemail from Maddie. Her voice sounded tense when she asked him to call her back. That couldn't be good. He immediately hit her number. "What's wrong?"

"We have a problem, Burke. Someone left a bouquet of dead roses for me. They put the flowers in front of your door. Whoever made that delivery got into your building and was standing right outside the apartment."

Fear ran through him. "I'm coming home. Don't answer the door for anyone but me."

"I am definitely not going to do that. I called Emma and she's going to fill Max in. She gave me the same instruction to stay put. I have to say I'm happy you're coming home."

"I'll be there soon."

While Maddie waited for Burke to arrive, she kept herself busy finishing off her next batch of meatballs and listening to music on her phone. Despite her best efforts at distraction, her mind kept going back to the flower delivery. The bouquet was obviously meant to be a warning of some nature—a scare tactic.

And it had worked. She was scared. Seeing her name on those flowers had made the threat really personal. She was glad she'd finally reached Burke. He'd know what to do. He'd protect her.

It bothered her a little that she felt she needed a man to tell her what to do and to protect her, but that wasn't the real truth. She just needed Burke. She was falling in love with him.

She smiled at that thought. She'd been falling for him since high school. She should have landed by now. Actually, she had landed, right in the middle of Burke's bed, and it had been the most amazing night of her life. She wanted another night and then one after that, and maybe every night for a long time. She didn't want to jinx it by saying forever, but in her heart she knew that's what she wanted.

She told herself to focus. Today they had other problems to deal with. Whatever was happening with them on a personal level would have to wait.

The sound of the door opening jolted her heart. She froze until she heard Burke's voice. Then she ran out of the kitchen.

He rushed over to her, worry and fear in his eyes.

"Are you all right?" he asked, cupping her face with his hands as his gaze raked over her face and down her body.

"I'm okay."

"Thank God." He pulled her in for a hard, hot kiss that they both really needed, and then said, "I'm sorry I didn't answer my phone. I had it on silent."

"It's fine. You're here now."

"Where are the flowers?"

She tipped her head to the kitchen table. "I wanted to throw them away, but Kate said I should make sure whoever needed to see them saw them."

"Kate was here?"

"She brought Joel over to taste some of my meatballs. They were leaving when I saw the flowers."

"Well, I'm glad you weren't alone."

"The flowers have to be connected to Paul, to the loan shark, don't you think? They're sending me a message that if I don't help Paul, I'm going to end up like those flowers."

His lips tightened. "I don't know. Maybe the Vegas police are still setting up their sting and they haven't been able to shut down the bookie's operation yet. You called Emma, so hopefully Max will be able to tell us what's happening in Vegas." He paused, his expression turning grim. "But those flowers might not have anything to do with Paul."

"Then who?"

"Mitch."

"Why would he send a warning to me? I'm not the one he hates."

"Because you're close to me. He knows me well enough to know that the best way to hurt me would be to hurt someone I care about. You've been staying here. You were at Brady's with me. You came to the firehouse. I'm sure he could have heard about that from his investigator or a buddy in the firehouse."

"He did warn me that day he came here that I should get away from you before I ended up like Leanne."

"This is going to end today, Maddie. I'm going to find him, confront him and talk it all out."

That had been her original suggestion, but now she didn't like it so much. "If he's crazy enough to find dead flowers and drop them off at your door, I don't think you should talk to him alone. I'll come with you."

"No possible way. You're not getting involved."

"I'm already involved."

"I can't take you with me, Maddie, and I'm not just trying to protect you. I think your presence would make things worse."

"Oh. Because he doesn't want to see you with another woman."

He nodded in agreement. "It might set him off. Let me drop you off with Nicole or Emma."

"And put them in danger? I don't think so. If you don't want to take me to Mitch's house, then you need to grab someone else for backup—one of your brothers or cousins."

"I don't want to put them in danger, either. And I can handle Mitch."

"I don't know that you can. He's not in his right mind."

She wanted to see indecision in Burke's dark blue eyes, but all she saw was determination.

"This is between me and Mitch. It always has been. I'll be back soon. I promise."

"I'm going to hold you to that." She pulled his head down for a kiss. "Be safe."

Twenty

───≫≫≪≪───

As Burke headed across town, he felt torn. While he needed to talk to Mitch, he hated leaving Maddie alone in the apartment. Despite her brave front, he knew the flowers had shaken her up. But the sooner he confronted Mitch, the sooner this would all be over.

His phone rang and he answered, playing the call through his car speakers. "Hey, Shelby."

"Hi Burke. I need to talk to you. Can we meet?"

"Uh, I can't right now. I'm going to see Mitch."

"Why? What's happened?"

"I have to talk to him."

"We should speak first. I was going through my closets, and I found the file I'd started with Leanne to plan your wedding. She used to send me notes when she saw something in a magazine or online that she thought she might want for her wedding. She'd jot down ideas wherever she was so she wouldn't forget. Anyway, she jotted something down on the back of a note she got from Kelly Hamilton. I don't know if you remember her."

"I do. What did it say?"

"You need to read it for yourself. Leanne wasn't the only

one who was involved with Mitch."

"What? Explain that."

"I really can't do it over the phone. When you're done with Mitch, why don't you meet me at Brady's? I'll bring the letter."

He didn't want to wait that long, but he was almost to Mitch's house. "All right. I'll call you when I'm leaving his house."

As he hung up, he wondered about what Shelby had said. Had Kelly lied to him earlier? Had she known more about Leanne and Mitch than she'd let on?

It was time to stop dancing around the source of all of his problems, and that was Mitch.

Mitch owned a small house near Lake Merced on the southern edge of San Francisco. The last time Burke had been to Mitch's home had been for a New Year's Eve party fourteen months before Leanne died. He'd never imagined then that the three of them would become entwined in a mystery and a tragedy such a short time later.

He walked up to the front door and rang the bell, following up the sharp peal with a pounding knock. It felt good to hit something, and while the door was no substitute for Mitch's face, at the moment it took a little of the edge off.

He hit the door again, then yelled, "Open up, Mitch."

No answer.

On impulse, he tried the door, surprised to find it unlocked. He pushed it open and stuck his head into the living room. "Mitch?"

Walking inside, he shut the door behind him. That's when he smelled smoke and saw the filmy whispers dancing through the air. He ran down the hall and through the half-open door to the kitchen.

Mitch was kneeling on the floor, struggling to get up as

fire burned around him.

Burke didn't understand why Mitch was having trouble standing up or why he was clutching his throat, giving him a panicked look.

He grabbed Mitch's arm and tried to get him on his feet, but Mitch's weight pulled them both back down to the floor.

"What the hell is wrong with you? We've got to get out of here," he said sharply.

Mitch's eyes were rolling around in his head. "Poison." The word came out like a desperate, pleading whisper.

He didn't know what was going on, but the fire was getting worse. He managed to get his shoulder under Mitch's chest, so he could lift him up and get him out of the kitchen. When he got to the front yard, he put him down and called 9-1-1.

"Help is on the way," he told Mitch.

Mitch was struggling to speak. Finally, he put together two words. "Leanne. Murdered."

Burke swallowed hard. "I didn't kill her. I swear I didn't."

"Not you." Mitch's eyes fluttered closed.

"Stay with me. Dammit, don't you die on me, Mitch!"

Mitch's chest heaved, then stopped moving altogether. Burke immediately began CPR. He heard sirens in the distance. He prayed they would be in time.

Finally, Mitch started breathing again, and his pulse was faint but still present.

The paramedics arrived and took over. He told them that Mitch had said he was poisoned, but he didn't know with what.

Then he moved to the sidewalk to speak to the battalion chief, Ron Carlos, as firefighters raced into the house.

He once again reported what little he knew. He had no idea about the cause of fire, but it appeared that it had been deliberately set. The chief called for a fire investigator, and Burke pulled out his phone to call Max. There were two cops already on the scene, but he wanted Max involved. His brother-in-law told him he was on his way and to stay put.

Burke drew in a long breath as he watched the paramedics load Mitch into the ambulance.

Mitch's words ran through his head: *Leanne. Murdered. Not you.*

He'd thought Mitch was the bad guy, the one threatening his life, but now it appeared that there was someone else involved.

Leanne. Murdered. Not You.

The words ran around in his head again.

His stomach turned over. Had someone really killed Leanne?

Why? Who would do that? And how had Mitch figured it out?

It had to be someone who knew Leanne, who knew Mitch, who would have some personal stake in their deaths.

Kelly?

Shelby had implied that Kelly and Mitch had been involved in some way.

Was it possible that Kelly had heard about Leanne and Mitch hooking up three years ago and flown into a rage? Had she rammed her car into Leanne's in anger? She'd certainly expressed some negative thoughts about Leanne in their earlier conversation. Kelly had obviously been a little jealous of Leanne. Had she finally gone too far?

But even if Kelly had been responsible for what happened to Leanne, she couldn't have poisoned Mitch and set his house on fire. There hadn't been time—had there?

Several hours had passed since he'd been at her house. But Kelly was pregnant. She was happily married. It didn't make sense, unless she was trying to protect her marriage? Was she afraid that Mitch could spill some terrible secret from her past?

He ran a hand through his hair in confusion and frustration.

Pulling out his phone, he called Maddie. He needed to hear her voice. He needed to talk things out with her. She could help him figure this out.

Her phone rang once then went to voicemail. She had to be on the line. As her voicemail came on, he left a quick message. "Call me back as soon as you get this."

He slipped the phone back into his pocket and paced restlessly around the sidewalk. He knew he should wait for Max. He should find out how the fire started, what kind of poison Mitch had ingested and how. But he couldn't focus on any one task. His stomach was churning, his pulse pounding. If Mitch wasn't the bad guy, then who was?

Should he go back to Kelly's house? Should he go to the hospital and wait for Mitch to wake up? Should he just go home and talk to Maddie?

—➤➤◄◄—

"I'm sorry, what?" Maddie asked, her hand tightening around the phone. She couldn't possibly have heard the words correctly. "Burke is hurt? St. Mark's Hospital? Yes, I'll come right now. How bad is it?" The nurse couldn't tell her. She just said to hurry.

Mitch must have gone after Burke again. She should never have let him go to Mitch's place on his own. She should have insisted on going with him.

Grabbing her bag and the keys to the apartment, she ran to the door and opened it. As she stepped into the hall and turned toward the elevator, she heard a heavy footstep behind her.

She hesitated for a split second, started to turn, then something hard and painful came down on her head.

Pain ripped through her skull.

She fell to her knees, her breath caught in her throat from the shock of the attack, her vision blurring. Whoever had hit her was now dragging her into the apartment. She tried to see who it was, but her mind was slipping away.

She'd made a big mistake by leaving the apartment.

She hoped it wouldn't be her last.

Maddie fought her way back to consciousness. Waves of pain were exploding in her head with every breath. She didn't know what was coming next, but she knew it was going to be bad. She heard the crackle of paper, a muttered swear, but it was the smell of smoke that brought her more fully awake.

She blinked, seeing a yellow-orange flame licking up the curtains by the dining room windows.

Fire!

She had to get out of the apartment. She tried to move, but her limbs felt weighed down. She finally rolled over onto her side. She tried to reach the edge of the coffee table. If she could push off that, she might be able to get up.

Her blurry vision made her head spin, and she had to take it way too slow. She heard someone coming down the hall…

She needed to get out.

She had made it onto her knees when her assailant came back into the living room.

The woman stared at her with hatred burning through her eyes.

Shelby!

"Why?" she asked in shock, unable to understand how Burke's friend, his coworker, could be setting fire to his apartment.

"He's mine. He always has been. I've been waiting forever for him to realize that. He was almost to that point, and then you came along and ruined everything. I'm not going to stand by and watch the two of you get together like I did before when he fell for Leanne. No, not again. I have worked too long and too hard." She pulled a syringe out of her pocket. "You're going to go to sleep now. Trust me, you won't feel a thing."

"No," she gasped as Shelby started towards her. She kicked out her feet and somehow managed to unbalance Shelby.

It was a momentary victory. Shelby jumped back up, murderous intent in her eyes, a deadly syringe in her hand.

Maddie struggled against the pain, the paralysis. She had to find a way to push past it.

Shelby grabbed her arm and at the same time she brought a heavy booted foot down on Maddie's leg, holding her in place.

"Don't make this hard," Shelby bit out. "It's just going to be more painful for you."

The smoke in the apartment was getting thicker. "Fire," she got out. "You're going to die, too."

Shelby shifted slightly to see how the fire was progressing and Maddie tried to slip out from under her, but Shelby immediately pushed her back down. As she lifted her arm to inject Maddie with the needle, the door flew open.

Burke ran forward. He grabbed Shelby and pulled her away from Maddie.

Maddie coughed and sat up as Burke and Shelby now

struggled together.

She wanted to help him. As she tried to get up, her movement distracted him.

Shelby shoved him aside, then sprinted out of the apartment.

Burke hesitated. "Maddie—"

"Go," she said.

He didn't listen. Instead, he grabbed her hand and pulled her into the hall. A neighbor gave them a shocked look.

"Where did she go?" Burke demanded. "The woman with brown hair."

"Stairwell."

"Get out of the building," Burke told the neighbor. He put Maddie over his shoulder and sprinted down the hall.

She wanted to tell him to wait, that Shelby might be lying in wait for them, but she couldn't get any words out. Fortunately, they made it downstairs and outside without running into her.

The fire trucks were just arriving when Burke set Maddie down on the ground. "Are you all right?"

She nodded, still not really able to speak. "The paramedics are going to take care of you," he said as two EMTs came towards them. "I need to find Shelby."

Burke stepped away as Maddie was examined by the paramedics. He looked around for Shelby. Where the hell had she gone?

Her car was parked down the block, but it was empty. He looked one way, then the other, and then something drew his attention upward.

Shit!

He ran back into the building, flying up ten flights of stairs until he broke through the door leading out to the roof. Shelby had climbed over the rail that surrounded the rooftop deck and was facing the street.

"Shelby," he yelled.

She turned her head, letting go of the railing with one hand to ward him off. "Don't come any closer, Burke. It's over. It's all over."

"It's going to be okay," he said, his training kicking into gear. "You didn't kill anyone."

"Yes, I did," she said flatly. "I killed Mitch."

"He's not dead. I got to his house in time. I saved his life."

"Why would you do that? Wait. I know the answer— because you're a knight in shining armor. You're just not my knight."

"Shelby—"

"Even if I didn't kill Mitch, I did kill Leanne. You know that now, don't you?"

"Why did you do it?" he asked, trying not to have an emotional response to her words. He would think about it all later. Right now he just had to keep her talking and get her off the ledge.

"Because we were supposed to be together," she said. "I've loved you for years." Her words were filled with pain, anger and bewilderment. "I've always been there for you, but you kept looking past me."

"We were friends. We still are friends."

"No, we're not. You're just saying that so I won't jump." She paused. "I want you to know that I was trying to help you. Leanne cheated on you with Mitch. She was going to have another man's baby. She didn't deserve you."

"You knew about the baby?"

The door behind him opened and a firefighter and a cop stepped out with Maddie coming out behind them. She was the last person he wanted to see right now. "Maddie go downstairs and both of you stay back."

The three of them didn't move. Well, he couldn't worry about them right now.

"I saw the way you looked at her," Shelby said, pointing at Maddie, tears now streaming down her face. "It was the same way you looked at Leanne. It wasn't fair. I waited three years for you to get over Leanne. I was there every day for you. Then *she* shows up in your life and I'm out. I couldn't lose you again, Burke. I just couldn't. She had to go. I told you to back off. But you couldn't do it, could you?"

He ignored that question, wanting to get her attention off of Maddie. "What about Mitch? Why did you go after him?"

"Because he knew I was the one who ran Leanne off the road. His investigator figured it out. He found a camera that caught a license plate a few blocks away. I thought I was safe after all this time."

He couldn't believe how calmly she talked about running Leanne off the road, about killing a woman she had once considered a friend. "Why did you run Leanne off the road? Why didn't you just tell me about the affair if you wanted to break us up? That would have done it."

Shelby shook her head. "I was trying to break you up when I sent her into Mitch's arms. But I didn't anticipate a pregnancy. I thought Mitch would surely use a condom."

"How did you send her into Mitch's arms?"

"I put a little something in her cocktail. Then he asked her to dance, and it all just happened. It was remarkably easy. It wasn't like she didn't like him. And he was in love with her."

Shelby really was twisted. He'd always admired her calm, but now he could see that calm came from a lack of compassion. She was completely detached and unapologetic.

"Leanne was going to tell you she was pregnant," Shelby

continued. "Once you knew there was a baby, you'd never let her go. So, I had to get rid of that baby. I didn't know Leanne was going to die, but maybe it was just as well. She cheated on you. She didn't deserve you. I was just trying to protect you, Burke."

"Don't put this on me."

"It's true. I made sure that no one got close to you, so no one could hurt you. I was the right person for you. I would have been the perfect wife."

He stared at her in shock, wondering if she'd hurt other women that he'd dated. How had he completely missed her obsession? He'd occasionally thought she was flirting with him, but she'd dated other men over the years. Apparently, none of those relationships had lessened her fixation on him.

He searched for something to say—the right words to get her off the ledge. But even as he did so, he wondered how he could want to save the life of the woman who had murdered his fiancée, an unborn child, and who had just tried to kill Maddie—the woman he'd loved for half of his life? How could he do that?

Shelby stared back at him. Her lips parted. "You don't care," she said, as if stunned by the idea. "You don't care if I jump—if I die."

He couldn't find the words to deny her accusation.

"Of course he cares," Maddie said, coming forward.

"I don't want to talk to you," Shelby said.

"Too bad. You tried to kill me, so now you can listen to me or you can jump, because I sure as hell don't care what happens to you." Maddie's voice rang across the roof. "But Burke does care. You're his friend. And he stands by his friends. If you truly love him, you're not going to make him live with the guilt of watching you die."

"I do love you, Burke," Shelby said brokenly. "I wish

you could believe that."

"Prove it," he said. "Come here." He extended his hand.

"I'll go to jail."

"You'll get help, and you'll be alive."

"What kind of life could I have now?" She looked from him to the street below.

He knew in that second that he'd lost the battle. She wasn't going to give herself up.

He did what he had to do, what his instincts as a firefighter—as a protector—demanded he do. He rushed to the ledge and grabbed her hand just as she let go.

Her weight almost pulled him over, but Maddie grabbed his arm, and the firefighter and cop were suddenly right next to him, helping him pull Shelby back over the ledge.

She fell to the ground, sobbing like a broken doll.

He stared at her as the cop cuffed her and got her to her feet.

Shelby gave him one last pleading look. "Don't hate me."

He didn't answer. He had no words.

As the cop took her away and the firefighter left the roof, Maddie put her hand on his arm. "Burke, are you all right?"

He gazed into her worried green eyes. "I can't believe it was Shelby."

"I know."

"I was completely fooled."

"She was very good at hiding her sickness, but it's over now."

He blew out an exhausted breath as Maddie rested her head on his shoulder.

He wrapped his arms around her and held on tight. "I almost lost you today."

She lifted her gaze to his. "You didn't. I'm okay."

"Are you? What did Shelby do to you?"

"She knocked me over the head. She was going to inject me with something, which would either kill me or send me into unconsciousness. Then she set a fire to either cover it up or finish me off." Maddie suddenly started."Your apartment. Do you think everything burned up?"

"I don't give a damn about my apartment. I'm just glad you're all right."

"You saved my life, Burke." Her eyes watered as she bit down on her bottom lip. "If you hadn't come in when you did, I wouldn't have made it. I was fighting, but I was losing."

"Don't think about it, Maddie. You're safe now, and if anyone saved anyone's life, it was you saving mine. I always thought I was on track, doing what I was supposed to do, but it wasn't until you came back that I realized I'd gone off the rails a long time ago. I'd been so focused on career and climbing every rung of the ladder I was supposed to climb that I couldn't see anything but the job. After Leanne died, I was stuck in a bad place. I didn't know how to get out of it. You showed me the way. You reminded me of the man I used to be. You opened my eyes to living in the moment, putting fun back into the day, laughing again, opening up my heart, taking a risk…"

"I did all that?" she asked in amazement.

"You did."

"I brought trouble into your life, too—the way I always do," she reminded him.

"The best kind of trouble." He paused, wanting to say the words that had been in his heart for a very long time. "I love you, Maddie Heller. I've loved you since the day you got me into detention."

"You hated me then."

"You scared me. I knew you could change my life. But not having you in my life has been boring as hell. I need you,

Maddie. I didn't think I needed anyone, but I do. You're the one."

Her gaze filled with emotional tears. "I love you, too, Burke. I think I always have."

"Thank God. We're finally on the same page," he murmured, giving her a tender kiss to seal their words.

"What happens next?" she asked.

"I have no idea, but that's what's exciting, right?" he asked, repeating her favorite line.

"Right," she said, giving him a watery smile.

"You need to go to the hospital and get checked out." He gently felt around the back of her head, wincing at the large, hard knot that his fingers encountered. "You probably have a concussion. Why didn't the paramedics take you to the hospital?"

"I wouldn't let them. I had to find you."

"I'm surprised they let you back in the building."

"I didn't ask. I slipped back in when no one was looking. I knew the fire was just in your apartment. I had to be sure you were okay."

"And now I need to be sure that you're all right, so we're going to the hospital."

"Fine, although following up *I love you* with a trip to the Emergency Room isn't really the most romantic of moments."

He laughed as he put his arm around her. "And yet it feels so appropriate for us, doesn't it?"

She smiled back at him. "Unfortunately, it does." As they walked down the stairs, she added, "What do you think is going to happen to Shelby?"

"She's going to go to jail for murder."

"I heard her say something about Mitch. What did she do to him?"

"Same thing she tried to do to you." The anger came back

as he remembered the panic he'd felt when he'd seen Shelby trying to inject Maddie with whatever she had in that syringe.

"Is he going to be all right?"

"I'm not sure. She managed to get the needle into him. He was going into cardiac arrest when I found him. I started CPR. His heart was beating again, but I don't know."

"You saved Mitch's life, too. It's been quite a day."

"I hope I saved his life. I don't know why I do, but I do."

She slid her hand into his and gave him a smile. "You're a really good man, Burke Callaway."

"I don't feel good right now, but I do feel lucky to have you," he said squeezing her fingers. He wanted to add the word forever, but he knew how much it scared her. So he would stay in the moment and hope that it lasted forever.

Twenty-One

When they got to Burke's floor, the smoke had diminished considerably. "Why don't you keep going?" Burke suggested. "I'll meet you out front. I want to check on the damage."

"I'll go with you," she said, feeling like she needed to see it for herself. The events of the last hour were surreal, the combination of adrenaline and her head injury making everything fuzzy.

A firefighter stood just inside the door. The windows in Burke's apartment had been opened, so there was now a cool breeze blowing the rest of the smoke away.

Maddie didn't recognize the man, but he gave Burke a relieved smile, and said, "I couldn't believe it when we got the call for this address. You all right?"

"I'm fine. Maddie, this is my cousin Hunter, one of Kate's older brothers—Maddie Heller."

"Hi," she murmured, still hanging on to Burke's hand. Of course Hunter was a Callaway. His blue eyes and dark hair should have been a giveaway.

"What's the damage?" Burke asked.

"Kitchen and bedroom. Emma is on her way over."

"You called Emma?"

"Captain called a fire investigator since there were obvious signs of arson. She was on duty."

"Great."

Another firefighter came down the hallway. "Chief," he said with a nod. "Glad to see you're all right. I heard you had a standoff on the roof. Is it true that Shelby did this?"

"It's a long story, Doug," Burke replied. "You'll hear it all soon enough."

"You're going to want to stay somewhere else tonight," Hunter told Burke. "Let the smoke clear. You know the drill."

Burke nodded, glancing down at Maddie. "Do you want to put a few things in a bag?"

"All right," she said, reluctantly letting go of Burke's hand.

Without Burke anchoring her down, she felt a little lightheaded. As she bent down to pick up the suitcase, the dizziness got worse. She quickly straightened, glancing back toward Burke, but he was engrossed in conversation with Hunter and Doug. That was good. She didn't want him worrying about her. She managed to put some clothing into the suitcase and grabbed her toiletries out of the bathroom. When she got back to the living room, Burke had stepped into the hall. She sat down on the couch and let out a breath.

Everything had happened so fast. One minute she'd been making meatballs and the next she'd been fighting for her life. She looked toward the kitchen, thinking foolishly for a moment that she should make sure the oven was off. But the charred curtains and blackened walls reminded her that there would be no meatballs left to save, and she was lucky to be alive.

As she glanced down at the carpet, she could picture herself lying there. She saw Shelby with the needle in her hand. She'd known that she was going to die if she didn't do something. She'd never been so scared in her life.

The memories made her shake, and cold chills ran through her body, drawing goose bumps along her arms. She pulled the blanket off the back of the couch and wrapped it around her shoulders, telling herself everything was fine. She was all right. Shelby was on her way to jail. They were safe.

She just wished she felt safe.

Then Burke came through the door, his gaze immediately seeking hers. And those blue eyes of his immediately steadied her. He sat down on the couch next to her. "I'm sorry. I shouldn't have left you alone."

"You were right outside the door."

"You're cold. You're in shock. Let's get you to the hospital."

Part of her wanted to argue, but the other part of her wanted to get out of the apartment so she could stop reliving Shelby's attack. "Shelby was so strong. It was like she had superhuman strength."

"You were dazed from the head injury."

"I was fighting to stay conscious," she agreed. "Maybe that's why she seemed so much bigger and more powerful than I was. I wasn't sure I could beat her."

"You were fighting hard when I came in," he said, admiration in his eyes. "You're something else, Maddie Heller. You don't give up, not even when the odds are against you."

"It was fight or die. I think I was losing. But you came him and pulled her off of me."

"I know you're going to go over it a lot in your head, and I want you to talk to me about every second of it," he told her. "But right now I want to get you to the hospital." He stood up and pulled her into a standing position. Then he put his arm around her. "Hang on to me, babe. I won't let you fall."

She had no intention of doing anything else.

Burke drove her to the hospital, and within minutes she was taken into an examining room. Burke insisted on accompanying her into the room. She sat down on the table while he hovered nearby, ready to make good on his promise to catch her if she was about to fall.

While they were waiting for the doctor to come in, Burke's phone rang. He pulled it out of his pocket to check the number. "Max."

"You should get it."

"Hello? Yeah, we're okay. We're at the hospital. Maddie is getting checked out." He paused. "We're at St. Mark's." He listened for a few moments, then added, "All right. Thanks."

"What's happening?" she asked.

"Max is on his way over here."

"Did he say anything about Mitch or Shelby?"

"Mitch is in intensive care, but he's holding his own. Max said he'd fill us in on everything else."

"It's weird that we're here at St. Mark's."

He gave her a questioning look. "What do you mean?"

"That's how Shelby got me to open the door. I didn't know it was her actually. I got a call on my cell phone. The woman identified herself as a nurse from St. Mark's. She said you'd been in an accident and wanted me to come to the hospital. I rushed out the door without thinking and bam, she hit me over the head. How stupid was I?"

Burke shook his head, his lips drawing into a tight line. "You couldn't have known. Shelby certainly had quite a plan going. She called me on my way to Mitch's house. She asked me to meet her after I saw Mitch. She made up some story about having something to show me. I guess she wanted to make sure I'd be out of the apartment. She was so calm on the phone. She sounded totally normal. But now that I think about it, she'd probably just finished poisoning Mitch and setting his house on fire."

"It's hard to believe anyone can be that evil."

"She's sick and very good at covering up that sickness. She's never had problems at work, never missed days for no reason, never acted out in any way. She's always been super calm, the kind of dispatcher who handles every crisis as if it's nothing. When I think about all the parties, all the dinners, all the days I spent talking to her, being her friend..." He shook his head in bewilderment. "It's beyond unimaginable. And Leanne befriended her, too. Shelby was helping to plan our wedding. But then apparently she decided to kill Leanne instead."

Maddie suddenly felt like it was Burke who needed her strength now. She put a hand on his arm. "It's going to take a while to sort through all the events and even longer to get through all the emotions. Don't try to do it all in one night."

As she finished speaking, the door opened and the doctor walked in.

Burke stepped off to the side while she was examined. The doctor asked quite a few questions that were meant to test her cognitive skills. Apparently, she didn't do a good enough job answering them to get her out of a CT scan.

"I'll be in the waiting room when you're done," Burke told her.

"I don't need this test. I'm fine. I have a hard head."

"I'm going to wait for the doctor's opinion. Do you want me to call your parents?"

"No, not yet. They'd just worry. Let's wait until all the tests are done, and I can honestly tell them I'm as fine as I think I am."

"Okay." He kissed her on the forehead. "I'll see you in a bit."

She nodded, wanting to get the test over with as quickly as possible so she could go home—wherever that was.

—➤➤◄◄◄—

When Burke entered the waiting room, he found Max and several members of his family waiting for him including Colton, his father and his mother.

"Burke," his mom said, coming forward first. "Are you all right?"

"I wasn't hurt at all," he assured her.

"How is Maddie?"

"I think she's all right, but they're doing a CT scan of her head to make sure there's nothing going on that we have to worry about."

His mom looked immensely relieved at his words. He turned to Max. "Did you fill them in?"

"On what I know," Max said. "Emma is investigating both fire scenes, but it appears that Shelby was working alone. I've gotten a brief statement from her but she's still being questioned."

"Is she at the station or the hospital?"

"She's at San Francisco General Hospital. She's in the Psych Ward, and she's cuffed to the bed. She's not going anywhere."

"Good."

"Why don't you tell us what happened, Burke?" Colton suggested. "We've heard bits and pieces."

He ran a hand through his hair as he took a breath. "Here's the short version. Shelby was apparently obsessed with me and has been for a long time. She ran Leanne's car off the road. And she waited for me to get over my grief and turn to her. But that didn't happen. Then Mitch got a new private investigator and started digging into the accident. He apparently found out that Shelby was involved. I don't know exactly how he figured that out." He glanced at Max. "Do you?"

Max nodded. "His investigator found some trace evidence, a partial license plate that led to a truck registered to Shelby's cousin. The investigator confronted the cousin and was able to get him to confirm that Shelby had borrowed his truck that day. I'll have more details when we finish getting Shelby's statement. But it looks like she lured Leanne to a meeting place near the firehouse. Apparently, as a dispatcher, she was aware of what intersections did not have security cameras or much foot traffic in the area. She set Leanne up to be on that street at that time and then she rammed Leanne's small compact car with her cousin's truck. It was not a match Leanne could win, especially since she was blindsided."

Burke felt another rush of anger at the explanation, followed by a wave of pain for Leanne.

"I don't think Leanne ever saw it coming," Max said. "If that helps."

"Nothing helps," he said. "So I guess once Mitch confronted Shelby, she decided to kill him. Once she'd gone that far, the only person left in her way was Maddie. Shelby saw Maddie and I together at the bar and other times. She knew we were getting close, so she went to Maddie's house with a syringe full of something and was going to kill her and cover up the murder with a fire."

"Oh, my God," his mother breathed. "How terrifying for Maddie."

"She was really brave. She was fighting Shelby when I got to the apartment."

"I never would have guessed Shelby was crazy," Colton said. "I thought she was totally normal."

"We all did," he said. "I must have missed some really big flags." He turned toward his father, expecting to see judgment in his dad's eyes. His father didn't suffer fools, and Burke certainly felt like a fool for never realizing Shelby was hurting the people around him. But all he saw in Jack Callaway's eyes was compassion. "I feel like I let everyone down," he muttered.

"You didn't let anyone down, son," Jack said. "You had no way of knowing what Shelby was capable of doing. And from what I understand, you saved her life today."

"He saved Mitch's life, too," Max said.

"I did what I was trained to do," Burke said with a shrug. "I hope Mitch recovers. He has some things to answer for, but he doesn't deserve to die. So that's all for now. I'm sure we'll know more in a few days."

"Where are you going to stay tonight?" Lynda asked.

"Probably a hotel."

"You can always come home. We have plenty of room— for both you and Maddie." She paused. "She's special to you, isn't she?"

"Very much so. She has been special to me for longer than I care to say."

Lynda smiled. "I'm glad. Let us know if you need anything."

"Take your next shift off," Jack said.

He hated to take off work, but in this case he did feel like he needed a few days." I will do that. Thanks for coming."

"We're always here for you," Lynda said, giving him a quick hug.

As his parents and Colton left, Max lagged behind. "I need to get a statement from you, Burke. Do you want to do that now?"

"I'm not leaving Maddie."

"Then we'll do it here," Max said, pulling out his notebook. "I think I know most of what went down, but let's run through it one more time."

They sat down in chairs by the window, and Burke painstakingly repeated every move he'd made that day, thinking as he did so that if he'd hit a red light or got delayed by traffic, two lives could have been lost. He was damn lucky, and he was going to make the most of the second chance he'd been given.

———————

"The Ritz Carlton?" Maddie asked as Burke pulled up to the valet in front of one of San Francisco's most beautiful hotels.

"Why not?" he said with a shrug.

"It's expensive."

"I want you to be comfortable tonight. You need to rest and recuperate."

"The doctor told you I'm fine."

"The doctor told me you had a mild concussion. That's not fine," he reminded her as they got out of the car. "So we're going to get you into bed and order up some room service."

"I can't believe it's almost eight o'clock. Where did the day go?"

"Let's not think about the day right now."

"Okay." She was more than happy to go along with that plan. Her headache was better after taking some medication, but she was really tired and also starting to feel quite hungry. Thinking about food reminded her of meatballs, which reminded her of Joel. As they walked up to the front desk, she said, "I should call Joel and tell him I'll still be ready to work on Friday. News of the fire at your place has no doubt spread through your family, so Kate has probably told Joel, and he's going to be worried that I'll bail on him."

"So you'll call him. After you get into bed. After we order room service." He handed his credit card to the clerk.

"You're being quite bossy tonight."

He gave her a smile. "Just tonight?"

She laughed. "Good point. It is your natural tendency to tell people what to do."

He shrugged, turning back to the clerk to finish checking in. Once they had their keys, they walked across a gorgeous lobby with marble floors, crystal chandeliers and elegant furniture. It felt nice to be out of the smoky apartment and away from the memories of what had almost happened.

Burke punched the button for the elevator. "You just need to accept the fact that I'm going to take care of you whether you like it or not, Maddie."

"I like it—I like it a lot."

He groaned. "Do not smile at me like that."

"Like what?" she asked mischievously.

"You know like what. You're going to rest tonight."

"You seriously think we're going to share a bed and go straight to sleep?" she asked as they got onto the elevator.

"I seriously think that. Your health is the most important thing."

"We'll see," she said lightly.

A few minutes later, they entered a luxurious oversized room with a king-sized bed, a love seat, a small table and chairs, and an amazing view of the city lights. Maddie wandered over to the window and looked out at San Francisco.

Burke came up behind her, sliding his arms around her waist, pulling her up against his chest.

"It's a beautiful night," she said, turning so she could face him. "I'm really happy I'm still here to see it."

Pain and anger moved through his eyes. "I'm so sorry I put you in danger, Maddie."

She quickly put a finger against his lips. "Hush. No blame, Burke."

"There's a lot you haven't heard Maddie."

"And I want to hear it all, but not right now."

"Okay. But I have to ask one thing."

"What's that?"

"Did it bother you that I saved Shelby's life? She'd just tried to kill you, and I was talking her out of taking her own life. I can't imagine what you were thinking."

She met his gaze head on. "I was thinking that I'd fallen in love with an amazing man, someone strong, noble, unselfish, and incredibly caring." Her eyes blurred with tears. "Watching you save your enemy just made me love you more. I just hope I can live up to you, Burke. I've made so many mistakes—"

"Hush," he said, repeating her earlier warning. This time his fingers came against her lips. "You make mistakes because you push yourself to the limits. You're adventurous and daring and you live your life the way everyone should live—the way I want to live. I always admired you, Maddie, even when you were pulling crazy stunts in high school. Every time we ran into each other during our twenties, I felt like I'd missed out on you. You were always with someone else."

"Or you were," she interrupted as he dropped his fingers from her lips. "It was never the right time for us."

"Until now," he said forcefully.

"You sound pretty certain about that."

"I am certain. I'm not letting you go, Maddie. If you

leave this city, I'll be at your side. If you want to move to India and study yoga and meditate, just make sure you buy two mats."

She smiled. "You would never want to give up firefighting. It's who you are."

"No, it's what I do," he corrected. "And I do it really well. But I'm done living for my job. I want more. I want you to live with me and marry me and have kids with me. I want us to cook together, and ride horses on the beach, and roll around in a hayloft with only the moon for light."

"We'll have to make sure my parents are on a trip for that one," she said, her heart overflowing with happiness. "But I love all those ideas. And you know I'll probably have some new ideas along the way."

He laughed and gave her a kiss. "I'm counting on that."

"Some of them will be bad," she warned.

"But some of them will be really, really good," he returned.

"I have an idea for right now."

He immediately shook his head. "No, you're going to eat. You're going to rest. That's what you need."

"Later," she interrupted.

"Maddie," he protested, but she could see his desire warring with his good sense.

"Love me, Burke. That's what I need right now. I need you."

"I need you, too," he breathed, then his mouth finally came down on hers.

Epilogue

Valentine's Day – Three Weeks Later

"What are we doing?" Maddie asked, a little breathless from trying to keep up with Burke's long strides. "I don't think there are any restaurants out here."

"Who said we were going to a restaurant?" he asked, a secretive smile playing around his lips.

"That's what most people do on Valentine's Day."

"Are we most people, Maddie?"

She laughed. "Well, you are—*usually*. Me, not so much."

He didn't bother to reply, just grabbed her hand as they walked quickly down the sidewalk. Then he took a turn, leading her along a path that led into Golden Gate Park, the city's largest park and one that sprawled across several miles of city land.

"Okay, we're at the park, so I'm guessing we're going to go to the De Young Museum. We're going to look at erotic art."

He grinned. "Wrong."

"Arboretum then. Instead of giving me flowers, you're going to give me an entire arboretum. Isn't it closed at night?" It was after seven, and the sun had gone down an hour earlier, but it was still somewhat light, with a full moon and a starry sky.

"Wrong again," Burke said with a laugh. "You're not

going to guess."

"I'm pretty good at guessing," she protested.

"Not this time."

She tried to think of what else they could do in the park. "We're going to the stables. We'll take a moonlit horse ride through the park. Wait, are there stables here?"

"Not that I know of. I think the only horses are on the carousel."

"That's it. You just gave it away. You're taking me on the merry-go-round."

"Would I be that crazy to give it all away? Who do you think you're dealing with?"

Apparently, she was dealing with a man who was much more imaginative and inventive than she had first thought, and she was more than a little happy that he was all hers. The past three weeks had been a whirlwind of love and romance mixed with more practical matters like working in the food truck and finding a new place to live—a place she and Burke were going to live in together.

They'd settled on a condo earlier that day and were supposed to be celebrating tonight—if they ever got to where they were going.

The path they were on wound through thick, tall trees, past green meadows and dense woods. And since she hadn't been in the park in years, she really had no idea where this walk was going to end, but she had a feeling it was going to be amazing.

"Almost there," Burke said, excitement in his voice.

They turned a corner and came out of the woods. In front of her was a small but beautiful fountain. She stopped in delight and astonishment, watching the effervescent pink streams of water splash into a beautiful moonlit pool.

"It's pink," she said, running over to get a closer look.

"Oh, my God. Did you do this, Burke? Did you dye the water in the fountain pink?"

"A Valentine's Day pink, like your mashed potatoes," he said, reminding her of that long ago day. "So that everyone can feel the love even if their locker isn't filled with valentines or flowers or candy hearts. They can feel the magic of love in the water."

He'd repeated her previous statement almost word for word. "I can't believe you remember my saying all that."

"I remember everything." He took both of her hands in his. "You changed my life the very first day we met."

"When I got you detention."

"When you showed me that there needed to be some fun mixed in with the work," he corrected.

"You know I got detention again for the mashed potatoes. You could get into trouble for this, Burke. You could get arrested for vandalizing city property. That wouldn't sit well with the Callaways."

He laughed. "I'll take my chances. You're worth breaking a few rules for. And I wanted to give you this, not just to show that I've changed, but that I'm not the stiff-necked, uptight, humorless person I used to be."

"I never thought that about you, Burke," she protested.

"Come on, Maddie. We tell each other the truth."

"Okay, you were a little bit like that. But the flip side was that you did everything really well. And you've made a tremendous life for yourself. You were on the right path all along. I was the one taking too many detours."

"Those detours were probably worth it."

"Some of them were."

"And some of them weren't even your idea," he reminded her. "You were living for yourself and for your sister, and I love that you fulfilled so many of her dreams. But it's your time now, Maddie. It's all you—it's what you want from life. That's all that matters."

She gazed into his eyes. "I didn't know what I wanted until you came back into my life. And then it was all so incredibly clear. I need you, Burke."

"And I need you."

He dropped to his knees, and her heart skipped a beat.

"What are you doing?' she asked with excitement.

He let go of her hands to pull a small velvet box out of his pocket. He flipped it open, revealing an oval-shaped diamond. "Will you marry me, Maddie Heller?"

Her eyes filled with tears as she dropped down to her knees. "Yes, Burke Callaway, I will marry you."

He put the ring on her finger. "If you don't like it, we can—"

"I love it and I love you," she said, giving him a long, passionate kiss. "We're going to be really happy."

He smiled. "I know we are." He helped her to her feet. "So this isn't the total surprise."

"No?" she asked.

"I'm taking you to dinner. You have two choices. We can join the rest of the family at my parents' house where there's a Callaway celebration of love going on, or we can have a more intimate dinner for two at a really good Italian restaurant. It's your call."

"That's a tough call, but I'm thinking the family dinner. Nicole told me that since it's so difficult to babysitters they've started a new Valentine's Day tradition of just getting together and letting love surround them. It seems like the perfect place to celebrate our love."

He blew out a breath of relief. "Good. I was hoping you'd say that, because your parents are already there."

"Burke, I can't believe you. What if I'd picked the

intimate dinner for two?"

"Then our parents were going to spend a lot of time talking about us tonight."

"You told my parents you were going to ask me to marry you?"

"I asked for your father's permission."

Her heart turned over again. "Oh, Burke. Really? He must have been so touched."

"He said he was glad you'd finally picked the right guy," Burke said with a laugh.

"He was right."

"And your mom gave me a suggestion on your ring."

"You really did plan everything out." As she said the words, she wasn't at all surprised. "I think I'm going to like being married to you."

"I think I'm going to like that, too. Shall we go?"

"Yes." As she took one last look at the pink watery spray, a thought occurred to her. "Hang on a second."

"What?"

"You got permission to do this, didn't you?"

"Who would give me permission?"

"Probably some park commissioner who is related or married to or friends with someone in your family."

"Does it matter?"

She smiled. "No, it doesn't matter."

He gazed into her eyes. "Be my valentine?"

"Forever."

"I thought you hated that word."

"I used to—not anymore. Now it's perfect." She put her arms around his neck and pulled his head down to hers.

THE END

Keep reading for an excerpt from Barbara Freethy's

DON'T SAY A WORD

12 weeks on the New York Times Bestseller List!

Everything she's been told about her past is a lie ...

Julie De Marco is planning a perfect San Francisco wedding when she comes face-to-face with a famous photograph, the startling image of a little girl behind the iron gate of a foreign orphanage -- a girl who looks exactly like her. But Julia isn't an orphan. She isn't adopted. And she's never been out of the country. She knows who she is -- or does she?

Haunted by uncertainty, Julia sets off on a dangerous search for her true identity -- her only clues a swan necklace and an old Russian doll, her only ally daring, sexy photographer Alex Manning. Suddenly nothing is as it seems. The people Julia loved and trusted become suspicious strangers. The relationships she believed in -- with her mother, her sister, and her fiance -- are shaken by new revelations. The only person she can trust is Alex, but he has secrets of his own. Each step brings her closer to a mysterious past that began a world away -- a past that still has the power to threaten her life ... and change her future forever.

Prologue

--->➤➤◄◄<---

25 years earlier

She took her bow with the other dancers, tears pressing against her lids, but she couldn't let those tears slip down her cheeks. No one could know that this night was different from any other. Too many people were watching her.

As the curtain came down one last time, she ran off the stage into the arms of her husband, her lover, the man with whom she would take the greatest risk of her life.

He met the question in her eyes with a reassuring smile.

She wanted to ask if it was all arranged, if the plan was in motion, but she knew it would be unwise to speak. She would end this evening as she had ended all those before it. She went into her dressing room and changed out of her costume. When she was dressed, she said good night to some of the other dancers as she walked toward the exit, careful to keep her voice casual, as if she had not a care in the world. When she and her husband got into their automobile, they remained silent, knowing that the car might be bugged.

It was a short drive to their home. She would miss her

house, the garden in the back, the bedroom where she'd made love to her husband, and the nursery, where she'd rocked...

No. She couldn't think of that. It was too painful. She had to concentrate on the future when they could finally be free. Her house, her life, everything that she possessed came with strings that were tightening around her neck like a noose, suffocating her with each passing day. It wasn't herself she feared for the most, but her family, her husband, who even now was being forced to do unconscionable things. They could no longer live a life of secrets.

Her husband took her hand as they walked up to the front door. He slipped his key into the lock and the door swung open. She heard a small click, and horror registered in her mind. She saw the shocked recognition in her husband's eyes, but it was too late. They were about to die, and they both knew it. Someone had betrayed them.

She prayed for the safety of those she had left behind as an explosion of fire lit up the night, consuming all their dreams with one powerful roar.

One

---→→»›«‹«‹←---

Present Day...

Julia DeMarco felt a shiver run down her spine as she stood high on a bluff overlooking the Golden Gate Bridge. It was a beautiful, sunny day in early September, and with the Pacific Ocean on one side of the bridge and the San Francisco Bay on the other, the view was breathtaking. She felt like she was on the verge of something exciting and wonderful, just the way every bride should feel. But as she took a deep breath of the fresh, somewhat salty air, her eyes began to water. She told herself the tears had more to do with the afternoon wind than the sadness she'd been wrestling with since her mother had passed away six months ago. This was supposed to be a happy time, a day for looking ahead, not behind. She just wished she felt confident instead of... uncertain.

A pair of arms came around her waist, and she leaned back against the solid chest of her fiancé, Michael Graffino. It seemed as if she'd done nothing but lean on Michael the past year. Most men wouldn't have stuck around, but he had. Now it was time to give him what he wanted, a wedding date. She didn't know why she was hesitating, except that so many things were changing in her life. Since Michael had proposed to her a year ago, her mother had died, her stepfather had put the family home up for sale, and her younger sister had moved in with her. A part of her just wanted to stop, take a few breaths, and think for a while instead of rushing headlong into another life-changing event. But Michael was pushing for a date, and she was grateful to him for sticking by her, so how could she say no? And why would she want to?

Michael was a good man. Her mother had adored him. Julia could still remember the night she'd told her mom about the engagement. Sarah DeMarco hadn't been out of bed in days, and she hadn't smiled in many weeks, but that night she'd beamed from ear to ear. The knowledge that her oldest daughter was settling down with the son of one of her best friends had made her last days so much easier.

"We should go, Julia. It's time to meet the event coordinator."

She turned to face him, thinking again what a nice-looking man he was with his light brown hair, brown eyes, and a warm, ready smile. The olive skin of his Italian heritage and the fact that he spent most of his days out on the water, running a charter boat service off Fisherman's Wharf, kept his skin a dark, sunburned red.

"What's wrong?" he asked, a curious glint in his eye. "You're staring at me."

"Was I? I'm sorry."

"Don't be." He paused, then said, "It's been a while since you've really looked at me."

"I don't think that's true. I look at you all the time. So do half the women in San Francisco," she added.

"Yeah, right," he muttered. "Let's go."

Julia cast one last look at the view, then followed Michael to the museum. The Palace of the Legion of Honor had been built as a replica of the Palais de la Legion d'Honneur in Paris. In the front courtyard, known as the Court of Honor, was one of Rodin's most famous sculptures, *The Thinker*. Julia would have liked to stop and ponder the statue as well as the rest of her life, but Michael was a man on a mission, and he urged her toward the front doors.

As they entered the museum, her step faltered. In a few moments, they would sit down with Monica Harvey, the museum's event coordinator, and Julia would have to pick her wedding date. She shouldn't be nervous. It wasn't as if she were a young girl; she was twenty-eight years old. It was time to get married, have a family.

"Liz was right. This place is cool," Michael said.

Julia nodded in agreement. Her younger sister Liz had been the one to suggest the museum. It was a pricey location, but Julia had inherited some money from her mother that would pay for most of the wedding.

"The offices are downstairs," Michael added. "Let's go."

Julia drew in a deep breath as the moment of truth came rushing toward her. "I need to stop in the restroom. Why don't you go ahead? I'll be right there."

When Michael left, Julia walked over to get a drink of water from a nearby fountain. She was sweating and her heart was practically jumping out of her chest. What on earth was the matter with her? She'd never felt so panicky in her life.

It was all the changes, she told herself again. Her emotions were too close to the surface. But she could do this. They were only picking a date. She wasn't going to say "I do" this afternoon. That would be months from now, when she was ready, really ready.

Feeling better, she headed downstairs, passing by several intriguing exhibits along the way. Maybe they could stop and take a look on the way out.

"Mrs. Harvey is finishing up another appointment," Michael told her as she joined him. "She'll be about ten minutes. I need to make a call. Can you hold down the fort?"

"Sure." Julia sat down on the couch, wishing Michael hadn't left. She really needed a distraction from her nerves. As the minutes passed, she became aware of the faint sound of music coming from down the hall. The melody was lovely but sad, filled with unanswered dreams, regrets. It reminded her of a piece played on the balalaika in one of her music classes in college, and it called to her in a way she couldn't resist. Music had always been her passion. Just a quick peek, she told herself, as she got to her feet and moved into the corridor.

The sounds of the strings grew louder as she entered the room at the end of the hall. It was a tape, she realized, playing in the background, intended no doubt to complement the equally haunting historic photographs on display. Within seconds she was caught up in a journey through time. She couldn't look away. And she didn't want to look away— especially when she came to the picture of the little girl.

Captioned *The Coldest War of All,* the black-and-white photograph showed a girl of no more than three or four years old, standing behind the gate of an orphanage in Moscow. The photo had been taken by someone named Charles Manning, the same man who appeared to have taken many of the pictures in the exhibit.

Julia studied the picture in detail. She wasn't as interested in the Russian scene as she was in the girl. The child wore a heavy dark coat, pale thick stockings, and a black woolen cap over her curly blond hair. The expression in her eyes begged for someone—whoever was taking the picture, perhaps—to let her out, to set her free, to help her.

An uneasy feeling crept down Julia's spine. The girl's

features, the oval shape of her face, the tiny freckle at the corner of her eyebrow, the slope of her small, upturned nose, seemed familiar. She noticed how the child's pudgy fingers clung to the bars of the gate. It was odd, but she could almost feel that cold steel beneath her own fingers. Her breath quickened. She'd seen this picture before, but where? A vague memory danced just out of reach.

Her gaze moved to the silver chain hanging around the girl's neck and the small charm dangling from it. It looked like a swan, a white swan, just like the one her mother had given to her when she was a little girl. Her heart thudded in her chest, and the panicky feeling she'd experienced earlier returned.

"Julia?"

She jumped at the sound of Michael's booming voice. She'd forgotten about him.

"Mrs. Harvey is waiting for us," he said as he crossed the room. "What are you doing in here?"

"Looking at the photos."

"We don't have time for that. Come on."

"Just a second." She pointed at the photograph. "Does this girl seem familiar to you?"

Michael gave the photo a quick glance. "I don't think so. Why?"

"I have a necklace just like the one that little girl is wearing," she added. "Isn't that odd?"

"Why would it be odd? It doesn't look unusual to me.

Of course it didn't. There were probably a million girls who had that same necklace. "You're right. Let's go." But as she turned to follow Michael out of the room, she couldn't help taking one last look at the picture. The girl's eyes called out to her—eyes that looked so much like her own. But that little girl in the photograph didn't have anything to do with her—did she?

◦━➤➤◄◄━◦

"It cost me a fortune to get you out of jail," Joe Carmichael said.

Alex Manning leaned back in his chair and kicked his booted feet up onto the edge of Joe's desk. Joe, a balding man in his late thirties, was one of his best friends, not to mention the West Coast editor of *World News Magazine,* a publication that bought eighty percent of Alex's photographs. They'd been working together for over ten years now. Some days Alex couldn't believe it had been more than a decade since he'd begun his work as a photojournalist right after graduating from Northwestern University. Other days—like today—it felt more like a hundred years.

"You told me to get those pictures at any cost, and I did," Alex replied.

"I didn't tell you to upset the local police while you were doing it. You look like shit, by the way. Who beat you up?"

"They didn't give me their business cards. And it comes with the territory. You know that."

"What I know is that the magazine wants me to rein you in."

"If you don't want my photographs, I'll sell them somewhere else."

Joe hastily put up his hands. "I didn't say that. But you're taking too many chances, Alex. You're going to end up dead or in some prison I can't get you out of."

"You worry too much."

"And you don't worry enough—which is what makes you good. It also makes you dangerous and expensive. Although I have to admit that this is some of your best work," Joe added somewhat reluctantly as he studied the pile of photographs on his desk.

"Damn right it is."

"Then it's a good time for a vacation. Why don't you take a break? You've been on the road the past six months. Slow down."

Slowing down was not part of Alex's nature. Venturing into unknown territory, taking the photograph no one else could get, that was what he lived for. But Alex had to admit he was bone tired, exhausted from shooting photographs across South America for the past six weeks, and his little stint in jail had left him with a cracked rib and a black eye. It probably wouldn't hurt to take a few days off.

"You know what your weakness is?" Joe continued.

"I'm sure you're going to tell me."

"You're reckless. You forget that a good photographer stays on the right side of the lens." Joe reached behind his desk and grabbed a newspaper. "This was on the front page of the *Examiner* last week."

Alex winced at the picture of himself being hustled into a police car in Colombia. "Damn that Cameron. He's the one who took that photo. I thought I saw that slimy weasel slinking in the shadows."

"He might be a weasel, but he was smart enough to stay out of jail. Seriously, what are you thinking these days? It's as if you're tempting fate."

"I'm just doing my job. A job that sells a lot of your magazines."

"Take a vacation, Alex; have some beer, watch a football game, get yourself a woman—think about something besides getting the next shot. By the way, the magazine is sponsoring a photography exhibit at the Legion of Honor. Your mother gave us permission to use the photographs taken by your father. You might want to stop by, take a look."

Alex wasn't surprised to hear his mother had given permission. Despite the fact that she'd hated everything about his father's job while they were married, she had no problem living off his reputation now. In fact, she seemed to enjoy being the widow of the famous photojournalist who had died far too young. Alex was only surprised she hadn't pressed him to attend. That might have something to do with the fact that he hadn't returned any of her calls in the past month.

"Why don't you check out the exhibit tonight?" Joe suggested. "The magazine is hosting a party with all the movers and shakers. I'm sure your mother will be there."

"I'll pass," Alex said, getting to his feet. He needed to pick up his mail, air out his apartment, which was probably covered in six inches of dust, and take a long, hot shower. The last person he wanted to talk to tonight was his mother. He turned toward the door, then paused. "Is the photo of the Russian orphan girl part of the exhibit?"

"It was one of your father's most famous shots. Of course it's there." Joe gave him a curious look. "Why?"

Alex didn't answer. His father's words rang through Alex's head after twenty-five years of silence: *Don't ever talk to anyone about that picture. It's important. Promise me.*

A day later Charles Manning was dead.

⮞⮞⮜⮜⁓

It didn't take Julia long to find the necklace tucked away in her jewelry box. As she held it in her hand, the white enamel swan sparkled in the sunlight coming through her bedroom window. The chain was short, made for a child. It would no longer fit around her neck. As she thought about how quickly time had passed, another wave of sadness ran through her, not just because of the fact that she'd grown up and couldn't wear the necklace, but because her mother, the one who had given it to her, was gone.

"Julia?"

She looked up at the sound of her younger sister's voice. Liz appeared in the doorway of the bedroom a moment later, the smell of fish clinging to her low-rise blue jeans and bright red tank top. A short, attractive brunette with dark hair and dark eyes, Liz spent most of her days working at the family restaurant, DeMarco's, a seafood cafe on Fisherman's Wharf. She'd dropped out of college a year ago to help take care of their mother and had yet to go back. She seemed content to waitress in the cafe and flirt with the good-looking male customers. Julia couldn't really blame Liz for her lack of ambition. The past year had been tough on both of them, and Liz found comfort working at the cafe, which was owned and run by numerous DeMarcos, including their father. Besides that, she was only twenty-two years old. She had plenty of time to figure out the rest of her life.

"Did you set the date?" Liz asked, an eager light in her eyes.

"Yes. They had a cancellation for December twenty-first."

"Of this year? That's only a little over three months from now."

Julia's stomach clenched at the reminder. "I know. It's really fast, but it was this December or a year from next March. Michael wanted December." And she hadn't been able to talk him out of it. Not that she'd tried. In fact, she'd been so distracted by the photograph she'd barely heard a word the wedding coordinator said.

"A holiday wedding sounds romantic." Liz moved a pile of CDs so she could sit down on the bed. "More music, Julia? Your CD collection is taking on mammoth proportions."

"I need them for work. I have to stay on top of the world music market. That's my job."

"And your vice," Liz said with a knowing grin. "You can't walk by a music store without stopping in. You should have bought some wedding music. Have you thought about what song you want to use for your first dance?"

"Not yet."

"Well, start thinking. You have a lot to do in the next few months." She paused. "What's that in your hand?"

Julia glanced down at the necklace. "I found this in my jewelry box. Mom gave it to me when I was a little girl."

Liz got up from the bed to take a closer look. "I haven't seen this in years. What made you pull it out now?"

Julia considered the question for a moment, wondering if she should confide in her sister.

Before she could speak, Liz said, "You could wear that for your wedding—something old. Which reminds me..."

"What?" Julia asked.

"Wait here." Liz ran from the room, then returned a second later with three thick magazines in her hands. "I bought up all the bridal magazines. As soon as we get back from Aunt Lucia's birthday party, we can go through them. Doesn't that sound like fun?"

It sounded like a nightmare, especially with Liz overseeing the procedure. Unlike Julia, Liz was a big believer in organization. She loved making files, labeling things, buying storage containers and baskets to keep their lives neat as a pin. Since taking up residence on the living room futon after their parents' house had sold, Liz had been driving Julia crazy. She always wanted to clean, decorate, paint, and pick out new curtains. What Liz really needed was a place of her own, but Julia hadn't had the heart to tell Liz to move out. Besides, it would be only a few more months; then Julia would be living with Michael.

"Unless you want to start now," Liz said, as she checked her watch. "We don't have to leave for about an hour. Is Michael coming to the party?"

"He'll be a little late. He had a sunset charter to run."

"I bet he's excited that you finally set the date," Liz said with a smile. "He's been dying to do that for months." Liz tossed two of the magazines on the desk, then began to leaf through the one in her hand. "Oh, look at this dress, the satin, the lace. It's heavenly."

Julia couldn't bear to look. She didn't want to plan her wedding right this second. Wasn't it enough that she'd booked the date? Couldn't she have twenty-four hours to think about it? Julia didn't suppose that sounded very bridal-like, but it was the way she felt, and she needed to get away from Liz before her sister noticed she was not as enthusiastic as she should be. "I have to run an errand before the party," she said, giving in to a reckless impulse.

"When will you be back?"

"I'm not sure how long it will take. I'll meet you at the restaurant."

"All right. I'll pick out the perfect dress for you while you're gone."

"Great." When Liz left the room, Julia walked over to her bed and picked up the catalogue from the photography exhibit. On page thirty-two was the photograph of the orphan girl. She'd already looked at it a half-dozen times since she'd come home, unable to shake the idea that the photo, the child, the necklace were important to her in some way.

She wanted to talk to someone about the picture, and it occurred to her that maybe she should try to find the photographer. After researching Charles Manning on the Internet earlier that day, she'd discovered that he was deceased, but his son, Alex Manning, was also a photojournalist and had a San Francisco number and address listed in the phone book. She'd tried the number but gotten a message machine. There was really nothing more to do at the moment, unless...

Tapping her fingers against the top of her desk, she debated for another thirty seconds. She should be planning her wedding, not searching out the origin of an old photo, but as she straightened, she caught a glimpse of herself in the mirror. Instead of seeing her own reflection, she saw the face of that little girl begging her to help.

Julia picked up her purse and headed out the door. Maybe Alex Manning could tell her what she needed to know about the girl in the photograph. Then Julia could forget about her.

Twenty minutes later, Julia pulled up in front of a three-story apartment building in the Haight, a neighborhood that had been the centerpiece of San Francisco's infamous "Summer of Love" in the sixties. The area was now an interesting mix of funky shops, clothing boutiques, tattoo parlors, restaurants, and coffeehouses. The streets were busy. It was Friday night, and everyone wanted to get started on the weekend. Julia hoped Alex Manning would be home, although since he hadn't answered his phone, it was probably a long shot. But she had to do something.

She climbed the stairs to his apartment, took a deep breath, and rang the bell, all the while wondering what on earth she would say to him if he were home. A moment later, the door opened to a string of curses. A tall, dark-haired man appeared in the doorway, bare chested and wearing a pair of faded blue jeans that rode low on his hips. His dark brown hair was a mess, his cheeks unshaven. His right eye was swollen, the skin around it purple and black. There were bruises all over his muscled chest and a long, thin scar not far from his heart. She instinctively took a step back, feeling as if she'd just woken the beast.

"Who are you and what are you selling?" he asked harshly.

"I'm not selling anything. I'm looking for Alex Manning. Are you him?"

"That depends on what you want."

"No, that depends on who you are," she stated, holding her ground.

"Is this conversation going to end if I tell you I'm not Alex Manning?"

"Not if you're lying."

He stared at her, squinting through his one good eye. His expression changed. His green eyes sharpened, as if he were trying to place her face. "Who are you?"

"My name is Julia DeMarco. And if you're Alex Manning, I want to ask you about a photograph I saw at the Legion of Honor today. It was taken by your father—a little girl standing behind the gates of an orphanage. Do you know the one I'm talking about?"

He didn't reply, but she saw the pulse jump in his throat and a light flicker in his eyes.

"I want to know who the little girl is—her name—what happened to her," she continued.

"Why?" he bit out sharply.

It was a simple question. She wished she had a simple answer. How could she tell him that she couldn't stop thinking about that girl, that she felt compelled to learn more about her? She settled for, "The child in the picture is wearing a necklace just like this one." She pulled the chain out of her purse and showed it to him. "I thought it was odd that I had the same one."

He stared at the swan, then gazed back into her eyes. "No," he muttered with a confused shake of his head. "It's not possible."

"What's not possible?"

"You. You can't be her."

"I didn't say I was her." Julia's heart began to race. "I just said I have the same necklace."

"This is a dream, isn't it? I'm so tired I'm hallucinating. If I close the door, you'll go away."

Julia opened her mouth to tell him she wasn't going anywhere, but the door slammed in her face. "I'm not her," she said loudly. "I was born and raised in San Francisco. I've never been out of the country. I'm not her," she repeated, feeling suddenly desperate. "Am I?"

About The Author

Barbara Freethy is a #1 New York Times Bestselling Author of 42 novels ranging from contemporary romance to romantic suspense and women's fiction. Traditionally published for many years, Barbara opened her own publishing company in 2011 and has since sold over 5 million books! Nineteen of her titles have appeared on the New York Times and USA Today Bestseller Lists.

Known for her emotional and compelling stories of love, family, mystery and romance, Barbara enjoys writing about ordinary people caught up in extraordinary adventures. Barbara's books have won numerous awards. She is a six-time finalist for the RITA for best contemporary romance from Romance Writers of America and a two-time winner for DANIEL'S GIFT and THE WAY BACK HOME.

Barbara has lived all over the state of California and currently resides in Northern California where she draws much of her inspiration from the beautiful bay area.

For a complete listing of books, as well as excerpts and contests, and to connect with Barbara:

Visit Barbara's Website:
www.barbarafreethy.com

Join Barbara on Facebook:
www.facebook.com/barbarafreethybooks

Follow Barbara on Twitter:
www.twitter.com/barbarafreethy

CPSIA information can be obtained at www.ICGtesting.com
Printed in the USA
BVOW06s0936081115

425791BV00001B/1/P